The kiss was brief. Insultingly brief.

"Better?" he asked, his expression blank, emotionless.

"Better?" she repeated, backing up a step, irritation overtaking her frantic pulse. "What do you mean, better?"

"Now you don't have to wonder anymore."

"I don't have..." Her confusion gave way to indignation as his meaning sank in. "*I* don't have to wonder? Heat rushed over her face. She took a menacing step forward. He didn't move. "*I* wasn't wondering." She jabbed a finger at him and came close to clipping his chin.

He stopped her hand and pulled her up close. His breath glided across her cheek.

"I was," he whispered, his face bent toward hers.

ABOUT THE AUTHOR

Debbi is originally from Kailua, Hawaii, but has lived in Cincinnati, Chicago, Detroit, Tulsa and Houston during the past fifteen years. She currently makes her home in Michigan with her husband, Peter, and their dog, Brandy. She's had a passion for books ever since she learned how to read her first one and quickly figured out that flashlights worked well for reading past curfew.

Books by Debbi Rawlins

HARLEQUIN AMERICAN ROMANCE
580—MARRIAGE INCORPORATED
618—THE COWBOY AND THE CENTERFOLD
622—THE OUTLAW AND THE CITY SLICKER

Don't miss any of our special offers. Write to us at the following address for information on our newest releases.

Harlequin Reader Service
U.S.: 3010 Walden Ave., P.O. Box 1325, Buffalo, NY 14269
Canadian: P.O. Box 609, Fort Erie, Ont. L2A 5X3

LOVE, MARRIAGE AND OTHER CALAMITIES

DEBBI RAWLINS

Harlequin Books

TORONTO • NEW YORK • LONDON
AMSTERDAM • PARIS • SYDNEY • HAMBURG
STOCKHOLM • ATHENS • TOKYO • MILAN
MADRID • WARSAW • BUDAPEST • AUCKLAND

For my sister, Earlette Benevedes
Thank you for your unconditional love and support.
You are the best sister (and mother) in the whole world.
I love you.

ISBN 0-373-16675-3

LOVE, MARRIAGE AND OTHER CALAMITIES

Copyright © 1997 by Debbi Quattrone.

Chapter One

"You got fired again, didn't you?"

Ignoring Gail's incredulous stare, Jolie Duval dropped her Bloomingdale's bag on a vacant chair at the table, crowded a Bergdorf Goodman tote beside it, then glanced around the small elegant bistro for her usual waiter.

"Have you ordered me an iced tea yet?" she asked, averting her gaze while sliding onto the burgundy leather banquette opposite her friend.

"You *were* fired." Gail shook her head. "How could you screw up flipping burgers?"

Jolie sighed. "Scratch the tea. I think I'll have a glass of wine."

Gail signaled the waiter, then turned her sympathetic blue eyes on her longtime friend. "What happened this time?"

"The manager and I had a misunderstanding." Ignoring every etiquette class that had been forced down her throat since she was a child, Jolie propped one elbow on the table, rested her chin on her palm and frowned. "Hey, do you think I qualify for some kind of record? Having four jobs in two weeks has to mean something, right?" She stared thoughtfully out the window at the lunch crowd rushing toward Wall Street.

"A record isn't going to help you out. You need a job." Gail made a face. "And you need to keep it for thirty days."

"I know." Jolie leaned back against the soft leather and huffed out a frustrated breath. "And I have less than two months to do it."

"You could ask Colette for a job at her gallery."

"I can't work for a friend, remember?" Jolie said, shaking her head. She looked disdainfully at the rolled-up want ads sticking out of her brown designer handbag. "I wonder if the Wadsworth Museum has any openings?"

Gail laughed. "Right. Have you forgotten you were asked not to come back after that last protest rally you organized?"

Heat climbed her neck and Jolie adjusted the collar of her white linen blouse. "That was almost three years ago."

"I seem to remember the words 'don't ever' being used." Gail grinned. "Besides, if you can't even flip a burger—"

"I can flip a damn burger," Jolie snapped. "It was the French fries that got me fired." She smoothed her hair and felt the ridge left by the ridiculous hat she'd had to wear at McHungry's this morning. Great. Not only did she have mousy brown hair, but right now her usual page-boy probably looked like a helmet.

A wide knowing smile spread across Gail's face. "How did the French fries get you fired?"

Jolie flipped open the leather-bound menu and buried her face in it. "I think I'll just have a Caesar salad."

"I'm not surprised," her friend said, laughter in her voice.

Against her better judgment, Jolie peeked over the top of the menu.

"Couldn't eat just one, could you?"

Jolie blinked, then raised her chin. "I thought it was my duty to assure product quality."

"Of course."

"That's what the manager said." She grimaced. "Right before he made me turn in my McHungry beanie."

Gail chuckled. "Too bad I didn't get to see you in uniform."

"You'll get your chance." Jolie sighed. Their waiter appeared and she gave her order, then said, "I've got to find another job and quick."

"You will," Gail assured her. "If you put your mind to it. You're smart and funny and pretty. Just stay away from places that make French fries. We both knew that was a mistake going in."

Jolie smiled ruefully at her friend. Her wonderful, loyal, lying friend. The only truth to Gail's words was her weakness for French fries.

Smart was not a term associated with Jolie. At least not in the same way it was used to describe her older sister, Monique. But she didn't care. She liked being a dreamer, being idealistic, and if her family thought she was a flake because of those traits, then she didn't care about their opinions anyway.

Her sense of humor, however, she would probably defend. But pretty? She'd never been accused of that. Her younger sister, Nicole, was the one who'd inherited the looks in the family. And that was all right, too.

Because that wasn't the kind of inheritance she was worried about. What *did* concern her was that if she didn't find a job in a hurry, she'd be broke. Busted. A street urchin. That was *not* okay with her. Not by a long shot. "I'm desperate, Gail. I'm going to be thirty years old in two months. I've got to find a job this week."

"Finding one isn't your problem," her forever practical friend pointed out. "You gotta be able to keep it."

For the first time since Jolie had found herself in this crazy situation, she felt panic blossom in her chest. She pinched the bridge of her nose and squinted as a headache started at her temples. "What am I going to do?"

"God, I hate this." Gail glanced at the ceiling as if looking for counsel, then met Jolie's curious gaze. "I have something you may be interested in." She reached into her purse, pulled out a piece of paper and shoved it across the table. "Read this before I change my mind."

She frowned, but took the paper and unfolded it. In the middle of the sheet was a neatly printed paragraph.

> Married Couples Only Need Apply
>
> Couple wanted to crew private yacht for one-month trip to Caribbean. Duties include cooking, cleaning, sailing and personal attendance. References required...

Jolie stopped reading and stared at her friend. "Are you kidding?"

Gail sighed. "It was Byron's idea. He has a buddy who'll play your husband."

"This is Byron's idea?" Jolie laughed. Somehow she couldn't picture Gail's fiancé coming up with a plan like this. The man didn't have enough imagination. Plenty of money, but no imagination.

Gail shrugged. "Actually, this friend of his brought him the ad and asked if he knew anyone who'd be interested. I told him it was ridiculous. But I promised to show it to you anyway."

"You're right. This is ridiculous."

Gail looked relieved and grabbed for the paper.

Jolie jerked it out of her reach. "You know, the timing is perfect." She studied the ad again, a smile tugging at her lips. "They can't fire me in the middle of the ocean."

"True, but there's another teeny, little detail."

"What's that?"

"You don't know anything about yachts."

Jolie's eyebrows shot up. "I was practically raised on one. Grandfather took us out every summer."

"Oh, silly me." Gail drew back and smiled at the young man replenishing her iced tea. As soon as he stepped away, she leaned forward and said, "I'd forgotten how many summers you'd spent being waited on hand and foot. I'm sure you know everything there is to know about actually sailing one of those things."

Jolie sniffed at the sarcasm. "I'll wing it. Besides, maybe the future Mr. Duval can take care of all that. Who's the guy anyway?"

Gail rolled her eyes. "You're not seriously thinking about this…are you?"

"Maybe. Tell me who he is and why he's willing to play husband for a month."

"I can't do that."

Jolie stared at the stubborn tilt to Gail's chin in disbelief. Gail had never denied her anything. They'd met in third grade after Jolie had painted Gail's cat purple. Even after the unfortunate incident, she had become her best friend. "You mean you won't tell me—"

"I mean I can't. I don't know anything about him except that he's a friend of Byron's."

"Great. The guy must be a preppy dweeb." Jolie winced, then mumbled, "Sorry." The mercenary Byron got on her nerves sometimes, but she liked him well enough. She had actually introduced him to Gail. And the fact that he'd fallen head over heels for the tall, spunky blonde, despite her lack of blue blood and fat trust fund, made him okay in her book.

"Part of the deal would be that neither of you know anything about the other. Apparently, this guy has his own reason for wanting this job," Gail said, ignoring Jolie's comment. "I told Byron that it was absurd and that you wouldn't go for the idea."

"You would've been right, if I hadn't been fired." She stared out at the gray spring day. "The Caribbean, huh?"

"I don't believe this." Gail grabbed for the ad but Jolie snatched it back. "You can't seriously be thinking about this. There are thousands of jobs in New York."

"I know. I've been fired from them all," Jolie said dryly, meeting her gaze. "Look, I've got to find a job, right? Why not go to the Caribbean? Besides, this phony marriage will probably be the closest I ever get to a wedding." She laughed.

Gail didn't. "That's not true. You're different from Monique and Nicole. That doesn't make you any worse."

It made a difference to her family. "I'm only kidding. Lighten up, will you? I just like the idea, okay?" Taking a deep breath, she leaned back in her seat. Whatever happened in the Caribbean had to be better than going home and telling her grandfather that she'd failed yet again. She smiled. "So, when do I meet the lucky guy?"

MIKE KRAMER PACED his friend's posh penthouse apartment, stretching his neck from side to side, trying to work out the knots from his having sat on a plane for ten hours.

"You're making me nervous," Byron said. "This deal better not be something weird or kinky. I can't have our friend involved in anything like that."

Mike gave him a dry look. "Right."

"Well, what am I supposed to think?" Byron fidgeted

with his bow tie. "You pop out of nowhere after five years, then won't tell me what the hell is going on."

"You don't need to know. In fact, it's better if you don't."

"And I'm not supposed to be nervous?"

"Relax, Byron, I'm not into anything illegal. Just into a free vacation in the Caribbean. That's all."

Byron reached into the wet bar's refrigerator, pulled out a bottle of wine and opened it. "I thought the security business paid well these days."

Mike's jaw tightened. Staring at the Gauguin painting over the fireplace, he forced himself to loosen up. "I hope you have a beer in that refrigerator."

"You *are* still in the business, aren't you?" Byron slid a bottle of imported ale down the length of the bar. He sent a tall, frosted glass behind it.

Ignoring the crystal pilsner, Mike picked up the beer and unscrewed the top. He took a long pull, then said, "You could say that."

"Hell, this conversation is about as enlightening as my damn stockbroker's market forecasts."

One side of Mike's mouth lifted as he slid his friend a hooded, unsympathetic look.

"Hey, don't blame me for being rich." Byron held up a manicured hand. "It doesn't wash with me anymore. I understand that, to some degree, you've joined our ranks."

"Not quite. Besides, I never blamed you."

"Right." Byron sniffed his cabernet. "Back in the old days, your disdain was as thick as vichyssoise."

He laughed. "Vichyssoise?" His friend would use that analogy. Mike would probably have used pea soup. Shaking his head, he admitted it felt good to laugh. It'd been a long time since he'd felt like doing that. "I rest my case."

Byron frowned, obviously bewildered.

"When are we going to know what this Joey's answer is?"

"Her name's Jolie," Byron corrected. "Gail is supposed to be talking to her even as we speak."

"And she's reporting back to you this afternoon?"

"That depends. If Jolie's been fired again, then she—" Byron stopped himself short, casting a quick glance at Mike. He took a healthy sip of wine, then consulted his gold Rolex. "I expect to hear from her at any minute."

"Fired again?" Mike set down his beer. "If this woman is some kind of flake..." He rubbed his jaw with agitation. "Why would she get—?"

"Uh-uh-uh." A smug smile inched across Byron's face, his green eyes crinkling in amusement. "You don't need to know anything about each other, remember? Those were your rules. All I'll say is that she's no flake."

"You'd better be right." Mike folded his arms and, facing the large glass window, stared down at Central Park. He couldn't afford any foul-ups. He had too much riding on this venture.

"I thought this was merely supposed to be a free vacation."

Mike stiffened at his friend's suspicious tone, then slowly exhaled. "That's right. But it won't be a very pleasant one if the woman's a fruitcake."

Byron sighed. "Look, we both know this has nothing to do with a vacation. I don't understand you. You've changed. I can't pinpoint it...." He spread a hand helplessly. When Mike said nothing and continued to stare out the window, Byron added, "I trust you. You were more than a bodyguard, you were my friend. But Jolie is a friend, too, especially to Gail. And I don't want to see her get hurt.''

Mike turned from the window to look at his friend. "She's not going to get hurt. I give you my word.''

Byron nodded. ''That's good enough for me.''

"Is it possible to meet her tonight? Timing is crucial. The ad goes into the paper tomorrow. I want to be the first in line.''

"I don't know how you managed to get your hands on it before publication, but I'm not surprised and I'm not going to ask. Assuming Jolie agrees to consider this proposition, let's plan on dinner and I'll make the introductions.''

"Good.'' Mike took a deep breath and picked up his beer again.

"I won't say anything too telling, but I'd better warn you. She's not your type.'' Byron took his time replenishing his wine, then slowly looked up. "She's nothing at all like Angela.''

Mike tried not to show any reaction as he loosened his white-knuckled grip on the sweaty beer bottle. Angela was history. Ancient history. He rarely thought about her anymore…not without feeling the anger and hurt threaten to explode. "That doesn't matter,'' he said calmly. "I'm not looking for involvement.'' One side of his mouth lifted dryly. "Believe it or not, I'm not looking for sex, either.''

His lips started to curve as he turned away to watch the fading fluorescent orange vest of a jogger disappear into the park. No, Jolie Duval's virtue was safe with him. He only needed her to get the diamonds.

JOLIE STEPPED out of the elevator and frowned when she saw Gail waiting outside Byron's door. Her friend looked up from the fingernail she was biting and gave her a weak smile.

"What's with the welcoming committee?" Jolie asked as she tried to smooth out her windblown hair. The chilly evening air had turned downright nasty, wreaking havoc on her once sleek pageboy, the cold nipping at her tingling cheeks. The Caribbean was sounding better by the minute.

"I just met Mike Kramer." Gail put a hand to her heart.

Jolie grinned and continued to swipe at her hair. "You mean the future Mr. Duval?"

"Somehow I don't think that remark would go over too well with him," Gail whispered, glancing over her shoulder at the heavy mahogany door to the apartment. "Wait till you see him. He's...he's gor—"

The door flew open and Gail almost fell backward into Byron's arms. "What are you doing out here?" Byron frowned at his fiancée, then looked at Jolie. He swung the door wide. "Hi, runt. Come on in."

Jolie's hand flew to her hip and she opened her mouth to deliver her usual wisecrack. But over Byron's shoulder, a pair of incredible blue eyes peered down at her and her smart retort made a U-turn down her throat. The man was standing far enough back that she couldn't see the rest of his face, only his probing eyes and shiny brown, sun-streaked hair tumbling lazily across his forehead. He swept it back with long, tanned fingers.

Her palm slipped off her hip. She recovered quickly, casually bringing her hand back up to tuck in her plum-colored silk blouse. She was pretty pleased with her swift reflexes, until she realized her mouth was still open. She clamped it shut.

Gail nudged her from behind.

Jolie jumped, then said, "Hello, Byron." As she swept

past him, she pointedly looked at his bow tie. "Nice wrapping, but Christmas isn't for another nine months."

He chuckled as she led with her lifted chin into his apartment. She shrugged out of the light coat draping her shoulders, carefully refraining from making eye contact with the stranger, who was undoubtedly Mike Kramer.

Quick as lightning, the man lifted the coat from her and passed it to Byron.

"Hi, you must be Julie," he said.

"Jolie," Gail and Byron corrected in unison.

"Oh, right. Sorry." He grinned. A faint dimple creased his right cheek. "I'm Mike Kramer."

When he pressed his palm into hers, it was warm and slightly callused. And big. Her fingers could barely curve around his hand. She let go and forced a smile. This guy was far too gorgeous to be taken seriously. He looked as if he'd just stepped off the pages of a calendar.

"So, you're looking for a pretend wife, huh?" She found she had to tilt her head back considerably to look up at him.

He blinked, surprise registering briefly in his eyes. Byron groaned and Mike glanced at him before turning back to study her. "Yeah. And I hear you need a husband." His gaze left her face to drift down to her chest, her waist, her hips.

She shifted her weight from one foot to the other. "About as much as I need a bad case of the flu."

His amused eyes met hers again, one corner of his mouth lifting. "Then we ought to get along just fine."

"I'll let you know." She slipped her purse strap off her shoulder so she'd have something to do with her hands.

"I'll take that," Gail said, and hurried to grab the leather bag, giving Jolie a furtive evil eye at the same time.

Jolie made a face back. She was going to kill her friend. She'd make sure it was a slow, painful death. Even if this guy was serious about this phony marriage, nobody would believe it. She'd look like Frankenstein's monster next to him. No way was she setting herself up for this.

"So…can I get everyone a drink?" Byron rubbed his hands together, his gaze darting between them as he headed to the bar. "The usual for you, Jolie?"

"A glass of Pouilly-Fuissé, please," she said primly.

He frowned and exchanged a surprised look with Gail. "I think there's a bottle in the kitchen. Gail, would you?"

"Sure," Gail said.

"I'll help." Jolie scrambled after her.

"Oh, no. You stay and—"

Jolie's squinty-eyed, meaningful stare stopped her cold.

"How nice of you," Gail amended right before she and her phony smile disappeared through the swinging doors.

Jolie glanced briefly at Mike, lounging near the plate-glass window, his expression watchful. She took a quick breath and pushed through after her friend.

"Are you crazy?" Jolie whispered loudly as soon as she was reasonably sure they couldn't be overheard.

Gail opened the state-of-the-art chrome refrigerator and yanked out a bottle of wine. "I tried to warn you outside."

"This isn't going to work." She grabbed the corkscrew out of one of the polished chrome drawers.

"I tried to tell you that this afternoon."

Jolie's mouth dropped open. "You'd already met him?"

"Of course not. I meant, I knew it wasn't going to work from the start."

"Yeah, well it's worse now." She took the wine from her friend and plopped herself down on a black lacquer bistro chair. After wrapping the chilled bottle with a linen towel, she tucked it between her knees and tackled the cork. "What is he, some kind of model or something?"

"I don't know, but he should be." Gail sank onto the opposite chair and, propping her elbow on the glass table, supported her chin with her palm. "Have you ever seen eyes that blue? And that cleft in his chin. God, if it weren't for Byron, that man could eat crackers in my bed anytime."

Jolie rolled her eyes. "He's probably dumber than a box of rocks."

"Who cares?"

Jolie groaned and tugged at the cork. It wouldn't budge at first, then, as she gave it an impatient yank, it exploded from the bottle with a loud pop. Tiny particles of cork crumbled and drifted back into the wine and onto her blouse.

"Great," she mumbled, dusting herself off. When she looked up, she saw Gail staring into space, a silly smile on her face. "Uh, excuse me, but could you save your erotic dreams for later and help me figure out what I'm going to say to this guy."

"What's keeping you two?" Byron poked his head through the swinging doors. "Dinner will be delivered any minute now."

Both women started at the unexpected sound of his voice. "We'll be right there," Gail said and rose from her chair.

Jolie reluctantly got up, too, and stopped to pull a crystal goblet out of the glass display case. She poured herself a healthy portion of the dry white wine, then, leaving the bottle behind, followed Gail back out to the living room.

Byron had been talking when they arrived, but he lapsed into a brief silence before embarking on a dissertation about the unusually cool spring they were having in New York.

Standing near the window overlooking Central Park, Mike indulged him for several minutes. But as soon as there was a break in the conversation, he sauntered over near Jolie. He pulled one of the dining-room chairs away from the table, turned it around and straddled it facing her.

"How much do you know about yachts?" he asked, forcing a stubborn lock of hair off his forehead, his intense blue eyes trained squarely on her.

Uncomfortable, she tried to look past him out the wide expansive window and succeeded only in noticing that his eyes were bluer than the sky framing his sun-streaked hair.

"I was practically raised on them," she said finally.

Frowning, he glanced at Byron. "Good." Then he ran his gaze down her body, his attention resting briefly on her small breasts. "What kind of shape are you in?"

She blinked. "Pardon me?"

"You look soft." He leaned forward, lifted a hand and, before she knew what was happening, he squeezed her biceps. "Not bad. Better than I thought. How tall are you? About five-one?"

Stunned, Jolie stared into his eyes. They were close. Too close. His long fingers easily circled her entire arm, and they lingered, pressing the silk of her blouse into her skin. Recovering her shaken senses, she twisted away, wine sloshing over the sides of her glass and blossoming into a wet spot on her cream-colored slacks. "What on earth are you doing? This isn't a slave auction. What next—checking to see if I have all my teeth?"

Mike's hand fell away. "Crewing a yacht requires a lot of physical work. I need to be sure you're up to it."

"You just worry about yourself." She slid a look at Gail. Her friend's eyes were the size of saucers. Byron pressed his lips together.

"Can you cook?" Mike asked.

Indignation stole her breath. "Of course."

Gail coughed.

Byron cleared his throat.

Mike's eyebrows furrowed. "Gourmet stuff?"

"You name it, I'll cook it."

He nodded. "Good. The Longfellows will expect full-course meals."

A buzzer sounded and Byron said, "Speaking of which, I believe our dinner has arrived."

He left to let in the delivery person, while Gail and Jolie finished setting the table.

Within minutes they were seated around plates of beef Wellington, parsleyed new potatoes and Caesar salad. Jolie noticed that although Byron and Gail carefully kept the conversation neutral throughout dinner, Mike seemed aware of every move she made.

She sipped her wine, feeling an awful lot like a laboratory rat. The intensity of his scrutiny made her wonder exactly why this job was so important to him. But the ground rules had been established early on. She couldn't ask the many questions buzzing around in her head.

Draining the rest of her wine, she stood. "Can I get anyone a refill?" Before Gail could decline, Jolie covertly angled her head toward the kitchen.

"I could use one." Gail jumped up and grabbed Mike's glass, too.

"None for me..." he said, his voice trailing away as she hurried after Jolie.

"It's not going to work," Jolie said, making sure the kitchen door was adequately closed.

"I've changed my mind. I think it will," Gail said.

"No, it won't." Shaking her head, she pulled out the bottle of Pouilly-Fuissé. "He wears earrings."

"No, he doesn't."

"He has a hole in his left ear."

Gail massaged her temple. "I didn't see anything. It's probably a mole."

"No. I'm sure it's a hole."

"So what?"

"I can't pretend to be married to a guy who wears earrings." Jolie refilled her glass and took too big a sip. Sputtering, she returned the wine to the refrigerator.

"He's not wearing one."

"Some day he will. And who knows what it'll look like. It may be some big obnoxious diamond."

Gail gave her a wry look. "Are you forgetting how your family made their millions?" She strode to the door. "I'm leaving now."

Jolie took another sip and hurried after her.

The conversation progressed amicably enough for the next ten minutes, considering how carefully everyone skirted around any information that would reveal too much. Jolie could tell Mike was consciously refraining from asking more personal questions, probably due to some counsel from Byron. She said very little herself. Although her thoughts were traveling at the speed of light and, no matter who was speaking, her gaze constantly ended up on Mike's slightly crooked but full mouth and the deep cleft beneath it.

"So, Jolie..." Mike finally turned his intense blue gaze on her again, and she raised her eyes to his, mentally bracing herself. "Think you can handle a month out at sea?"

"No problem."

"I understand we'll stop at only three ports."

She sipped, nodded.

"I imagine the yacht is pretty large, but we'll be in fairly cramped quarters." He propped his elbow on the table and rested his chin on his palm, his eyes watchful.

She shrugged, unconcerned.

"Of course they'll expect us to share a cabin."

She drained her glass and stood. The room did a half spin. "Anyone care for a refill?"

Mike narrowed his gaze on her and shook his head.

Gail caught Jolie's look and automatically got up to follow her, while Byron frowned in confusion.

"It's not going to work," Jolie said as soon as they were in the kitchen.

"Why not now?" Gail got the bottle of wine out of the refrigerator and handed it to her.

"He wears a ponytail."

Gail cast a long-suffering glance at the ceiling. "How would you know?"

"His hair is long enough. Besides, I think I see a ridge where a rubber band may have been."

"That doesn't mean he wears a ponytail."

"Yeah, but some day he may wear one." Jolie poured, shook her head, then sipped. "I can't pretend to be married to a guy who wears a ponytail."

"Enough wine already. You're getting sloshed. He's not the ponytail type." Gail turned for the door. "I'm leaving now."

Jolie stared pensively into her glass of pale yellow liquid. She watched a remnant of cork do the back float. Gail was right. She was getting drunk. Or so it seemed. She'd never been drunk before.

She looked up at the swinging doors and, spilling half her wine, she scrambled after her friend.

Mike was the first to look her way as she swayed back to find that they had moved into the living room. Distaste clouded his handsome face as he looked her up and down. Her chin came up and she nearly tripped over the Oriental rug.

Mike jumped to his feet and grabbed her upper arm. She allowed her arm to go limp and angled her head back to stare up into his sinfully beautiful face.

"Are you all right?" he asked.

"I, uh—" Her vision shimmied, then settled on the cleft in his chin. When she stared a moment too long, his lips started to curve. "I'll be right back." She set down her goblet on the glass end table and made a full turn in the direction of the kitchen.

Gail dutifully leaped to her feet over Byron's protest and followed.

"What now?" her friend demanded as the kitchen doors swung shut behind them.

"It's not going to work."

"Why?"

"He's too tall."

Gail grinned. "For what?"

Jolie blinked. "I'm leaving now." She grabbed the partial bottle of wine and pushed through the doors with Gail close behind.

Mike hadn't returned to his seat. His hands were stuffed into the pockets of his khakis, his eyes narrowed on her.

"Mr. Kramer?" she began, then realized she was waving the bottle of wine around. She set it next to her glass. "Mike, about this phony marriage…"

"Phony marriage?" Mike frowned at Byron. "Lady, that's about the only thing that won't be phony. If you're in, we have an appointment with a justice of the peace tomorrow."

Chapter Two

"Justice of the peace? Tomorrow?" Jolie sank onto her chair. Slowly, she raised her gaze to his expressionless face. "You mean I'd have to say 'I do' for real?"

"For a month anyway." Mike withdrew his hands from his pockets and went behind the bar to pull out another beer.

"Why? We can just say we're married." She glanced at Gail, who shrugged.

He shook his head. "I don't want to take any chances. They may ask for proof and I don't want any foul-ups that could knock us out of the running."

"What if they don't offer us the job?"

"They will."

Jolie watched him tip the bottle to his lips, and couldn't help but wonder about him. She envied him his confidence and poise. The way he seemed so certain of himself, of achieving his goal. Of course, with looks like his, some of that confidence was probably automatic. She wouldn't know.

Even in his slightly faded, navy blue shirt, he would have been a better match for either of her sisters. Not plain-Jane Jolie. But Monique and Nicole didn't need jobs. Grandfather hadn't threatened to withhold their trust funds. Jolie figured her beautiful, charming sisters had earned their financial security by merely existing.

"What makes you so certain we'll get the job?" she asked.

"Let's just say I managed to stack the odds in our favor."

"How?"

Mike set down his beer, the corners of his mouth lifting wryly. "You don't need to know that. Are you in or out?"

Jolie moistened her suddenly dry lips. It wasn't as though she had a whole lot of choice. She needed her inheritance. She didn't know how to do anything that could earn her a living. Working at the shelter didn't count. Besides, her family didn't—and couldn't—know about her moonlighting there.

She looked at Byron and Gail for reassurance. His wary eyes trained on Mike, Byron fidgeted with his bow tie. Great. That was certainly confidence-inspiring. Gail gave her an enthusiastic nod. But then again, Gail was all agog over Adonis here, Jolie thought as her eyes returned to Mike.

He was rubbing his jaw, his long, lean fingers looking entirely too sensual as they stroked the beard-roughened skin. Oh, hell. Could she blame her friend? She retrieved the glass she'd abandoned and took a long satisfying sip. The wine skipped her stomach and went straight to her head.

"Okay," she said. "You've got yourself a deal."

"Good." Mike nodded, all business. "We meet at the courthouse tomorrow morning at ten. Since the ad will appear tomorrow night, we'll respond first thing the next morning. In the meantime, I suggest we get to know each other."

Jolie nearly spit out her next sip. "What do you mean?"

"Like maybe you cook dinner for me tomorrow night so I can check out your culinary skills."

"You let me worry about that," Jolie snapped, ignoring Gail's coughing attack.

"In fact, I think we ought to spend the day together. The last thing we need to do is to act like strangers during the interview."

"I suppose you're right." She took another sip.

Mike lifted an eyebrow. "And you've got to lay off the wine."

She defiantly tipped her glass to her lips and drained the contents, then started to get up. "You'll learn very quickly, Mr. Kramer, that telling me what..."

The room spun in slow motion and Jolie grabbed for the arm of the chair. Only it didn't have one. She wobbled uncertainly for a moment, and then his large hand gripped her forearm.

"I'll take her home," she vaguely heard Mike say, "and sober her up."

She thought briefly about protesting, but when he scooped her up in his arms and cradled her to his chest, Jolie sighed, closed her eyes and snuggled against him.

MIKE OPENED the last cupboard and shook his head. Either the woman couldn't cook worth a lick or she never ate. The sum total of her supplies was a pot, a skillet, two plates and two glasses. In the pantry sat a lone jar of peanut butter—extra chunky—and small, restaurant-style packets of strawberry jelly. He was glad he hadn't found any wine. The last thing he needed was a lush blowing things, though Byron had assured him he had nothing to worry about in that department.

He supposed it wasn't fair or ethical to go through her things while she slept off the wine, especially in view of their agreement to ask no questions of each other, but he'd gotten one too many mixed signals from Jolie and that had him worried. He couldn't afford to screw up this opportunity to get his hands on the diamonds.

When he'd first seen the small snapshot of her, he'd figured she'd be the perfect candidate to pose as his wife. Lola Longfellow didn't like competition. If a woman was too pretty or too sexy, she didn't have a chance at working for the Longfellows, temporarily or otherwise.

Now that Mike had met Jolie in person, he was a little concerned. Pictures didn't do her justice. Although she wasn't pretty or sexy in the usual way, she was cute, with intelligent brown eyes and enough spirit for three women.

He smiled, thinking about how she'd tried to explain to him how capable she was of getting herself home…right before she fell sound asleep against his shoulder in the cab.

It had taken little effort for him to carry her slight body up to the simple third-floor apartment and deposit her onto the plain white sheets of her sofa bed. Although the apartment was on a fairly decent side of town, it was obvious that Jolie spent all her money on rent. The efficiency was sparsely furnished with one yellow director's chair and a foldout bed. Merely a half dozen items hung in her tiny walk-in closet, although the few things she did have were quality pieces. He knew that for certain. Hell, it was his business to recognize that kind of thing. He needed to know if items were worth stealing or not.

He poked around a little more, wondering how she knew Byron. The rich usually stuck to their own kind. The ones Mike knew were more interested in manipulating the have-nots than befriending them. Byron had been different, he reminded himself. Although Mike had been dirt poor when he'd met Byron nearly twenty years ago, he'd had something Byron wanted. Which pretty much brought everything around full circle. The rich were a different breed, oblivious to those less fortunate, unless they served some function for them.

Best-forgotten memories clutched at his insides and Angela automatically came to mind. Muttering a curse, he leaned over the sink. He turned on the tap and splashed his face with cool water. Calm down, he ordered himself. Reliving the past did no good. He had to stay focused, find Lola's diamonds and make his move.

THE INSIDE of Jolie's eyelids felt like sandpaper. Her dehydrated tongue felt even worse. She tried to swallow but every formerly working part in her mouth felt freeze-dried in place. If she hadn't known better, she might have thought that someone had stuffed her full of cotton balls.

She took a deep breath and allowed one eye to squint open. The window blinds were partially slanted and graypink light streamed across her face and pillow. She inched back so that a strip of dawn fell across her nose rather than her too sensitive eyes. Only then did she force her other lid open.

Arching her back, she stretched toward the low, unfamiliar, white ceiling and then it dawned on her where she was. She was in the small studio apartment she'd rented only a month ago. The one her family didn't know about.

She frowned.

The one she'd used for only one night before now.

Warily, she pushed herself to a sitting position, searching her foggy memory. The scene at Byron's apartment began forming. Mike Kramer. The cab ride.

Swallowing painfully, her throat still horribly dry, she

picked up the cover sheet, peeked underneath and groaned. A plain cotton bra and unimaginative white panties were all she wore.

"Oh, God." Her brain scrambled for recollection. Had he put her to bed? Or had she undressed herself? How was she going to face him today without remembering?

She looked around the bed for her clothes, a clue. Nothing. Then she saw the pillow. Not her mangled pillow. The other one. The one perfectly shaped, except for the indentation. Of someone's head.

The breath left Jolie's lungs with a whoosh. She tried to swing out of bed, but her legs tangled in the sheets, her hands getting caught in the mess. Before she was able to disengage herself and get to the closet, she heard whistling coming from the small kitchen.

She stilled for several seconds, listening, sniffing the aroma of coffee wafting from the direction of the sound, then made a beeline for the bathroom. She was going to strangle Mike Kramer...if the pounding in her head didn't get her first.

After taking a shower in record-breaking time, she slipped into an old pair of jeans and a peach cashmere sweater. She didn't bother with makeup or blow-drying her hair. Instead, she stormed out of the bathroom and ran smack into Mike's broad chest.

"Watch out." He drew back the plastic-foam cup he was holding. Some of the dark java splashed onto his hand and he uttered a succinct but colorful word.

"What do you think you're doing?" One hand installed itself on her hip.

"Too much, obviously." He thrust the cup at her and winced when another dark wave surfaced over the rim and splattered his knuckles. "Here's your damn coffee."

Lifting her chin, she folded her arms across her chest.

She was one of those people who could take or leave coffee.

He opened his other hand. Two white tablets sat in the middle of his palm. On the other hand, aspirin she couldn't afford to thumb her nose at.

Another annoying pain pulsed in her temples and she meekly uncrossed her arms and accepted both offerings.

She took a tentative sip and frowned. "How can I take these? This coffee is too hot."

"Blow."

His gaze rested on her mouth, and Jolie felt an unreasonable, hot trill of excitement shoot through her. The look wasn't sexual exactly. It was basically unsympathetic. But its intensity knocked her equilibrium off by ten degrees.

His attention wandered up to her eyes. "Did you just move in, or what? You don't even have coffee. I had to go to the corner to get this."

"Had I invited you in the first place, I might have been prepared."

Mike grinned at her clipped tone. It took her aback and she realized she hadn't actually seen him smile yet. Not in good humor, anyway.

"Had I known I had to baby-sit, I'd have brought my toothbrush. But don't worry." He held up a hand. "I got that at the corner store, too."

She flushed, then blurted, "You slept with me."

His gaze briefly ran the length of her body. "There was only one bed."

"No one asked you to stay."

"True enough. Not that you were capable of it."

His attention fell to her mouth again, and for the first time it occurred to her that something physical could have happened between them last night.

She shoved the thought away. The idea was ridiculous. She wasn't his type. She didn't have the kind of looks that would hold his attention for a nanosecond. She was merely annoyed that he'd been so bold and presumptuous by undressing her and putting her to bed. Still, the way he was looking at her…

She ducked from his obsession with her mouth and fiddled with the hem of her sweater. "About last night," she began, "did anything, um, you know, did anything…"

She looked up to find him staring blankly at her. His brows furrowed together, and he rubbed his unshaved jaw. Then, as recognition dawned, his eyes widened briefly before crinkling at the corners, and he laughed.

"Of course not." He put a hand out to her. She wasn't sure why. Probably to take the coffee.

But she slapped it away and dived for the bathroom, afraid he'd see the humiliation brimming in her eyes. How stupid could she be to think that someone like him had been attracted to her?

"Jolie?" Mike rapped at the closed bathroom door. "I swear nothing happened."

"I believe you. Go away." She looked into the mirror and scrubbed at the smudges of black she missed earlier beneath her lower lashes.

"Jolie?"

She didn't answer.

After several minutes of humbling silence, she heard the front door close. She took a few more shaky minutes to collect herself, then calmly proceeded to get ready for her wedding day.

"I WONDER IF he'll bring you flowers," Gail said as she fussed with Jolie's collar.

"Oh, please." She glanced at the courthouse clock and

wondered if he were going to show up at all. "Are you sure Byron didn't say anything about last night?"

Gail's hands fell away from the collar and she stared solemnly at Jolie. "That's the third time you asked me that. Are *you* sure there's nothing you want to tell me?"

"Not a thing." She looked away. "I still don't understand why you let him take me home."

"He was very persistent. Anyway, Byron trusts him. At least we remembered to give him directions to your apartment. He doesn't know anything about your family."

"Thank God. Can you imagine how many questions he'd have had thrown at him if he'd taken me to Grandfather's?"

"I don't understand why you don't move out of the old coot's estate once and for all. You can certainly afford a better apartment than the one you've rented," her friend said, doing nothing to hide the sarcasm in her voice.

"If I don't get this job, I won't even be able to afford the efficiency," Jolie shot back. "Besides, I like being near the shelter and it's enough space for only me. And don't call Grandfather an old coot. He's the only sane person in my family."

"Right. Marrying you off just so you can keep your trust fund?"

"He doesn't know about the marriage part. No one can know. As far as my family is concerned, I'll be on vacation."

"They'll wonder why you aren't working instead."

"Are you kidding? When have they ever given me a second thought?" Jolie clamped her mouth shut. She hadn't meant to say that, although there was hardly a secret between them.

Gail smiled sadly, and tactfully let the comment slide. "Just think. Within ten minutes, you'll be a married woman.'' At Jolie's grimace, her smile widened. ''Couldn't you have found something a little nicer to wear for your wedding day?''

Wedding day? The words sounded strange to Jolie as she suddenly recalled Monique's lavish church affair last year, complete with adoring groom and approving parents. She shoved aside the unexpected wistfulness crowding her good sense and rolled her eyes. But she couldn't help peeking down at her plain gray slacks and burgundy sweater.

''This is fine,'' she said, dusting off her pants, not because they needed it, but because she couldn't quite look Gail in the eye yet. A stupid, irrational melancholy had stolen over her, and she suddenly hoped Mike did bring her some token flowers.

''Here they come.'' Gail tugged at her sleeve.

Jolie looked over her shoulder. Mike strolled purposely down the corridor toward her with Byron a step behind. They were nearly the same height, which put Mike a hair under six feet, but he was far broader in the shoulders than Byron, and his hair was unfashionably long. His khakis were a little too lightweight for the chilly March air, and she noted he wore no socks.

He also had no flowers.

It didn't matter. This was business. She knew that.

''I hope you weren't waiting long.'' Mike stopped beside her and held out his hand for her to precede him. If he was upset about what had happened earlier this morning, he showed no sign. He merely smiled and added, ''I forgot how nasty New York traffic can be even at this time of the day. Shall we?''

Jolie nodded, and was glad that Gail automatically fell in step beside her as they headed into the justice of the peace's office.

The local magistrate was not a him but a her. Nor was she the older, gray-hair so often depicted in movies. She looked to be in her mid-thirties with flaming red hair and black-rimmed, no-nonsense glasses. As soon as the four-some entered her office, she looked up from her paper-work and smiled, her eyes quickly finding Mike.

"I'm Margaret Wilcox. I'll be performing the cere-mony. Who is the lucky couple?" she asked, her gaze scanning their faces, a frown beginning to pucker her fore-head.

Mike immediately stepped forward, dragging Jolie with him. "We are," he said, smiling as he stuck out his free hand. "I'm Mike Kramer."

Margaret Wilcox smiled back, whipping off her glasses at the same time. The scene was so comically cliché it made Jolie want to gag. So, Gail wasn't the only woman he could make a fool of. And here he was, about to be a married man.

Jolie stood a little straighter and waited for the woman to let go of his hand. When she did, Jolie shook hers as well, while Mike finished the introductions.

She was glad, Jolie told herself as she signed some papers and nodded at the instructions given her, that this wasn't a real marriage. Being married to someone as good-looking as Mike would be difficult at best. It'd been trying enough living in the shadows of her sisters most of her life. Having such a stunning husband would be the final insult.

She tried to remember that, as the justice recited words of love, commitment and honor. She didn't dare look at Mike. If she did, she might tell him to forget the whole thing. Because as much as she would have liked to deny it, she was one of those silly women who found him dan-gerously attractive. And for that reason alone, she was not only going to stay at arm's length from him but at ship's length if she could manage it.

"You're now husband and wife," the magistrate said, closing her book. "Kiss all you want."

Jolie blinked at the woman. She didn't even remember saying "I do." She felt Mike's gaze on her, felt him take her elbow, and her pulse burst into erratic chaos. Swallowing a lump of nerves the size of Manhattan, she slowly turned toward him.

He smiled down at her, his eyes bluer than the azure shirt he wore beneath his navy jacket. His sun-streaked hair was swept back from his face, the bottom long and curling, resting on his collar.

She lifted her chin, her tongue darting out to moisten the corners of her mouth.

His smile widened slightly until the dimple appeared. He ran his hand up her arm to her shoulder...and patted her sleeve. Then he gave her arm a light squeeze, and turned back to the justice. "We have more papers to sign now, don't we?"

Margaret Wilcox flicked a perplexed look between them before moving to her credenza. "Right this way."

Jolie bit her lip. The nausea she'd felt earlier from last night's overindulgence threatened her coiled stomach. Was she really that big a fool? What had she expected him to do? She slid a sideways look at Gail but her friend was talking to Byron.

"It's your turn." Mike held up a pen to her.

She covered the short distance between them with surprising poise and took the pen. She leaned over the official document and paused.

Misunderstanding her hesitation, the justice pointed to the line below Mike's lazy scrawl. "Right here, Mrs. Kramer."

Jolie straightened, and cast a quick glance at Mike. "I'm keeping my name," she murmured.

"What?"

Her eyebrows rose. "This is the nineties."

"Not as far as the Longfellows are concerned. You're using Kramer."

"As long as we have this piece of paper, I don't see that it matters," she insisted, her voice raising a notch.

"Would you excuse us?" Charm oozed from Mike's smile as he nodded to a frowning Margaret Wilcox. He grabbed Jolie's arm and gently pulled her to the side. The smile disappeared when he turned his impatient blue eyes on her. "Why are you being so stubborn? It's only a name. And for chrissake, it's only temporary."

"Then change yours."

"Mine?"

"Sure." She folded her arms. "It's only temporary."

Pursing his lips, he stared out the window for a full minute. Although there was nothing to see but an ugly, gray, soot-covered building across the street. "Okay," he said finally and plucked the pen from her fingers, then headed toward the credenza.

Within seconds he'd added Duval behind Kramer and handed the pen back to her.

Dazedly, Jolie signed her name below his.

"Now..." He turned to her, his smile returning, its brilliance reaching his eyes. "Time for the honeymoon."

Chapter Three

Mike had no idea why Jolie was so jumpy. She had been ever since the ceremony this morning and right on through their lunch with Gail and Byron.

When he'd asked her to go for a walk with him in Central Park shortly after they'd eaten, she'd nearly torn his head off. Then she haughtily informed him that she did have a life to get back to.

He rubbed his tired eyes and sank onto the hotel bed. He had time for a quick nap, which he seriously needed after the restless night he'd had. Jolie's bed had been small and uncomfortable and, frankly, he knew he'd had no business helping himself to her unoffered hospitality.

His only defense was that he'd hung around hoping she'd get up, giving them time to plan their strategy. He'd also been dead tired and jet-lagged. Except that once he'd lain down beside her, his brain and body fell out of sync, and his thoughts started buzzing like summer lightning.

He wondered if she knew that she sighed in her sleep. That they were low, sensual sounds that whispered in the dark. Except when she'd rolled close, snuggling up to him. Then she'd begun purring like a well-loved cat.

Mike had taken her unconscious seduction pretty well. Until she'd stripped.

He'd known at the time that the apartment seemed warm. But he'd figured it was him. But then Jolie had started kicking off the covers, pulling at the neck of her blouse until she'd finally stripped down to her underwear. Remembering that she was no fan of Frederick's of Hollywood, he smiled.

He knew for certain that she'd been sleepy and slightly inebriated and totally unaware of what she'd been doing. But that didn't erase her well-defined calves, her toned thighs, the firm swell of her breasts, from his memory.

Damn. Sighing loudly, he punched his pillow. The last thing he needed was to be attracted to this woman. What he did need was an hour's nap before he went back to her apartment for dinner. He only hoped that she cooked as well as she slept.

He jabbed at the alarm clock button, then rolled over. He had serious work ahead of him...stealing diamonds was no laughing matter.

"WHERE ARE YOU GOING with that silver platter, young lady?"

Jolie had great reflexes. She could stop on a dime, and she did. She turned toward Sylvester Pillbury's tobacco-roughened voice and gave him an angelic smile. "Hi, Grandfather. Why aren't you taking your nap?"

"Good thing I wasn't. What are you sneaking around with that for? Pretending you can cook?" He howled at his less-than-entertaining joke.

"I'm not sneaking around. And don't worry. I'm not stealing the family silver. I need this for my new job."

"I don't give a hoot about the family silver," he grumbled as he came closer, peering at her over his round, wire-rimmed glasses.

Jolie knew that much for sure. He didn't give a hoot

about money, period. He just happened to have a lot of it. But that was what puzzled her so much. Why was he suddenly making her scramble for the few million Grandmother had left her?

"Sorry I can't stop to chat..." she began, and knew she'd made a mistake when he narrowed his eyes and stroked his long white beard. He'd keep her for a good fifteen minutes longer just because he thought she was hiding something. And all because she'd used the word chat. Damn. She never used that word.

"Gertrude," he bellowed down the long hall that led to the kitchen. "Bring us some tea."

"You know Mother doesn't like you yelling," she reminded him, hiding a grin.

"Then she should have married someone with money, instead of more blue blood than common sense. Then she could afford her own damn house and wouldn't have to listen to me yell. Sit down, girlie." He pointed toward the sitting room, then cupped the side of his mouth with one hand. "Gertrude? Did you hear me?"

"The whole block heard you, sir." Gertrude bustled past, coming from the east-wing guest rooms. She slowed when she saw Jolie. "Your bed wasn't slept in," she said in a bland voice, then kept walking toward the kitchen.

Jolie hesitated, facing the French doors to the sitting room, and stared at the white marble fireplace. She'd never lied to Grandfather before and she hated starting now. But she was too embarrassed to admit to what extreme she was going in order to gain her trust fund. Especially since, after dinner tonight, the entire deal might be off. Posing as Mike Kramer's wife was too...

Her thoughts skidded, then somersaulted. She grinned to herself. Mike *Duval*'s wife, she amended. In any case, the whole mess was beginning to sound as appealing as a cold shower in subzero temperatures.

"Why not?" Her grandfather walked past her, frowning all the way to his favorite leather recliner.

She started, then remembered he was asking where she'd been last night. "I was with Gail."

"All night?"

This time her only hesitation was a deep breath. "We went to a film fest."

"That pay anything?" he asked, leaning back and resting his hands on his plaid-flanneled paunch.

She sighed. "I have a job."

"When did you start this one?"

"You don't need to know that." She gripped the edges of the silver platter. "You only need to know when I've completed my thirty days and I bring you my pay stub."

He nodded. "You haven't got much time."

She didn't need to be reminded. She studied the marks her fingers made on the silver, trying to keep herself from asking why he was doing this to her. Why he wasn't issuing the same ultimatum to Monique and Nicole?

Jolie and her grandfather had always been close. If it hadn't been for him, she would have wondered if she'd been adopted. While her mother and sisters had attended one social event after another, she and Grandfather had been content to amuse themselves with checkers and card games. Although he'd made a fortune mining diamonds, he was a simple man who still remembered the Louisiana shanty where he was raised some eighty years ago.

So why was he testing her? Did he think she took his money for granted? That thought hurt. Surely he knew that wasn't the case. He knew her better than anyone. Yet she had her secrets and reasons, too. So she had respected his and asked no questions.

"You're right, Grandfather." Instead of taking a chair, she bent to kiss his cheek. "I don't have much time. I've got to run now."

"Wait a minute. What about your tea?"

"No time." She blew him another kiss from the doorway and hurried down the hall.

"Fudge. Gertrude is gonna chew my hide...."

She laughed at his mutterings as she made her escape before her sisters returned from their pedicures. While she waited for a cab near the corner, she pulled out her cellular phone and dialed the number she knew by heart.

"Roberto?" She smiled when her favorite waiter immediately recognized her voice. "I need to have dinner delivered no later than six-thirty." She paused while he wrote down her usual order and wondered if she had time for a crash cooking course tomorrow. At the least she'd pick up a couple of cookbooks. She already knew how to flip burgers. "No," she said. "This time, make that for two."

She grinned as she disconnected the call. And Mike thought she didn't know how to cook.

As soon as Jolie opened the door to let him in, a whiff of butter and garlic greeted Mike. He sniffed the heavenly-scented aromas and his sudden hunger was overcome only by a sense of relief. The woman obviously knew her way around the kitchen.

"Italian?" he asked as he entered the tiny apartment and shrugged out of his jacket.

She lifted a shoulder. "A little Italian. A little French."

He followed her to the kitchen that was really too small for the two of them. She looked nervous, making him wonder if he was crowding her. He stepped back a little. "Need any help?"

"I've got everything under control." She opened the oven and peered inside.

He craned his neck to get a look but she slammed the door shut. Then she reached into the cupboard, on tiptoes, her cream-colored skirt riding high on her thighs.

Mike vaguely realized that he should offer to help her, but he was too stunned to form the words. For a short little thing, she had surprisingly long—and very shapely—legs. True, he'd gotten a peek at them last night, but it had been dark and she'd been curled up and he'd honestly tried not to take advantage of the situation by looking at her as much as he'd have liked to.

But now, standing there in her three-inch heels, those sleek, toned legs were giving his heart a hell of a good workout.

"Uh, Mike? I think I pushed the plates too far back. Could you…?"

He tore his gaze away from her legs. Barely. Her cheeks were tinged with pink and he knew he'd been busted. "Sure."

He advanced and reached over her before she could step away. Her hair had a fresh herbal scent to it.

"Thanks." She moved to the far end of the narrow room and gestured for him to leave the plates on the counter.

"Can I do anything else to help?"

"No. We can eat in five minutes. I'm afraid it'll have to be on our laps though."

"No problem." He looked around at the immaculate counters. Only a pot sat in the sink. "You sure are a neat cook. You've cleaned up already."

She blinked. "Yeah, I like to clean up as I go. Uh, you want a beer?" She spun toward the refrigerator, opened the door and pulled out his favorite import—the same kind he'd drunk at Byron's. "If you want wine, you'll have to go to the corner market."

He grinned. Good sign. "Right. I know the one."

She scowled at him before passing him the green bottle. He didn't blame her when she shoved it at him. He supposed he deserved that for bringing up last night. But she deserved the ribbing, too. She wasn't supposed to have great legs. Damn it.

"So...how does it feel to be married?" He twisted the cap off and opened the cupboard door under the sink.

"Hold it." Jolie's eyes rounded as she stood frozen, both hands up, her gaze darting to the lower cabinet.

Mike froze, too. Though he wasn't sure why. Only his eyes moved as he looked from side to side. "Why?"

"It's so...so messy down there." She scooted toward him and grabbed the cap out of his hand.

"Isn't that where you keep the garbage?"

She nodded.

He cocked his head to the side and frowned. "It's supposed to be...messy."

"That doesn't mean company has to see it." She tugged at his arm, her short, well-manicured nails digging into his cotton shirt. "Now, go sit down before dinner is burned."

"Shouldn't we serve ourselves from here?" He trudged slowly toward the door while she put a considerable amount of weight into pushing him out.

"I'll serve you."

"Hell, I should have gotten married a long time ago."

She glared at him, then smiled...a forced one to be sure. As soon as they cleared the doorway, she gave him a final nudge, then let go and said, "I'll be right back."

Mike ignored the yellow director's chair in favor of the pullout bed, which had been returned to a couch. He arranged himself on the uncomfortable piece of furniture and wondered what was making Jolie so edgy. Probably the interview tomorrow, he reasoned. And then he remembered that he hadn't told her it had actually been set up. He had called the Longfellows' secretary after they'd parted that afternoon.

No wonder she was jumpy. She didn't know what was going on. He looked around the sparse apartment. The poor kid probably really needed this job. He got to his feet and at the door to the kitchen was about to tell her the news when she saw him.

She dropped the Mickey Mouse pot holder. And with her body, blocked a silver platter heaped with pasta. "What do you want now?" she snapped.

"Excuse me for living. I thought you'd like to know that we have an interview set up with the Longfellows tomorrow morning." He shook his head. "What the hell is wrong with you?"

"Here. Your plate is ready." She passed him a dish with mounds of mouth-watering food on it.

The aromas dancing under his nose were enough to do some serious damage to his thought process, and he decided to drop the subject. "This looks and smells incredible." He glanced at her with awe and admiration. "Too bad the interview doesn't include a cooking sample. We'd get the job hands down."

"Yeah." She cleared her throat. "Too bad."

"Are you coming?"

She reached behind her and grabbed another plate. "I'm right behind you."

After they'd settled down and were well into dinner, he brought up the subject of the interview again. "I'm not really sure what they'll ask. Questions that pertain to the yacht itself, I'll field."

Jolie poked at her pasta. He noticed she still had a considerable amount of food on her plate, whereas he'd polished off most of his. He only half hoped she'd made dessert. He was nearly filled to his limit. Although a little chocolate would be nice. Nah. She wouldn't have had time.

"I know a lot about yachts, too," she said.

"I bet not as much as you know about cooking." He set his plate on the small antique end table and was vaguely surprised to realize it was an expensive piece. "I've got to say you outdid yourself. That was a fantastic dinner. Where did you learn to cook like that?"

She jumped up. "How about dessert?"

"I underestimated you."

She smiled.

"Can we wait a little while? Then I'll go get some coffee to go with it."

"Sure." She hesitated a moment instead of resuming her place on the director's chair.

Mike moved over and patted the couch next to him. "Why don't you sit here?"

"This is fine." She dropped to the chair like a concrete anchor.

He sighed. Just as he'd thought, she was afraid of him. He cursed himself for his poor judgment last night. He'd had no business staying in her bed. She didn't know him. She didn't know that he would have never taken advantage of her. He'd been amazed this morning that she'd even thought he'd be capable of forcing himself on her when she'd been too woozy to consent. But other than the fact that he was Byron's friend, she knew nothing about him. So what was she supposed to think?

As sorry as he was about her misconception, he was even more concerned about their interview. If she didn't start relaxing, she was going to telegraph her uneasiness to the Longfellows.

"Okay. Let's go over our story again," he said, once she'd settled herself into the chair, her legs crossed, her skirt inching up on her thigh. He leveled his gaze on her face. "We've been engaged for two years. We only just got married and can't afford a honeymoon."

She nodded. "That's why we want this job. To have a sort of working honeymoon." Then she frowned.

"What's wrong? You don't buy the working honeymoon part."

"No. It's not that. I think maybe we ought to say we'd only been engaged for six months, or maybe even less."

He leaned back, absently scraping a knuckle against the shadow starting to darken his chin. "You have a point. A shorter engagement would explain why we don't know each other very well." He shook his head. "Still, stability would go a long way with Howard Longfellow."

"As long as we have a marriage license, I don't see why that would matter."

"The last thing I want is for it to look like we got married specifically to get this job."

"Why would they think that?" Jolie's mouth twisted wryly. "We practically answered the ad before it made it to the classifieds. How did you get the ad before it hit print, anyway?"

"Why were you fired?"

She blinked. Her lower lip quivered, then thinned angrily. "That's a personal question. You want to change the rules?"

Mike watched her uncross her legs and straighten her skirt with a jerking motion that broadcasted her annoyance loud and clear. "Okay. I withdraw the question."

"What do you know about my being...about that? What did Byron tell you?"

"Nothing. He started to say something and caught himself." He smiled. "Is this our first married spat?"

"First of many, I'm sure." She rolled her eyes heavenward.

"Is it time for the making-up part yet?" he asked in a low, teasing voice.

Jolie abandoned her divine counsel, her gaze skidding back to his. "Look, Kramer—"

"It's Duval."

She took a deep breath and left her chair to pace the tiny, combination living room and bedroom. "There are a few things you need to know about me." She held up a hand and ticked off one finger. "First, I'm a no-nonsense kind of gal. I know my, uh, let's say limitations. More importantly, I've accepted them. And I don't fool myself. You got that?"

He nodded, even though he had no earthly idea what she was talking about. But for some reason, with her restless mood, he decided that going along with her was his best bet.

"Second, although I really do need this job, I—" She stopped midstride as she swiveled back toward him. "What are you looking at?"

Mike quickly raised his gaze from her legs. "Nothing."

She glanced down and tugged her skirt hem toward her knees. It ended up several inches shy of its target.

"What were you saying?" he asked.

She frowned, giving a small shake of her head. "Um...I..." She shrugged. "What do you wear for this kind of interview?"

"Anything that..." His attention snagged again on her shapely calf and he scowled. "No skirt. And for God's sake, no shorts.'' Lola Longfellow would flip if she got a look at Jolie's legs. ''Wear some sort of wide, gauzy pants.''

''You're kidding,'' she said, following his gaze. When she brought her eyes back to him, her face was flushed with anger. ''Sorry I'm not up to your standards.''

She turned and snatched their plates from the end table.

He grabbed his empty beer bottle and followed her to the kitchen. ''What the hell are you talking about?''

She glared at him while she scraped their dishes into the sink.

Shaking his head, he reached around her to discard his bottle. His hand made it as far as the lower cabinet handle, pulling it open an inch before she slammed it shut with her knee.

''I told you to stay out of my garbage.''

Mike yanked back his hand in hope of keeping his fingers. He straightened and stared down his nose at her. The top of her head barely made it to his chin. What in the hell was she so mad about?

But when she tipped her head back to center her chocolate-brown eyes on him, it wasn't anger he saw there. It was fear.

And then he understood.

A slow smile tugged at his mouth. He knew what the problem was, what was causing all this tension between them. And he knew how to fix it. ''What do you say we solve the mystery?''

Her eyes narrowed, then widened as he lifted a hand to brush the hair from her pinkening cheek. Curiosity was a simple human trait. So was the solution. His hand slipped to cup her neck, and he lowered his face to hers.

He heard her gasp as their lips met.

Chapter Four

Jolie widened her eyes on him, her mouth frozen beneath his. But when he dragged his lower lip across hers, rubbed his thumb along the sensitive skin at her neck, her eyelids fluttered closed and her mouth automatically softened. He increased the pressure, his mouth beginning to slant, the heat his body was throwing off searing her chest, her belly.

And then she felt nothing.

The kiss was brief. Insultingly brief. He pulled away roughly. His hand, at her nape, tightened before it loosened, and she blinked as she stepped back a respectable distance.

"Better?" he asked, his expression blank, emotionless.

"Better?" she repeated, separating them by another step, irritation overtaking her frantic pulse. "What do you mean, better?"

"Now, you don't have to wonder anymore."

"I don't have..." Her confusion gave way to indignation as his meaning sunk in. "*I* don't have to wonder?" Heat rushed over her face. She took a menacing step forward. He didn't move. "*I* don't have to wonder?"

He put up both hands in surrender. "Okay. I meant we don't have to wonder."

"*I* wasn't wondering." She jabbed a finger at him and came close to clipping his chin.

He fisted a hand around hers to stop her, and pulled her arm straight to her side. The motion brought her up close. His breath glided across her cheek.

"I was," he whispered, his face bent toward hers.

She didn't believe him. Not for a minute. She reared her head back. "Let go of me."

His eyes briefly left hers to stare down at her mouth, and he released her hand.

Jolie sucked in a breath. "I think you'd better go."

Mike frowned slightly. "You're making too much of this."

Was she? Obviously he was used to quick, meaningless kisses. He probably had women lined up just to take a number. "It's late."

"We only get one shot at that interview tomorrow. Do you understand that?"

"I understand." She left the kitchen and headed for the door. He didn't follow right away, and she wondered if she'd have to race back to keep him out of her garbage. Of course, his finding out that she'd ordered dinner from a restaurant wasn't exactly at the top of her worry list anymore.

No. She had far graver things to consider. Like how she was going to get through the next month. He was playing her, no doubt like he played many women, to get what he wanted. She figured his success rate was phenomenal. But she refused to be one of his statistics.

He and this job were probably the last chance she had to keep her inheritance, and Jolie wasn't so foolish that she didn't realize that her money was the most she had going for her. She had no skills. She couldn't even keep a job. And ladling soup at the homeless shelter got her nothing more than a free meal and satisfaction. But she had several shreds of dignity left. And playing pushover for Mike was not in her cards.

He came around the corner from the kitchen, his wary blue eyes seeking her out. She noticed that he'd pushed back the sleeves of his shirt, exposing tanned, strong forearms, liberally sprinkled with dark hair. She wondered when he'd done that. Her gaze flew to his. Or *why* he'd done that.

She grabbed his jacket from the small table where he'd left it and pushed it toward him, her pulse leaping along with her imagination. She didn't know this man. Only that Byron had vouched for him. But right now, that didn't seem good enough.

Mike watched her, amusement replacing wariness in his eyes. He took the jacket and tossed it back on the table. "I'm not leaving."

Even standing in her high-heeled shoes, Jolie saw that he towered over her by nearly a foot, which did little to inspire her confidence. She casually shifted out of reach, carefully keeping her sights on him.

She had known immediately that Mike was different from the other men she knew, the ones she'd met in prep school, or the Armani suit bunch who ran her grandfather's company. Oh, he was polished and smooth as silk, his artfully beautiful yet rugged face designed to disarm a woman.

But he was dangerous, too. His entire presence fairly radiated a sense of warning. It was like a high-pitched sound that no one heard. Except Jolie could hear it. Almost as loud as the inner voice that told her this business marriage had been a huge mistake.

He had a hard edge to him that could shred and maim the unsuspecting. Luckily, her glass house had already sustained the bulk of life's stones. He couldn't touch her. No one could.

"You can't keep looking like you're afraid I'll pounce. How do you think the Longfellows will interpret that?" Mike asked.

"Just keep your hands off me and that won't be a problem."

One of his brows shot up. "We're supposed to be newlyweds."

"Then save your role-playing for when it counts." She placed the director's chair between them and held on to the back with both hands. "And for the record, I'm not in the least afraid of you."

His gaze traveled to the whitening of her knuckles before returning to her face. He smiled.

"I'll see you tomorrow," she said, loosening her grip.

"I want to help with the dishes."

"I can handle them."

His smile widened slightly before it slowly faded and he tugged down his sleeves.

She watched him, feeling a little light-headed. "Where and what time shall I meet you tomorrow?"

"I'll come by for you around nine-fifteen. Our appointment is at ten-thirty." He moved toward her and it took all her willpower to stand her ground.

Her stomach fluttered when he leaned forward, his tanned cheek grazing her hair. Then he reached around her and picked up the hotel key he'd left on the table.

He straightened, stepping away, and resumed buttoning his shirt cuffs. "Be ready on time. We'll have coffee first."

"Anything else, *Captain?*"

"Yeah." A slow mocking smile lifted the corners of his mouth. His eyes leveled with hers before he ran a brassy yet indifferent gaze down her legs. "Remember to wear long pants."

She mentally flinched, even though she already knew she wasn't up to his standards. She'd always thought her legs were one of her better attributes. But of course, he'd had the best. "I assure you I'll dress appropriately," she said stiffly and moved to the door. She unlocked it, then pulled it open. "Good night."

He stared at her a moment, his eyebrows slightly knitted. She wanted to laugh at his bewildered expression, the one that clearly told her that he wasn't used to feminine indifference.

He transferred his attention to slowly smoothing out the creases left in his shirtsleeve. Then he lazily sauntered to the open door, lingered with his palm on the cheap tan wood and turned his eyes on her. There was no warmth, no vulnerability in their blue depths…only steely intent that sent a shiver across her shoulders and reminded her that maybe she should be afraid of this man.

"Tomorrow is important to me," he said distinctly.

His gaze slowly left her as he pushed the door wide with the heel of his hand, his scuffed boots toeing the threshold.

"What about dessert?" She bit her lip, her breath swirling into a lump in her throat. What was she doing? She wanted him to leave.

He stopped to stare at her again. A slight smile lifted one corner of his mouth. "I'll be back," he said with a determined look that made her stomach flutter. "With my bags. I'm moving in."

MIKE SKIPPED the elevator to Jolie's apartment and took the stairs instead. Neither his duffel bag nor the carry-on slung over his shoulder was very heavy. Not that it mattered. He had a lot of restless energy to burn.

They weren't prepared to meet the Longfellows tomorrow. Dinner hadn't gone the way he'd planned. Jolie had been skittish for some reason, maybe from worrying about the interview. At least, he hoped that was what was causing her jitters. That he could fix. If she was wary of him, well, he wasn't sure what he'd do about that. Moving in would help. She'd get used to him being around.

It was obvious she needed this job badly. Her budget certainly hadn't allowed for any extra apartment decorating. Hell, the place was barely furnished. He thought again about the first night he'd brought her home and how bare her closet had been.

Maybe the poor kid didn't have anything to wear to the interview tomorrow. Mike slowed his steps, going back to taking one at a time. That was it. That was why she'd been so prickly when he'd suggested she wear long pants.

Rubbing the back of his neck, he glanced at his watch. The stores were already closed. And they wouldn't be open in time before the interview tomorrow. He massaged the knot of tension forming at his nape. There wasn't much he could do right now but hope the interview went well. Later, after they'd aced the job, he'd take Jolie shopping.

And they would ace the job, he told himself as he brought his knuckles up to her door. For him, there was no alternative.

He waited a long time after the first knock before rapping again. When she still didn't answer, he used the heel of his hand and hoped he hadn't awakened the entire floor.

"All right," she muttered, swinging the door open. She'd changed her clothes. The short cream-colored skirt she'd worn earlier had been replaced by oversize gray sweatpants. The sleeves of the matching sweatshirt ended near the tips of her fingers. She was drowning in all that stuff. He wondered briefly if she'd appreciate his pointing out that he was a certified lifeguard.

"The latest in honeymoon wear, I presume," he said dryly.

Her lips pulled into a thin line of irritation. "Dessert was fabulous. Too bad you missed it."

She started to slam the door but he stopped it with his foot. "Trying to find out how many neighbors we can wake up?" he asked as he slid the carry-on off his shoulder. He let it drop at a strategic point between the door and frame.

She held her ground, not backing up so much as an inch. "You don't seem bothered that you woke me."

He glanced at the sofa. It was pulled out into a bed, the sheets and blanket still tucked neatly in place. He smiled at her.

She glared back. "You're not staying here."

"It makes perfect sense."

She pushed back the ridiculously long sleeves as if preparing to do battle. "That's absurd. It makes no sense at all." Her gaze started to sweep the room but riveted to the bed. "Look at the size of this place. It's too small."

"For what? We're only going to sleep here."

She straightened and gave him a look that told him she'd gladly strangle him if given half the chance. Well, so much for his making her uneasy.

"Look," he said calmly. "Once we go to the interview, we're going to have to stick together anyway. Why not take advantage of making sure we're prepared for tomorrow?"

Someone opened a door down the hall. Jolie started to duck her head for a look but before she or Mike could investigate, a man's voice called, "Would you let him spend the night already?"

With that the man slammed his door with an earthy curse.

Jolie grabbed Mike's arm and hauled him inside.

"Now, that's the kind of enthusiasm I like to see." He kicked the carry-on aside to keep from tripping over it.

"I'd give you the couch but I don't have one. You get the floor." Glancing down to see that she still clung to his arm, she dropped it as if she'd been stung. "But only for tonight."

"I'm not sleeping on the floor."

"It's either that or the director's chair." She hurried over to the bed, picked up a pillow and threw it at him.

She'd flung the peach-colored pillow hard and it hit him in the chest. He caught it, then advanced on her, silently daring her to back up. She didn't. She stood stone-still, her chin lifted, her eyes flashing a warning he didn't heed. When he stopped, only the pillow he held at his waist separated their bodies.

"You're going to have to get used to us being together. This is business. Nothing more." Brushing the pillow aside, he let it drop to its place on the bed. He wasn't going to let her blow his chance at grabbing the diamonds. And he was not going to get worked up, he told himself. He was going to remain calm, cool and confident. After all, he was good at that. That was why the rich trusted him. That was why he was good at his job.

"We'll sleep together tonight," he said in a reasonable tone, a sense of renewed control cutting a path through his discomfiture. A benign smile eased the tension around his mouth. "In the same bed, just like we'd do on the ship."

She opened her mouth to refute him, her lips parting

slightly. They were full and pink, and with startling clarity, memory of the earlier kiss they'd shared assaulted his hapless brain. Heat filled the pit of his stomach and so unexpectedly charged his body, that he stumbled back half a step.

Muttering a succinct and audible curse, he grabbed the pillow and threw it on the floor.

MIKE GULPED down the last of his morning coffee, then eyed Jolie's full cup rapidly cooling on the side table. From the bathroom, the low hum of a blow-dryer stopped and started again. He glanced at his watch and sighed. He'd already made two trips to the corner market for coffee and to give her privacy. But it seemed she was going to be late anyway.

That thought didn't help his foul mood. He'd barely gotten any sleep last night. The floor had been hard, his nerves shot to hell. None of that seemed to have bothered Jolie, however. Clearly besieged by dreams, she'd shifted and tossed in bed, her whispery soft moans taunted him half the night. And they made him wonder what fantasies her subconscious had woven.

Letting out a tired sigh, he leaned forward and shrugged out of his tan windbreaker, preparing to get comfortable when he heard the bathroom door open.

He only caught a flash of her as she ducked into the closet and slammed the door. But within two minutes, she popped out, her arms hooked up behind her as she fidgeted with the back of her navy linen dress. Her *short* navy dress.

"I'm ready," she said a little breathlessly.

He narrowed his tired eyes. "You're wearing *that?*"

Her face fell. She looked down at the simple but elegant dress. "What's wrong with this?"

"I told you to wear long pants."

"Tough." She reached behind once again and jerked her arm, and he realized she was having trouble with the zipper. "This is perfect for an interview."

"Turn around."

She eyed him suspiciously.

"We're married, remember?" he said dryly. "Turn around."

She gave him a long-suffering look, then slowly did as he asked, sweeping her hair up with one small, manicured hand. Her neck was slender, slight enough that he could almost slip his fingers entirely around it.

The zipper was only halfway up, caught on a piece of thread. At the gap, a horizontal strip of delicate black lace lay against slightly tanned skin.

He frowned as he tugged at the metal. How had she gotten that tan? Winter was barely over. Surely, she couldn't have afforded a sunny vacation. Visits to a tanning salon maybe? Still, by the looks of her apartment, she could hardly afford such a luxury.

His attention snagged on the fine quality of her dress, and he frowned again as he finally disengaged the zipper and slid it up to her nape. His index knuckle brushed the skin of her neck. It was incredibly soft. He promptly drew back.

"Thanks." She let go of her hair and it swished back into place, glossy with health and care. When she turned to look at him, he saw unexpected wariness in her brown eyes.

"Well..." he said, his gaze wandering down to her legs. He considered for a moment if he should insist on her not wearing a dress. She didn't know about Lola as he did. He'd done his homework well. The woman wouldn't welcome the competition. Maybe he ought to level with Jolie. He didn't have to tell her too much and it would make life simpler.

"I'm not changing." She turned away from him and ducked into her closet again.

He followed to the doorway and stole a quick look around. About half a dozen items hung there.

She snatched a tan coat off a hook and, arching an indignant brow at him, raised a palm to his chest and pushed him back into the tiny living room. With her other hand, she jerked her closet door closed behind her.

"This is a great interview dress. Trust me on this," she said as she scurried past him, shrugging into her coat, and opened the entry door.

"I thought jobs were a problem with you." He followed, grabbing his own jacket off the couch and sending a regretful look at the now-cold coffee.

"Not getting them," she snapped. She barely allowed him to make it over the threshold before she slammed the door. He felt the motion at his backside and grinned.

"What are you smiling at?" She squinted at him. "Byron did tell you something, didn't he?"

"Not a thing." He held up a palm. "I swear."

"Yeah." She looked him up and down before sidestepping him and punching the elevator button. Then she presented him with her back, her gaze purposely avoiding his. "How do I know your word is any good?"

He surprised her from behind, banding his arms around her, pulling her back up against his chest and bringing his mouth close to her ear. She let out a small squeal of alarm, but he didn't let go. She was far too stiff around him. The Longfellows would spot her uneasiness in a minute.

"Because we're supposed to be married. And you'd better start remembering that," he whispered darkly. "I already warned you. Don't screw this up."

Her body softened in his arms and he loosened his hold slightly. He inhaled a large breath, sucking in the clean, herbal scent of her.

Right before she stomped hard on his foot, her high heel connecting soundly with his second toe.

"Damn." He jumped back, and looked down at his throbbing foot. Hazy stars obscured the brown leather. "What the hell did you do that for?"

"What's the matter? Married life not agreeing with you?" The elevator chimed. The doors opened and with her chin lifted, she got in and quickly pressed a button. The pale green metal doors slid closed before he could get his feet and mind in the same gear.

Swearing under his breath, he raced for the stairs. The first three flights down were easy, but anger and clenched teeth eventually served to undermine his stamina. By the time he reached the ground floor and entered the lobby, he was taking quick, shallow breaths.

Jolie pushed off the wall from a leaning position and tugged up the collar of her coat. A slow, sly smile lifted the corners of her mouth. "What kept you?"

His temper rose above the simmering level. He wrenched the tangled jacket free from around his arm, plowed his hands through the sleeves and yanked it up over his shoulders.

I won't let her get to me.

Mike repeated his silent mantra three times before grabbing her arm and ushering her out into the brisk morning air. He hailed a Checker cab and urged her inside, ignoring the smirk playing around her irritatingly full pink lips.

He barked the address to the driver as he slid in beside her, and managed to ignore the shapely calves she crossed and angled to the side. Almost. Rotating a tight shoulder, he gave her a brief and final look before forcing his attention out the window to the crowded street.

"Are we going directly to the interview?" she asked sweetly.

"Coffee first."

"Oh." She adjusted her hem. He opened the car window. "So that's your problem."

Slowly, he turned to look at her.

"Not enough caffeine?" She raised her eyebrows.

I'm not going to let her get to me.

He took a deep breath and forced a smile. She flicked at her hair and lifted her chin to high heaven, a grin spreading across her smug face.

"Lady. *You* are my problem."

A cacophony of car horns accompanied his words. Sirens wailed for several seconds, punctuated by a flashing blue light a block away.

"Pardon me?" She angled slightly in his direction.

"I guess you don't need this job all that much, huh?"

She straightened, blinked. Any trace of a smile faded from her lips. "Yes, I do."

"You don't act like it. Maybe we ought to kiss this idea off." He shrugged indifferently, his gut as tight as a sailor's knot. He hadn't meant it, of course. He merely wanted her reaction.

She fidgeted with the strap of her purse. Her expensive purse, he noted once again, peering a little closer. It wasn't one of those knockoff designer bags. It was the real thing. Several hundred dollars worth of the real thing, unless he was mistaken. He frowned at her anxious face.

"I really do need the job, Mike. I can't afford..." She stared off into the distance before bringing her wounded gaze back to him. "I promise I won't mess up the interview."

"Okay." He shrugged again. "Let's do it."

She smiled tentatively. Her shoulders visibly relaxed as apparent relief turned the color of her eyes to pure milk chocolate.

Something inside him responded at a level purely alien to him. A warm fluttery feeling expanded his chest. He hadn't been wrong about her needing the money, and although he was sorry she was in that predicament, he was inexplicably glad to be part of her solution.

He started to smile back and take her hand. Then he realized what he was doing and sharply turned his body away to stare out at Central Park coming up on his left.

He was a sucker. He muttered a curse under his breath. A damn big sucker without the good sense God gave a jackass. His entire financial future was wrapped up in this interview and the outcome of this job. But was he adequately focused?

Hell, no.

He was too busy worrying about his new *partner*'s financial security. He cast a censorious glance at her purse. Not that he should be. She obviously wasn't concerned enough herself. The few things she did have, she'd obviously spent a small fortune on.

The cab pulled up in front of a neighborhood diner for which Mike had given the driver the address. Two blocks down was the town house where the Longfellows were staying and conducting the interviews. If Mike's scheme was on track, he and Jolie would be their *only* interview.

She slid out of the car while he paid the driver. When he joined her on the sidewalk, she wrinkled her nose at him.

"This is it?" she asked, tossing a disdainful look at the small, shabby diner.

He regarded her for a silent moment. She looked quietly

elegant in her tailored tan coat, her posture erect, her hair falling perfectly into place...a touch of haughty reserve coating her like a fine layer of perfumed lotion. She confused the hell out of him.

"We have coffee here and review our story." He pointed down the street where the high-ticket addresses started. "Then we go meet the Longfellows."

She nodded, and without hesitation, headed for the restaurant's door.

"Hey, Jolie!"

A large booming voice came from somewhere behind them. Mike started to turn toward its owner the same time she did, but he stopped when he saw the look on her face.

She smiled at first, as though pleasantly surprised by a friend. And then her eyes widened, darted to Mike's, panic etching itself between her eyebrows.

"I ain't seen you all week. You got new digs or something?" the male voice continued as it got closer, his words followed by a rusty chuckle and sickly cough.

Mike reluctantly tore his gaze from her shocked face to check out her friend. But when he glanced over his shoulder, all he saw was a bum in a tattered army-surplus jacket, one sleeve held on by an inch of stitching.

As the man stopped to root through a trash can, Mike blinked and looked around some more. No one was there. The bum straightened and continued toward them. A horrific cough rattled his bony body.

Mike's eyes slowly returned to Jolie. How the hell did she know this guy?

Her gaze darted between him and the approaching man. He saw her swallow. Then she grabbed Mike's arm and shoved him into the diner.

Chapter Five

Her back was to him for most of her brief conversation with the older man. Mike had purposely chosen a table near the window, and after he'd ordered coffee for himself and Jolie, he did nothing to hide the fact he was more than slightly interested in her friend.

But after she'd pushed Mike in the door and muttered that she'd be with him in a minute, she'd not once given him so much as a glance. He could still tell she was uneasy, though. By the way she fiddled with her earring. He'd identified that nervous habit early on.

She smiled warmly at the thin man, apparently oblivious to the spittle that caked his gray scraggly whiskers. She touched his arm, her glossy, nude nails looking out of place against the filthy green sleeve. Then she dipped into her purse and passed the man some money.

He smiled with the three teeth he had left. She kept her palm pressed to his a long moment before stepping away and hurrying into the diner.

Mike wasn't sure how much money she gave him. He knew it was more than a single bill. He frowned, watching her slip into the vinyl booth opposite him.

"Thanks for ordering my coffee." She picked up the cup and sipped, avoiding eye contact.

"Who was that?"

She looked at him then, and made a face. "That's very rude."

"I just asked who he was."

"None of your business," she answered pleasantly. "Now, about the Longfellows." She casually took another sip. And touched her earring.

"What did that guy mean about new digs?"

Her fingers stopped fidgeting and her brows shot up. "How about I start asking you some questions? Like why you couldn't talk one of your many girlfriends into playing your wife?"

He glanced around the semicrowded restaurant to see if anyone had overheard them. Damn her. The last thing they needed to do was create a scene so close to the Longfellows' apartment. "Would you keep your voice down?" he warned, his attention slowly swinging back to her. She was as red as the cracked vinyl behind her. He frowned. "What girlfriends?"

Her cheeks grew impossibly redder. She picked up the menu the waitress had left and buried her face in it.

"We don't have time to eat. We'll grab something later," he said, a grin starting to form at her sudden discomfort. "What girlfriends?"

She peered over the top of the coffee-stained menu. "My point is, you don't have any business asking personal questions."

"I'll temporarily waive my rights. Let's discuss the 'many girlfriends.'" He smiled at the dirty look she gave him. Right before she glanced at her watch.

As much as he enjoyed flustering the hell out of her, and as curious as he was about her speculations concerning him, now wasn't the time. He had a job to do. And the only woman he needed to be interested in was Lola and her million-dollar baubles.

"Let's go over our story one more time," he said, removing the menu from Jolie's hands.

She nodded. "We want this job as a honeymoon. We've crewed yachts before. I'm a trained chef." She looked away.

"Look, I know that's a small lie, but after the great meal you cooked..." He smiled. "I'd buy it."

She glared at him.

What the hell was that for? He'd meant that as a compliment.

He watched her take a deep breath before she asked, "How do you know Mrs. Longfellow used to be a Las Vegas showgirl?"

He shrugged. "It was in the newspaper."

"I don't remember that."

He frowned. He didn't expect she would, unless she followed the society pages...or the tabloids. "It was a while back. Anyway, that's not important. We have our hands full trying to keep our stories straight."

"I've got everything under control." She smiled sweetly and added, "Darling."

He'd been reaching for his wallet, but he looked up in time to catch her lips twitch. "'My hero' would be okay, too."

"Oh, please." She rolled her eyes. "Save that for one of your girl—" She stopped herself, snatched up her pocketbook and lit out of the booth. "We have ten minutes."

"I'm right behind you." He threw some money down on the table, including a vastly inflated tip. With the way Jolie tore out of there, he didn't have time to wait for change.

As soon as he caught up with her outside, he experimentally slipped an arm around her shoulders. She didn't jump exactly, but she started to shrink away.

He held her tighter. "Uh-uh, *honey*. We're newlyweds, remember?" he whispered close to her ear.

She gave him a nod, as grudging as it was, and although she no longer pulled away, she was as stiff as a board.

He stroked her upper arm with his thumb, trying to get her to loosen up. He watched her breasts rise and fall, felt her body relax slightly against him.

Progress.

He shot another quick glance at her breasts, wondering how they'd feel cupped within his hands. He nearly dropped his arm to his side at the unexpected thought.

Instead, he reminded himself of what was at stake and kept on walking, Jolie tucked under his arm, his eyes straight ahead.

They stayed that way, walking close, touching, her herbal-scented hair teasing his senses the rest of the way to the Longfellows' town house.

Her legs were much shorter than his and he had to adjust his stride to accommodate her. One thing he knew for certain was that she sure as hell wasn't about to adjust her stride. She was an independent woman. Mike had recognized that fact early on. It was a refreshing change from the self-absorbed socialites he too often came into contact with—the kind interested in money and social status and eager to attach themselves to a man with both.

Jolie was the first to reach the doorbell. In a matter of seconds, a uniformed butler answered. As soon as they gave him their names, he ushered them to a large oak-paneled library off the parlor.

Howard Longfellow sat behind a large antique desk, a paper airplane poised between his thumb and forefinger.

As soon as they stepped into the room, he let it fly, smiling as it soared toward the light streaming in from the open French doors. The plane made it as far as the balcony, then nose-dived into a tangle of ivy crawling up the ancient red brick.

Longfellow narrowed his blue eyes in irritation and shook his snow-white head. "They don't make them like they used to," he muttered, before transferring his gaze to them.

Mike stared hard at the man. It was difficult to push aside the animosity he felt toward him, but he managed to bite back the sarcastic remark that teetered on his tongue. After all, grabbing the diamonds would be his best revenge.

He smiled, stepped forward and extended his hand. "Mike Kr—Duval, sir."

The older man grunted. He rose halfway to his feet and accepted Mike's handshake from across the desk. "Howard Longfellow here. But then, you already know that." His frown melted into a chorus of chuckles.

"This is my wife, Jolie." Mike stepped back and guided her forward while giving her one last meaningful look. Which she meaningfully ignored.

She barely glanced at Mike but gave Longfellow an engaging smile. "I'm pleased to meet you." Her hand disappeared into Howard's massive one.

He squinted at her. "Do I know you, young lady?"

"No." She said the word too quickly. Then she pulled from the man's grip, her eyes widening a fraction while her fingers found her earring.

What the hell?

Mike grabbed her hand. "My wife hears that all the time," he said, tightening his hold and smiling through thinned lips at her. If there was something she'd neglected to tell him, he was going to kill her. "Don't you, sweetheart?"

She shrugged and smiled. "All the time."

Mike's thumb strayed to her pulse. It raced.

Her chin lifted, her gaze remaining on Longfellow. Her fingernails dug into the back of Mike's hand.

He casually shook free. She was hiding something, all right. And he was going to rip it out of her at the first opportunity.

Howard nodded, dragging his narrowed eyes off Jolie to look past them. A moronic smile lit up his face. "Lola," he said before slipping into an off-key song that celebrated the name.

They both turned to follow Howard's gaze.

Lola Longfellow stood at the entrance of the library, pausing under the elaborately carved door frame as if posing for a photographer. Light from the crystal chandelier bounced off the waves of her long flaxen hair. Her cleavage was endless.

"Hi," she said in a small breathy voice, her red lips returning to a practiced pout. She was tall and leggy and just Mike's type, and he briefly wondered if he would have found her attractive under different circumstances.

She took a series of tiny little steps across the room, her tall spiky heels doing a number on the polished wood floor. He wasn't sure if the small steps were for effect or because her tight white leather dress wouldn't allow for a decent stride.

"I'm Lola," she said, stopping in front of him. She held up her plum-tipped fingers as if she expected him to kiss them.

He briefly shook her hand and met her measuring green eyes. "Mike Duval." Then he stepped aside. "This is..."

He looked down at Jolie. She was nearly a foot shorter

than Lola. Her head was tilted back, watching them, her large brown eyes warm and inviting and entirely too mischievous. His gaze dropped to her mouth and the lift at the corners. And he suddenly remembered that this sexy, sneaky little package was hiding something. He frowned into the silence.

A panicked look crossed Jolie's face, then she turned to Lola. "I'm Jolie." She smiled at the other woman's perplexed look. "We're newlyweds," Jolie explained. "I guess I still make my husband tongue-tied."

Damn it all to hell.

Mike took a quick breath before he smiled, too. First at Jolie, then at Lola. He turned back to his wife and tried not to grit his teeth. "Yes, *sweetheart,* you certainly do."

Only she wasn't paying any attention to him. Her gaze seemed hopelessly snagged by Lola's multiringed hand, her eyes rounding like those of a child ogling a hot fudge sundae. And then she blinked, her fascination quickly disappearing behind a cool mask.

A siren went off in Mike's head. The sound, loud and clear, strummed his nerve endings, reminding him something wasn't right. Had she only ogled the stones, he would have been okay. But the careful show of indifference had the hairs on the back of his neck reaching for the ceiling.

"Won't you sit down?" Lola asked, spreading her sparkling hand.

This time, Jolie didn't so much as give Lola's hand a fleeting glance. She merely sank into the chair to which Lola had gestured. Mike followed her lead, dropping into the chair beside her, then wondered if he were going crazy. He watched Jolie tuck a strand of silky brown hair behind her ear. Her fingers were bare save for the thin gold band he'd given her to seal their charade.

Unconsciously, she smoothed the surface of the shiny metal with her thumb. A small, nearly imperceptible sigh breached her lips.

Mike almost sighed himself, the relief he felt was so great. He rubbed the back of his neck and settled more comfortably in his chair. Her only interest in Lola's diamonds was that they sparkled. She was merely admiring and maybe coveting the hideous baubles. He was the one who was acting strange.

Howard Longfellow snorted loudly, snaring everyone's attention. But when all heads turned toward him, he was busy folding another paper airplane.

"Oh, Howard." Lola shook her head, her spiked heels clicking loudly as she hurried around the desk. Everything that could jiggle on the woman jiggled.

"Come, Lola." Smiling, Longfellow patted his lap.

Lola arched a brow. Her gaze slid briefly to Mike. "We have an interview to conduct, remember?"

"Interview?" Howard frowned. "I thought we already hired them."

Lola frowned, too, her gaze finding Jolie. "Can you cook?"

Jolie stared.

Mike elbowed her, and she nodded.

"Actually, she's a trained chef," Mike added.

Jolie gave him a faint smile.

"Really?" Lola's eyes lit up. "With which restaurants have you been affiliated?"

Jolie hesitated, her startled expression somewhere between scared-spitless and flustered modesty. When the silence lasted a moment too long, Mike decided to play up the latter. "Go ahead and tell them, honey." He squeezed her cold hand and smiled at the Longfellows. "She's way too modest."

"Well..." She blinked. No, batted. She actually batted her eyelashes, then rattled off a string of impressive New York restaurants.

Lola's eyes widened in surprise. So did Mike's. He quickly noted that Howard was more interested in his new paper plane. Lola was still enthralled with Jolie's claim, so Mike took the opportunity to look long and hard at his wife as he waited for the bottom to fall out.

"And I spent two years at school in Paris," she added, not smugly but with such cool elegance that he believed her.

He frowned. She was polished. No doubt about that. He'd been around enough finishing-school types to know. Maybe she'd had money at one time and fell on hard times. He mentally shook his head.

"I'm certainly impressed," Lola finally said, "but why would you want a temporary job?"

"We haven't been married long and we're still trying to decide where to live. Besides, this way we get to be together." Jolie looked adoringly at Mike.

Only he caught the wry gleam in her eyes, but he dutifully smiled back. "I'm such a lucky guy."

"Yes, you are." Jolie patted his knee and turned back to the Longfellows.

Howard put down his plane and narrowed his eyes on them. "Most young people don't get around to tying the knot these days. Are you two really married?"

"Absolutely," Jolie said quickly, "or I wouldn't sleep with him."

Howard slapped Lola on the fanny and howled at the ceiling until his eyes teared. Still chuckling, he dabbed the moisture away. "Good for you, young lady."

"How quaint," Lola said, annoyance lacing her tone. "But Howard is right. We do insist that the couple we hire be married.'' She leaned speculatively toward Jolie, her gaze taking in the short brown bob, the navy linen dress.

Mike sat up straighter, ready to defend their legal status, when he realized that Lola wasn't challenging them. The once-over she gave Jolie had been brief, and, now smiling at Mike, she had already dismissed Jolie as competition.

Irritation swept him. Lola was an idiot. Why else would she overlook Jolie's appeal? The blonde obviously hadn't seen his wife's legs, or looked closely into her expressive brown eyes. He tried to shake his exasperation, reminding himself that this was good. The last thing he needed was for Lola to feel threatened.

''So, now that we have that settled, can we get on with the interview?'' Mike asked, and at his brusque tone, all eyes turned to him.

He took a deep breath and forced a smile. He aimed it at Lola in particular. ''I'm sure you want to get this matter of crewing the ship taken care of.''

Lola tilted her head to the side and assessed him with an eagle eye. ''Of course. So tell us about you.''

Jolie's sudden interested gaze clung to him like chocolate to a candy bar. She propped an elbow on the chair arm and rested her chin on her palm, her entire body angled toward him.

Mike focused his attention on Lola, while Howard refolded his plane. ''I've crewed on a variety of ships for the past ten years. My last job was on a fifty-six-foot Sportfish. Before that I captained a sixty-foot ocean yacht. Most of my experience has been in the Pacific, but I've worked the Caribbean, too.''

Lola glanced at Howard who appeared to be paying not a scrap of attention to the conversation. She scrunched up her mouth and chewed on her lip in a most unattractive way. Clearly she was at a loss as to how to interpret the information he'd just given.

Everything he'd said was true, except that he hadn't worked on those vessels. He owned them. "I can handle the job," Mike assured her, throwing in a few more details to add to her confusion. Again, Howard declined to look up.

Lola had her husband wrapped around her little finger, Mike knew. He'd bet his last dollar that the decision would be her call. The man would have no say. Mike could almost feel sorry for the old coot. Except he suspected Longfellow wasn't quite as daft or senile as he let on.

Leaning forward, Mike rested his forearms on the edge of the desk and gave Lola an engaging smile. "What do we have to do to get this job?"

Lola's gaze roamed his spread hands, up his arms, across his chest, and he knew how it felt to be mentally undressed. He shifted uneasily.

"Well, Mike..." Lola lifted a hip onto the desk and leaned toward him.

Holy... He swallowed hard, slowly sinking back into his chair, carefully keeping his eyes level with hers. Enough cleavage flooded over her V neckline to sink a damn battleship.

Jolie stood suddenly. Her chair flew backward, its rear legs clearing the Oriental rug and grating against the wood floor. With a toss of her hair and a lift of her chin, she partially wedged herself between Mike and Lola.

Their potential new employer jumped, totally ignoring Jolie's outstretched hand. Then a slow smile lifted the pout from Lola's lips as her narrowed eyes seemed to receive a silent message from Jolie's.

Mike watched in awe. Jolie was a magnificent actress.

Anyone would have taken her for a jealous wife. He grinned, enjoying his role as the endangered husband.

"Thank you for your time, Mrs. Longfellow," Jolie said sweetly, pulling her hand back and clasping it with her other one. "I'm sure you have a busy day scheduled."

"Yes," Lola said, sliding Mike a mournful look that evolved into a sly smile, and he promptly recovered from Jolie's abrupt interruption. "But the other interviews shouldn't take long."

"Hire us and I'll make you a memorable first dinner," Jolie said, her smile widening.

She was doing a terrific job, Mike thought, as he stood and slipped his arm around her shoulders. If she kept up the good work, she'd deserve a bonus, something a little more than that thin gold band. Especially if he did his job well. "Mr. and Mrs. Longfellow, we appreciate your consideration."

Lola waved a dismissive hand as she edged her hip off the desk. "Don't call me Mrs. Longfellow. It makes me feel old." She cast a quick, apologetic glance at her preoccupied husband before returning her gaze unerringly to Mike. "Call me Lola," she said, shoving back a heavy swath of platinum hair...and giving him an unencumbered view of mounding flesh.

Jolie sighed. "When will we hear from you?"

"What?" Mike dropped his arm from her shoulders and turned to stare dumbly at her.

She gave him a dirty look.

"Oh, yeah." He smiled purposefully at Howard, who remained oblivious to his wife's flirtations. "Can we expect to hear from you within the next couple of days?"

"Count on it. Right, pumpkin pie?" Lola turned briefly to Howard, dusting his grinning face with a kiss, before sashaying around the desk to slip a hand through Mike's arm.

"There's paperwork that needs to be filled out in order to give you further consideration. Joey, you tell Howard about—"

"Jolie," they both corrected at once.

Lola gave them a patronizing smile. Jolie looked as though she had something to give Lola, too. And it wasn't going to be pretty.

He stepped back, drawing Lola with him, his eyes speaking volumes to his wife. "Good idea. *Honey,* why don't you tell Howard some of your menu suggestions while I tackle the paperwork?"

He raised a hand to ruffle her hair, but the look she gave him made him think twice. He touched her cheek instead.

Her skin was soft, rose-petal soft. It was warm, too, tinted pink, whether from irritation or nerves he wasn't sure. He only knew that the color dipped to her neckline, and her skin was flawless there, too....

A totally inappropriate thought startled him back to reality.

Slowly, he met her glare. Dropping his hand, he cleared his throat. So much for that fantasy. "Okay?" he prompted.

"Sure," she said, then pressed her lips together.

When he turned back to Lola, he noticed that she was watching them with keen interest.

"Shall we?" He spread a hand for her to precede him, anxious to draw her attention elsewhere.

But she continued to stare at Jolie, a frown drawing her finely shaped eyebrows together. "Have we met before?"

Jolie blinked twice. "No." She shifted the strap of her

purse...her very expensive purse, he noted once again, his earlier uneasiness returning with conviction.

"You look so familiar but I just can't place you." Lola wagged a long, plum-tipped finger.

Again, Jolie's eyes were riveted to the woman's rings. Then they narrowed to a gleeful, wicked gleam that made no sense.

Mike got a sick feeling in his gut.

"May I?" Jolie asked suddenly, reaching for Lola's hand.

Their new employer looked confused for a moment, then smiled when she realized that Jolie only meant to look at her jewelry. Lola proudly presented all ten fingers.

One finger in particular held Jolie's attention. The one with the emerald-cut diamond. Although it wasn't the largest stone on Lola's fingers, or the most eye-catching, it was by far the most expensive. Only an expert would know that.

"Absolutely gorgeous," Jolie said, closely studying the diamond and its mounting.

Lola sighed. "Isn't it? Pumpkin gave it to me for our anniversary last month. He has such exquisite taste." She looked at Pumpkin, but he was too busy trying to get his plane to fly. So she transferred her gaze to Jolie's fingers, all of them bare except for the thin gold band. "Know anything about diamonds, hon?"

It was a petty and deliberate question, Mike thought, and he mentally cringed waiting for Jolie's choice response.

But she merely shrugged. "Not much."

Lola's lips curved in a smug smile.

Mike exhaled softly.

"Except that this one is quite rare, discovered in the late 1800s, if I'm not mistaken," Jolie continued. Lola frowned slightly at Howard, appearing to seek confirmation. When she didn't get it, she gave a small shrug and stared at her ring.

Mike didn't need any affirmation. Jolie was right on the money. He wondered how the hell she knew that obscure piece of trivia. With increasing dread, he wondered how she'd recognized that damn stone.

Before he could step in to conduct damage control, she added, "But I was actually more interested in the setting." She smiled sweetly. "Clever knockoff. I believe Pastorelli designed the original ten years ago?"

Mike didn't know if he should be angrier that she'd probably insulted Lola and cost them the job or that Jolie...

He felt the breath whoosh out of him as he stared incredulously at her suddenly angelic face.

God help him.

The little witch was running her own scam.

Chapter Six

"Where are you treating me to lunch?" Jolie asked, buttoning her coat as she stepped out onto the sidewalk. Though the wind had picked up while they'd been inside, the weather had nothing on the chilly way Mike was treating her.

And as much as she'd rather get away from him, having lunch beat sharing the same air of her small apartment while she tried to think. Last night had been nerve-racking. Now that the interview was over, she needed to ditch him.

"What the hell were you doing in there?" Mike signaled a cab. "The object was to *get* the job. Not lose it."

"You're overreacting. We did fine." Okay, so maybe she'd gone overboard in pointing out that Lola was wearing a knockoff ring. But the woman had pushed one button too many. Not only had she treated Jolie like an invisible, mindless twit, she had all but thrown herself at Mike.

And did he ignore the overtures?

No-o-o…

Personally, Jolie didn't care. But if he was going to pretend to be married to her, then he'd darn well better act as if she existed.

A Yellow cab screeched to a stop. Jolie slid in. He followed, crowding her toward the opposite door. She turned her face out the window, her back partially to him.

Mike gave the driver an address, then heaved something between a grunt and a groan. "You wanna tell me how come you know so much about diamonds?"

She slowly faced him. "What?"

His expression was totally unreadable. His eyes, though, were the color of anger. She started to duck, but his hand shot up and held her chin. "Diamonds, Jolie. What's your interest in them?"

"Nothing." She reared her head slightly back, but he held firm, his middle finger extending to trail her jaw, the side of her neck.

"Wrong answer, sweetheart."

"Take your hand off me."

He blinked, and the blue crept back into his eyes. She held his gaze for a moment, then his dropped to her mouth.

She moistened her parched lips.

He smiled. "Tell me about the diamonds."

"Go to hell."

"No doubt I will." He stroked her jaw again.

His touch was so light and smooth, she was amazed to feel heat pool in her belly. "My grandfather," she said, swallowing, "he was a jeweler before he retired."

Mike frowned. His hand slackened at her chin. "And you were his protégée?"

"Not exactly." Her sisters had filled those shoes. She slipped away from his touch. He didn't seem to notice. He stared past her out the window, his forehead creased in thought.

After a full minute, he looked back at her, and asked, "What's his name?"

"That's personal, remember?"

He lifted a hand and Jolie shrank back a fraction. But he used it to rub the back of his own neck. He looked really tired all of a sudden, almost discouraged, and the burst of apprehension she'd felt a moment ago dissolved.

Then he looked her squarely in the eyes again, and said, "You'd better not be screwing with me."

"I have no idea what you're talking about."

His gaze didn't waver for several long moments. "Don't bring up the subject of diamonds again."

She shrugged. "I'm just the cook."

He nodded slowly. "How did it go with Howard?"

"Great. He seemed impressed." She suppressed a shudder, thinking about the extensive menus she'd foolishly suggested. "He said we should hear from them soon."

Her confident tone apparently appeased him because he seemed to relax. His shoulders pressed back against the uncomfortable seat, his long legs sprawled out, cramping her space.

"Do you mind?" She grumbled, tugging at the hem of her coat, which was being pressed by his thigh. "I can tell you've never been married before." As soon as she freed herself, she drew an imaginary line with her finger between them. She pointed first to one side. "This is your space." Then the other. "This is mine."

All the earlier tension faded from his eyes. An amused grin tugged at his mouth. "So, you know all about being married, huh? How many times have you taken the plunge?"

"I was a virgin until I met you."

His laugh was strangled. "I beg your pardon."

She sighed dramatically to keep from laughing herself.

"You're my first." The cabdriver's eyes met hers in the rearview mirror, then flickered away. "Husband, I mean."

"Really?" Mike cracked open his window.

"How about you?"

"Another virgin."

"I see." She heard the smile in his voice but kept her attention directed at the people rushing down Fifth Avenue. "Now, about lunch?"

"We're headed there now. After that we'll do some clothes shopping. I want to be prepared when they call."

Gritting her teeth, she glanced at him. "For you?"

He shook his head.

"Look, I don't know why you think you need to play den mother, but I've been dressing myself for nearly thirty—" She stopped herself and glared out the window. He didn't need to know how old she was. He didn't need to know anything about her. And if he didn't like her taste in clothes, then he could go...go...

"This isn't charity. You can pay me back when the Longfellows pay us." He paused. "How's that for optimism?"

"Charity?" Her gaze flew back to him.

"Look, you don't have the proper wardrobe for this trip. We both know that. I've been around your apartment enough to know money's been tight for you." His gaze slipped to her purse and his look could only be described as disapproving. "But there's no shame in that. We've all been there."

Jolie had to keep herself from gaping. He thought that she was poor. Which, of course, she would be if she didn't keep this job. She pulled herself together. "Thanks, Mike. That's very kind. But I have everything under control."

"Come on, kid. Let me give you a hand, will you?"

Kid? Her blood pressure soared a point. Next thing she

knew he'd try to ruffle her damn hair again. It was obvious she paled next to Lola. That didn't bother Jolie. She'd been compared to her sisters all her life. And she'd always come out short. But she was a viable half of their partnership and he'd better recognize her as such.

She took a deep, calming breath and reminded herself she needed this job. She told herself that his opinion didn't matter, that she had nothing to prove to him.

Then she decided to max out his credit cards.

MIKE SPOTTED Jolie in the cookbook section and peered over her shoulder at the appetizing picture of duck à l'orange she had open. "That looks good."

She jumped. Her head bopped him in the chin. She slammed the cookbook closed, her hand shooting up to rub her head. "I thought you were making a phone call," she grumbled.

He moved his lower jaw back and forth. It still worked. Barely. "I thought you were going to the sportswear...."

She was already walking away from him. Briskly. Toward the women's department. He hurried after her.

"I don't have much time," she said. "I'll try things on at home."

"What's the rush?" He picked up a red T-shirt coupled with long, matching striped shorts.

She rolled her eyes and kept walking.

She'd done that a lot in the past half hour, ever since they'd finished lunch and hit the stores. Although he admitted that the things he'd been looking at weren't to his taste either, they were conservative items designed to keep Lola from bearing her claws.

Mike casually sneaked a look at Jolie's legs while she riffled through a rack of clothes. The shapely calves were heart-stopping enough, he didn't need her exposing any thigh…for his sake and Lola's.

He brought the red T-shirt number along with him. As she pulled out an assortment of shorts and tops, he flipped through the bathing suits. He found a nice black one-piece that looked as if it could cover some major territory. When he saw the tiny lemon yellow bikini, his pulse skipped a beat.

"I'm ready." Jolie's arm had disappeared under a mound of clothes. She eyed the black suit and red T-shirt set. "Buying a gift for your mother?"

"You found all that already?"

"This?" She shrugged. "Child's play."

"We'll only be gone for a month."

"I'll have the clerk wrap them. Will that be cash or charge?" She smiled.

Mike walked past her toward the dressing room and lowered himself into a chair stationed near the pink dividing curtains. "Let's have a look."

"What? You want me to model for you?"

"You got it." He tried passing her the black swimsuit and the shorts set. She ignored them.

"Go ahead and exhale. It's not going to happen."

He grinned. "Shy, are we?"

Then he signaled a salesclerk. When the young blond woman spotted the haul in Jolie's arms, an eager smile split her face. She grabbed the bulk of the hangers before Jolie could protest and headed for the dressing rooms.

Jolie dug in her heels. Although she didn't say anything, he saw the stubborn glint in her eyes. And then it vanished, and to his amazement, she grinned. It wasn't a sudden smile, it was slow and calculated, clearly the product of a newly hatched idea. It bugged the hell out of him.

"Okay," she said. "No problem. I'll try them on." She

reached into a rounder of swimsuits and grabbed something else before trailing after the salesclerk.

He settled into the plush, green brocade seat and occupied himself with watching the other shoppers. They were a well-heeled bunch, designer purses slung casually over their shoulders, expensive shoes covering their feet. Anxious salesclerks hovered. One woman had brought a uniformed maid to carry her purchases.

Had he actually accused Jolie of being shy? Hell, she sure hadn't been shy about choosing a store to shop at. He'd winced at more than one price tag already. But he wasn't about to quibble over a few bucks, especially when he was this close to the diamonds.

As he waited impatiently, his mood slipping several notches, he realized that the money wasn't what bothered him. He had enough of that. It was the store itself that annoyed him. With its expensive fragrances, the damn thick carpet that wouldn't dare show a footprint, the fawning clerks, who hadn't approached him and Jolie because they hadn't been dressed the part. They were all stinging reminders of Angela and her upper-crust friends.

And how, in the end, Mike wasn't good enough.

And for a reason that was probably too far out in left field for him to comprehend, he was disappointed that Jolie had chosen this store.

Someone loudly cleared their throat and he looked up.

Jolie stood near the entrance to the dressing room. She wore a pair of white drawstring pants. They were long and baggy and...resting on her hips an inch below her navel.

He wouldn't have known that except her striped nautical T-shirt ended just under her breasts, showing off her tan, bare midriff. The neckline was scooped and fitted tightly. The tops of her breasts rounded high and firm above the scalloped blue edge. He swallowed hard. "What is that?"

"Cute, huh?" She looked down. "I could wear this top with white shorts, too."

"What happened to the red outfit I found?"

She looked up, her eyes widening innocently as they strayed toward the tangled heap of black and red sitting beside him. He glanced at the forgotten clothes. Damn.

"I thought they were for your mother. Anyway, I've found plenty of things. Be right back."

She disappeared before he could tell her that outfit was totally unacceptable. That it played havoc with his body temperature. That it reduced his brain to seaweed. That it...

Damn.

He flagged down the clerk who'd shown Jolie to the dressing room and shoved the clothes he'd selected at her. The woman frowned at his gruff instructions to make sure Jolie tried them on next. But he didn't give a rip. He had to stay focused. He had to remember that this wasn't a vacation, as he'd led everyone to believe. He had to concentrate on his plan and not his smart-mouthed *wife*. He had to...

"What do you think of this?"

He looked up at Jolie's voice.

And wished he hadn't.

Two flimsy strips of hot pink kept her from being totally nude as she slowly advanced on him. The legs of the bikini were cut up high, bypassing her thighs to rest on her hips. Her top left little to the imagination. Not an inch of pale skin was visible. She was tan from top to bottom.

Breath got trapped in his chest and a funny noise emerged from his throat.

Focus, he told himself. He had to concentrate. He had to...

"Do you like it?" She started to spin around to give him a back view.

He jumped from his chair and reached for his wallet, while keeping his gaze averted. Pulling out a credit card, he pushed it into her hands.

"I'll see you back at your apartment," he mumbled, then made tracks faster than a New York cabdriver.

THE BIG WEASEL.

Jolie jerked her own clothes back on. She had half a mind to go ahead and buy the awful bikini and crop top. So what that she didn't have a body like Lola. She didn't exactly have anything for him to be *that* embarrassed about.

The jackass.

Sighing, she picked up the two more conservative outfits that she had decided on. She wasn't even in the mood to put his credit card through the wringer anymore.

It served her right, she scolded herself. For having had the sudden silly urge to get him to notice her. But she was tired of being called "kid" and having her hair ruffled. It wasn't just Mike. Men had done it as far back as she could remember. Right before they fell like a ton of testosterone for one of her sisters.

She'd never coveted Monique's or Nicole's luscious curves or height...well, maybe a couple of times while still in high school. But she did now. And she hated Mike for causing her to feel that way.

After paying for her purchases, she stopped to browse through the cookbooks again. A couple of them looked rather idiot-proof and she snatched them up in a hurry. A third one showed her how to fold napkins and prepare garnishes. The books were fairly expensive with large glossy pictures, and she took perverse delight in charging all three to Mike's credit card.

As Jolie made her way to the front of the store, she realized that she had a lot to do if they did get the job. Not the least of which was to make arrangements with Father Martin to have her shifts covered at the shelter.

When she'd unexpectedly bumped into Wishbone Jones this morning, she'd asked him to warn the director. But Wishbone was only reliable when he hadn't tipped a gin bottle. And as much as she hoped the ten dollars she'd given him had been spent on breakfast, she wouldn't have bet her inheritance on it.

As soon as she stepped onto the sidewalk she saw Mike, several yards away, standing in the shadow of a towering redbrick building. Her heart reeled at his unexpected appearance and she had to consciously slow her breathing.

His shoulders were hunched forward, his face slightly angled away in deference to the wind funneling between a string of skyscrapers and the row of brownstones across the street.

With his head cocked to the side, she got a clean shot of his strong chiseled jaw, and noticed that his nose was slightly crooked. She smiled wryly. Big deal. One tiny, irrelevant imperfection, which on him, looked darn good.

He hadn't seen her and she wondered whether she should just hail a cab and leave. The same gust of wind that shot through her thin spring coat sent a lock of hair tumbling across his forehead. He swept it back, then stuffed his hand into his pants pocket. The other hand held a cigarette.

A cigarette?

Okay, two imperfections. Jolie frowned as she stepped

toward him. "I thought you were going to my apartment."

He'd been in the process of bringing the cigarette up to his mouth, but stopped midway. It was then that she saw he didn't have a cigarette at all, but what looked like a short straw. Then he did an amazing thing. He put the straw between his lips and drew on it.

He briefly shut his eyes, and when he opened them again to meet her gaze, sheer frustration marred the normal crystal blue. "I quit three years ago."

"Sucking straws?"

Irritation crossed his face for a moment, and he grabbed two of her packages. She held tight to the one with the cookbooks. "I see you were never a smoker," he drawled. "I'm not going to get any sympathy from you."

"I know quitting is tough," she said, relinquishing some of her crummy mood. "My grandfather has tried for forever."

"The jeweler?"

"Yeah, the jeweler." She folded her arms. She didn't like the way he narrowed his eyes, as though he didn't believe her. Huh. As if it mattered what her grandfather did anyway. "Why are you still here? And what's with the twenty questions?"

"First, I figured you'd need some help carrying things home. Second, I figured I'd get to know you a little more."

She gave him a long, skeptical look before craning her neck to spot a cab. "Sorry to disappoint you, but there's not much to know. I'm just your normal, everyday person."

"Jolie! Jolie, darling, over here."

She recognized her sister's voice immediately. Even over honking horns, screeching brakes, the throaty, sensual purr of Monique's cultured resonance reached Jolie's disbelieving ears. She thought seriously about not turning around, about sprinting for the nearest available taxi. She even briefly considered throwing herself in front of the next car. But with her luck, she'd end up in the hospital, and she'd still have to explain who Mike was.

Slowly, she turned toward her sister's voice, and cringed as Monique stepped out of Grandfather's stretch limo.

"Who's that?" Mike asked.

Her sister huddled into her mink coat, her long blond hair shimmering over the black fur. She glanced down the street before making her way through the stalled traffic.

"Jolie," Monique called out, while casting several interested looks Mike's way. "How about a lift home?"

Jolie groaned. How was she going to explain Mike? Oh, hell. How would she explain Monique? She took a deep breath and muttered half under her breath, "I have something I need to take care of. See you back at the apartment." Then she plowed heedlessly between two moving cars toward her sister.

Mike watched her go with not so much as an apologetic glance at him. When she reached the decked-out blonde, she swung the woman around toward the waiting limo and nearly pushed her back inside. The blonde was no more surprised than Mike was, as within seconds, the shiny black car merged into traffic, the operator either unconcerned or unmindful of the two angry drivers he cut off in his haste.

Mike absently reached into his pocket for the pack of carefully trimmed and simulated straws he kept for emergencies. And damn, if this wasn't an emergency.

His wife starts the day by hobnobbing with the homeless, and ends it by speeding off in a limo. Late model. Stretch. Expensive.

Damn.

But she was just a normal, everyday person.

Mike leaned against the cold brick, sucking his straw.

Yeah, right.

Chapter Seven

"Jolie Antoinettc Pillbury Duval, put down that valise immediately and explain yourself."

Cringing, Jolie tightened her grip on the leather bag and slowly turned to face her mother. Looking younger than her years, Simone stood at the entrance to the parlor, her blond hair neatly coiffed in its usual French twist. Her pink Chanel suit was one Jolie hadn't seen before.

"Mother, I thought you were at a meeting concerning the new hospital wing," she said with a conciliatory smile. If she wasn't out of here in the next two minutes, she was going to be late. Seriously late.

Her mother raised a perfectly arched brow at the small bag her daughter had refused to relinquish. "Going on a trip?"

"Well, yes...I thought I'd..." She transferred the bag to her other hand. "Yes, I am."

"Oh?" Simone Duval crossed the foyer and glanced out the beveled-glass windows. "You're taking a *cab?*" She made it sound like a dirty word.

Jolie sighed. "I'm only going to the airport, Mother." It was a small, harmless lie that she felt only marginally bad uttering. The less her family knew about what she was doing the better.

"My driver would've taken you." Her mother turned back to her, such an unexpected look of hurt on her face that it stopped Jolie. "When were you going to tell me about this?"

"Well, I left you a note."

"A note." That hurt look again.

"The trip is kind of sudden."

Her mother stared at her for a silent moment. "Does this have anything to do with your grandfather?"

She forced a laugh. "Why do you ask that?"

"His behavior has been peculiar lately." Frowning, Simone shook her head, then stared intensely at her daughter. "Monique says *you* were acting strange earlier today, too. But you wouldn't tell her what was wrong." Her expression softened. A nervous hand fluttered to the top button of her suit. "Anything you want to talk about, darling?"

A lump bloomed in Jolie's throat. She couldn't remember the last time her mother had singled her out to find out how she was feeling. Her grip around the bag handle slackened.

"Well, I—"

Outside, the impatient cabdriver leaned on his horn. Jolie reflexively jerked her attention toward the noise, before returning her eyes to her mother's anxious face. Jolie's heart constricted, and with it a rush of childish longing. But in a split second, the cool Duval mask her mother had perfected over the years slipped into place and the moment was gone.

"I'll call, okay?" Jolie hurried over, stretched up on tiptoes and brushed a kiss on her mother's cheek. Despite the fact that Simone elected not to meet her daughter halfway.

MIKE ALTERNATED between pacing the corridor outside Jolie's apartment and looking at his watch. How could he have forgotten to get a key from her?

Within the thin apartment walls, the phone rang for the second time. And rang. And rang. It was the Longfellows calling. He felt it in his gut.

Letting out a sound of disgust, he slammed his palm against her door. In desperation he'd finally called Byron, and once again he'd been assured of Jolie's reliability. However, the one question that bothered him the most, he couldn't ask his friend without raising more questions.

Was the little minx planning a scam? Although he'd just about let go of his suspicions by the time they'd gone shopping this afternoon, her running off with the blonde in the limo had him in a tailspin again. How the hell did she know people like that? How the hell did she know Byron? None of it made sense.

Mike shook his head. And how had he gotten so wrapped up in this Longfellow scheme that he'd gotten sloppy? A man in his line of work couldn't afford sloppy.

It might be too late to change the rules of the game but it wasn't too late to watch her like a hawk.

If she ever showed up.

He glanced at his watch again, but jerked his head up when the elevator dinged. The doors slid open, and Jolie stumbled into the corridor. A small designer bag was tucked under one arm, while she dragged a larger version behind her.

She looked startled to see him, her large brown eyes widening before her gaze darted to her apartment door as if she thought about outrunning him.

Then she shook back her hair and with an irritatingly dismissive air, she said, "Grab this for me, will you?"

She dropped the larger bag and marched past him, fumbling in her purse.

"The phone's been ringing off the hook." He frowned at the luggage. "Where have you been?"

"I went to borrow this from a friend." She concentrated on inserting her key.

"The blonde?"

She unhinged the lock and hurried inside.

He snatched the remaining suitcase and lunged forward to stop the door from closing in his face, and narrowly missed getting his nose broken. It wouldn't have been the first time. But this would have ticked him off twice as much.

"I need my own key," he said, trying to control his temper as he watched her head for her closet without a trace of apology. She had purposely kept him waiting, knowing he'd be locked out. He was tired of her attitude.

She stopped, glanced at him over her shoulder and inclined her head toward the table next to the couch. Near the spot where he'd left his wallet last night was a small brass key. "I left it there while you were in the shower."

Rubbing the back of his neck, he let out a weary sigh. "Thanks."

Unsmiling, she nodded, and continued toward the closet.

"Hey, how about we make dinner together tonight?"

She dropped her bag. "I was thinking," she said, spinning around with a bright smile, "that you'd have far more room at Byron's, and besides, we don't know when the Longfellows are going to make a decision."

"I have a feeling it'll be soon." He knew for certain that they were anxious to cast off. He just couldn't tell her why. "Now, how about dinner? I'm getting hungry."

She toed the bag she'd discarded over the threshold and

into the closet. "Go ahead and get something at the corner. I'm on a diet."

He laughed. "With all those French fries you ate at lunch?"

Her chin lifted. "That's why I can't eat dinner."

Leaning past her to deposit the suitcase he'd carried in, he cupped the side of her waist for balance. He dropped the bag, then straightened, looking down at her, his hand still molding the indentation, two fingers gently stroking the curve of her hip. "Doesn't feel like you need a diet to me."

Her startled gaze rose so abruptly that a lock of hair whipped up and clung to her face. "What I don't need is false flattery. I'm already in this up to my neck."

He stared harder at her, frowning. Strange choice of words. "I wasn't trying to flatter you, false or otherwise."

She studied him with equal intensity. A glint of anger sparked then died in her eyes. Finally, sighing, she stepped back, shoving the hair away from her face.

She missed several strands. He brushed them off her cheek. His knuckles trailed over the satin smoothness of her skin. She drew in her lower lip. He ran his thumb over her top one.

"Go get your dinner," she murmured against his hand.

"Kiss me."

"Not a good idea."

"Why?"

"Because we're married."

He laughed, his hand working its way around to her nape.

A faint grin displayed white teeth against her pinkening face. "I mean, we need to keep this business."

"Then consider it a business kiss." He stroked the skin behind her ear.

"You really should go to Byron's." Her eyelids briefly fluttered closed.

"I like it here." He lowered his mouth to hers.

Although she stiffened when their lips first touched, her body swayed toward him. He circled his other arm around her waist and pulled her more snugly against him. Her mouth softened, her head tilting farther and farther back to meet his kiss, her hands clutching his shoulders.

He realized he was too tall for her and that she had to be uncomfortable. So he slowly crouched, the friction of her soft pliant body rubbing against him, causing an unbearable sensation in his groin.

A groan rumbled in his throat. He was hardening, and he knew she could feel it. But she didn't pull back. She clung to him, kissing him with an intensity that should have sent him running for the next plane out of here.

He reached a blind hand out to the wall to steady himself, and her body shifted against the movement. When she started to loosen her grip on his shoulders, he swept her up in his arms. He'd made it to the couch when the phone rang.

Neither of them acknowledged the summons. Mike couldn't get enough of the eager way her tongue dueled with his, the way her palms pressed heat into his shoulder muscles.

The phone rang again as he loosened his hold to lower her onto the couch. She gained her footing, then stumbled backward, her bare neck still arched, spotted red from his thumb, his mouth.

She reached for the phone. Her hand froze above the mouthpiece, and she took a deep breath, visibly trying to compose herself, her bewildered gaze ebbing from his. Exhaling, she grabbed the instrument.

"Hello?" After a long pause, she leaned a hip against

the arm of the couch, and smiled. "He'll be as delighted as I am, Mrs. Longfellow." As she continued to listen her smile faded to a frown, and she shook her head. "Tomorrow?"

Mike was in the process of subtly adjusting the front of his too-tight slacks when her eyes found his. She followed the movement and blinked. Then her wary gaze slowly moved to the hideaway bed.

"Tomorrow is perfect," she said, and held out the phone to him with a slightly trembling hand.

"NOT A GOOD WAY to start a new job," Lola said, pointing to her diamond wristwatch. "You're three minutes late."

Still several feet away, Jolie glanced at the gaudy timepiece and muttered, "Gee, it's not even digital."

When Mike glared at her, she cleared her throat and said in a louder voice, "Sorry, Lola. I'll make it up to you by fixing a nice lunch." She grinned.

Appeased, Lola smiled back. Except her flashing white, capped teeth were aimed a little higher. At Mike. "It's okay, really. Howard still hasn't decided which hat to wear." A flicker of impatience glittered in her dramatically made-up eyes before she turned toward the open limo door and gave her husband an indulgent look.

"Almost ready, dumpling?" she called sweetly.

Howard bobbed his head out of the car, his captain's hat glaring white and a size too big. "What about this one?"

"Wonderful." Lola waved him toward her. "Come along, sweet pea. I've instructed Miles to bring them all, anyway."

"That's not necessary," Howard grumbled. "I only have one head, you know."

Lola sighed with annoyance, but not so her husband could hear. "Back in a minute." She hurried over to the limo and whispered something to him. He grinned like a child promised a praline ice-cream cone, then meekly climbed out.

She steered him toward Mike and Jolie. "You go along with the Duvals. I'll personally see to your hats."

Jolie saw her husband start at the use of *Duvals*. "It's got a nice ring to it, don't you think?" she murmured before preceding him toward the dock. She was still irritated with the stunt he'd pulled last night. If he thought he could kiss her any time he wanted, he had another think coming.

Her fingers automatically went to her sensitive throat, drifted across her tender lips. She wasn't one of those sappy women who fell easily for a great face and tight butt. Her steps faltered as she considered how tight his butt probably was.

Mike cupped her elbow to steady her.

She jerked her hand away from her mouth, her arm away from his touch.

"You're not still mad about last night, are you?" Mike's voice was so close to her ear she felt the vibration of its deep resonance along her nerve endings.

No way would she let him think she placed any importance on one kiss. Her look was all innocence. "What happened last night?"

"You're right. It was more like what didn't happen."

She wanted to ignore him, but a confused frown formed before she could intercept it.

"You're still mad because I slept on the floor again."

His arrogance stopped her cold. Her grip on the suitcase handle slackened and she turned to scowl at him.

Mike glanced over his shoulder at Howard, who trailed

behind and was still fidgeting with his cap. "I honestly didn't want to, but I thought it best to keep some distance. Let's say we forget it."

"You really are something." Shaking her head, she resumed speed, dragging her suitcase with her, and realized that she didn't know which yacht they were headed for. Then she saw the white monstrosity with *Lola II* scripted in gold near the end of the pier.

He kept up with her. "So, are you going to keep treating me like pond scum or are we going to call a truce?"

"I don't know if this news bulletin will penetrate your thick ego, but I did *not* want you in my bed last night. I didn't even like the kiss."

"So the heavy breathing was just special effects?"

She stopped again and glared at him, not even squinting into the midmorning sun. Then she casually ran her gaze down to his fly. Where she got the nerve, she had no idea. "And speaking of props."

He shrugged. "I never denied liking it."

She could have easily pushed him into the water, just to see the arrogant expression get washed from his face. The Atlantic sparkled around them as if taunting her, waves slapped against the wood columns supporting the planks beneath their feet.

"Don't even think about it." He grabbed her wrist and guided her toward *Lola II*. "I'm not letting you screw up this deal, *sweetheart*. Besides, it would be more sensible to admit the attraction and get on with our *honeymoon*."

She let him hold her arm until they got the few yards to the yacht, because Howard was gaining on them. When they got to the gangway she pulled away. "I have no intention of *screwing* anything up."

"I like it when you talk dirty," Mike whispered in her

ear just as a uniformed crew member reached across to offer her a hand onto the ship.

She refused to look at her husband. Hearing the amusement in his voice was enough. Letting out a small huff of exasperation, she hustled herself and her suitcase over without anyone's help.

Mike waited for Howard to meander across, while he balanced her second bag in one hand, his misshapen duffel in the other.

It was a small issue, but she wished she hadn't accepted his help with her things, she thought as she watched him navigate the gangway. Beneath his blue polo shirt, chest muscles bunched in his effort to maintain balance. His forearm was corded beneath a dusting of dark hair and tan skin.

And his hands. God, he had incredible hands, his fingers so long and lean...and entirely too capable of circling her neck. She shuddered.

She wanted to have as little to do with him as possible. Life would be easier that way, she decided as she turned to follow the man who'd greeted them and was now signaling for them to accompany him. She didn't bother to wait for Mike, and although he made not the slightest sound, within seconds she sensed him behind her.

She'd noticed before that his movements were quiet and graceful. That he was unusually observant. His manner put her in mind of a jungle animal stalking its prey. She didn't much care for the feeling. But it did make her wonder again about his line of work. And how he knew Byron.

Jolie had quit trying to wheedle information about him out of Gail, who'd gotten nowhere with her fiancé. Byron was being tight-lipped. He'd only say that he owed Mike.

Well, she didn't. As long as she fulfilled her part of

their bargain, that was all he could expect from her. Any marital bonuses were out of the question.

Taking a deep breath, she wobbled down the few steps to go below deck. The mere thought of being physical with her new husband made her knees as stable as tapioca pudding.

The crewman, who'd identified himself as Tom, gestured toward the parlor and dining salon at the end of the narrow passageway. Jolie concentrated on the opulent features being pointed out, trying to ignore the fact that Mike was so close she could feel his heat at her back.

The yacht was well-appointed, with no comfort spared, including several crystal ice buckets scattered throughout, stocked with bottles of French champagne. Plump gray sofas swept the corners of the main salon. Their burgundy-and-gold velour cushions were too gaudy for Jolie's taste, but she nastily figured they made Lola feel right at home.

In the dining salon, two seascape watercolors hung side by side. She recognized them as originals. All told, the Longfellows' yacht was quite nice. Not as luxurious or as roomy as Jolie's grandfather's ship, but then her mother always made sure the Pillburys and Duvals had the best.

As they passed the galley some of her bravado slipped. It looked modern enough...and as familiar as a UFO. She eyed the row of polished brass pots with dread, her steps lagging. Something bumped her fanny.

"Sorry, sweetheart." Mike's voice was a soft rumble. Close. Over her left shoulder. She didn't even want to think about which part of him made contact. "Nice, huh?"

She wanted to laugh. "Great."

She sped up to Tom, thinking that the galley might not be such a bad place. She did have several idiot-proof cookbooks. And time spent cooking meant time away from Mike.

She'd have to get things straight with him immediately, establish the rules. They were better off apart.

Tom stopped suddenly in front of her, causing Mike to crowd her from behind once more. His scent cocooned her, his breath stirred her hair. A shiver slithered down her spine.

Apart. Definitely better apart.

"Here you go," Tom said, winking as he threw open the door. "Best guest room aboard."

Jolie stared into the room.

One lone double bed, the size of a peanut, stared back.

Chapter Eight

"We need two beds," Jolie said.

Tom's eyebrows drew together as he glanced at Mike.

"Jolie?" Mike kept his tone neutral. He calmly set her bag on the floor beside him, and cupped her elbow in warning.

She wouldn't look at him. "He snores. Loud. Right when I'm about to fall asleep. Every time." She raked a hand through her hair, causing it to spike out.

"Jolie?" Mike forced a smile, his grip tightening on her elbow.

"Then he starts tossing and turning." She shrugged. "The sheets are practically off the bed by the time we get up in the morning. That is, if I finally get to sleep."

"I'm not sure what we can do about this," Tom said, his anxious gaze darting between them. "There's no extra stateroom. FiFi only has one bed, too."

"FiFi?"

"Jolie?" Mike still couldn't get her to look at him.

"Lola's terrier."

"Oh." She frowned. "Well, maybe—"

"Will you excuse us, Tom?" Mike grabbed the suitcase and none too gently pushed her into the room. He managed to close the door without slamming it. Barely.

"What the hell are you doing?" He dropped her bag before throwing down his duffel. "Why don't you just wear a sign that says 'Mike is really not my husband'?"

"Lots of husbands snore. I thought I sounded convincing." She swiped at her wayward hair.

He picked up his duffel and slammed it onto the bed. After roughly unzipping it, he started yanking clothes out. "No wife of mine is going to sleep in another room. Or bed."

"Is this an ego thing?" She grinned. "Interesting."

"What's that suppose to mean?" He squinted at the smug tilt of her head. He didn't like this conversation. "Never mind. I'm going on deck."

"Hold it. No husband of mine is going to run out on an argument."

He'd reached the door but turned to scowl at her. She was laughing at him. "There's nothing to discuss."

She rolled her eyes toward the ceiling. "Did you take Husbanding 101 to come up with that intelligent remark?"

Watching the satisfaction inch across her face, he released the doorknob. "Yeah," he said, slowly heading toward her. "Wanna see what I learned in Husbanding 202?"

That wiped the grin from her lips. She casually slipped around the bed to stand near the teak dresser. "I'll see you on deck in a few minutes."

"What? No longer interested in my education?" He strolled around the pale pink upholstered chair, past the foot of the bed.

"Did I tell you *I* snore?"

He laughed, and moved closer. "Thanks for the warning, but I've already slept with you. Remember?"

Her face darkened. "I hog the covers, too."

"I'll get an extra blanket."

"I sleep diagonally."

He stopped a breath away from her. Reluctantly, she tilted her head back to look up at him. He grinned and said, "I'll sleep on the bottom."

She opened her mouth, but no sound came out. He heard the quick and shallow breath she took, saw the shadow of apprehension cross her face.

Then she smiled sweetly. "Only if you remembered the condoms."

She couldn't have surprised him more if she'd ripped open her blouse and flashed him. Well, maybe... His blood surged at the idea. "Gee, why didn't I think of that?"

Her groan was low with disgust. She shouldered past him, pushing up the sleeves of her lime green pullover, and heaved her bag onto the bed.

His lips twitched at the way she tried to divert the subject by riffling through her things. But at her sudden strange behavior he frowned.

Her hands had stilled. She squinted at something she had tucked under a peach sweater, then darted him a sidelong glance. Her cheeks blossomed like two pink roses.

As if unsure whether to withdraw it, she toyed with the corner of what looked like a blue foil box. "I've got something for you," she said, looking unusually bashful.

Condoms?

The thought leaped into his brain. His heart inflated like a helium balloon. It crowded his lungs, cut off his air. "Yeah?" he croaked.

Her shy smile broadened as she produced the box. "It's gum," she said. "I heard it helps when you quit smoking."

He stared silently at the blue package, initially disappointed. The feeling passed quickly and surprise set in. When he looked up, he saw her smile waver.

"If you don't want it, no problem. I don't chew the stuff myself." She shrugged and started to toss it aside.

He touched her shoulder to stop her, then trailed his fingers down her arm to the offering. "Thanks."

"Sure." She released it. "What? Why do you look so funny?"

He shook his head, not willing to admit how touched he was by her thoughtfulness.

She waited expectantly, her eyebrows drawing together.

"I was hoping they were condoms," he said, and she blinked. He had to swallow the urge to retract his deliberately brash comment. It was only half a lie. Condoms would have been a whole lot simpler.

Her worried frown faded to a look designed to kill. "Okay. That does it." She reached for the quilt, yanked it off the bed and separated the two pillows.

"This is your side," she said, sweeping her hand down the center of the bed and nodding to the left. "And this is my side. Any questions?"

"No," he said, regretfully. "But I liked the diagonal idea better."

MIKE SNIFFED the air. Something was burning. He was almost sure of it. A bad feeling coiled in his gut. They'd cast off more than two hours ago. If anything *was* burning, it meant trouble on the yacht.

Foolishly, he'd just begun to relax, just started to believe he was close to grabbing the diamonds. What an irony it would be for all his well-constructed plans to literally go up in smoke at this point.

The last he knew, Howard and Lola were still in their stateroom. Jolie was below deck, as well. Tom, the only other crew member on board, was on the flybridge. Hoping not to alert him, Mike quickly, yet nonchalantly, strolled the deck, while keeping a careful eye out for the trouble.

After a quick perusal, he headed below. But before he reached the steps, a stream of black smoke ribboned through the hatch.

Swearing under his breath, he raced below. Another large cloud of the sooty stuff billowed from the galley. Coughing and sputtering from within followed the acrid haze.

Jolie.

She was trapped inside.

All rational thought escaped him. Sucking in a staggering breath, he rushed through the darkening fog.

He saw nothing at first. Metal banged against metal above the low hum of a vent. An oily, putrid aroma stung his nostrils. Then something wet slapped him in the face.

"Who is that?" Jolie coughed again.

He pushed the soggy, smoke-scented rag away. "Jolie? Are you all right?"

"I will be as soon as I get this damn stove to—" Her words dissolved into more coughing.

"Give me your hand." He groped the rag she continued to cling to, until he felt his way to her wrist. He yanked her toward him. A small fire extinguisher hit his chest. He pried it from her other hand, then guided her to the doorway.

The smoke had subsided enough that he could see some of it being sucked into a vent near the stove. More of the gray stuff was funneling out the door into the hall.

A large frying pan sat on a burner, scorched beyond repair. He knocked it to the side before continuing out the door with Jolie tucked under his arm.

Once he got her clear of the galley, he dropped the extinguisher, grabbed both her shoulders and forced her to face him. "Look at me," he said, his gaze traveling her face. "Are you okay?"

A black smudge streaked across her jaw, another smeared her cheek. "I'm fine," she grumbled. "It's that damn stove that's the problem."

By the tone of her voice, he knew she really was fine and his pulse started to return to normal.

"Where are the Longfellows?" she asked, scanning both sides of the hall with wary eyes.

"They're still in their room. But don't worry about them. If something is wrong with the stove, it isn't your fault."

"Right." She looked away…a little too quickly.

"What's going on down here?" Tom's voice startled them both as he poked his head down the passageway.

"Small grease fire," Mike said smoothly. "It's under control. Nothing to worry about."

Advancing, the crewman waved at the hazy air. "That's an awful lot of smoke."

"It looks worse than it is. I'll help Jolie clean up and be up top shortly."

Tom frowned and cocked his head for a better look at the galley area. Mike blocked his view. "Okay," he said reluctantly. "You be sure and let Mrs. Longfellow know if there's any damage."

"Got it." Mike waited for him to disappear up the steps before he turned back to Jolie. "What exactly did happen?"

She shrugged, her fingers fumbling for her gold hooped earring. "I'm not sure. I was making quiche for lunch and all of a sudden the stove started smoking like crazy."

Something niggled at his mind. Something that made

him uneasy. Maybe it was because she looked nervous. But then again, the fire had given her a scare. Hell, it had nearly given him a coronary. He smiled and put an arm around her shoulders. "Let's go take a look. I'm sure after all the smoke settles, things won't look so bad."

"No." She shrugged away. "You go back up on deck. I can handle it."

"Look, that was quick thinking to grab the fire extinguisher, but you're probably still a little woozy from all the smoke. I'll just—"

"I said I can handle it. I *am* capable, you know."

He frowned at her sharp tone. "I never said you weren't. I merely want to help." Without waiting for a response, he entered the galley.

She sighed loudly, but followed without further argument.

Black soot streaked the upper cabinets. Yellowish-gray clouds blotched the cream-colored ceiling. The smell of burned food hung heavy in the stagnant air. He looked down at the source—the large skillet he'd pushed to the side. Hideous clumps of black, charred food clung to the hopeless metal.

"Lunch, huh?" he said lightly, trying to make her smile. She didn't. But that was okay. He was relieved she was all right. Probably far more than he should be. "Looks like a couple of rags will do the trick. The vents will take care of some of that smell. And time."

She nodded slowly and reached underneath the sink to get some rags. At the same time she grabbed a book off the sooty counter and tossed it below.

Mike pursed his lips. Had she been so busy reading a novel that she'd let lunch burn? He didn't care for that idea and decided to give her the benefit of the doubt.

"Wanna grab me a spatula while you're at it?" he asked. "Who knows? Maybe I can salvage this skillet."

He moved the pan into the sink and ran some water over it. When she hadn't come through with the spatula, he glanced up to see her frowning in concentration at the row of silver and wooden utensils dangling from a copper rack. She nibbled her lower lip.

"The spatula?" he reminded her, and grinned. "You do know what that is?"

Her eyes widened. "Of course I do," she snapped. Her hand hovered over a ladle for a second, then she snatched the spatula and passed it to him.

"Thanks," he murmured.

The triumphant look in her eyes might have been comical. Instead, it renewed that uneasy feeling he'd had earlier.

On impulse, he touched the oven door. It was cool. "I thought you said you were making quiche for lunch."

"That's right," she said slowly, her gaze straying warily to his palm held flush to the cool metal door.

"What were you making it in?"

Her gaze darted to the skillet. "Why?"

His eyes followed her warily. "Jolie?"

"I thought you were going to help me clean this place up." She threw a rag at him. It hit his chin. He caught the piece of white terry before it slid to the floor.

He watched her through narrowed eyes for several pregnant moments. Ignoring him, she started wiping down the counters. "I'll tackle the upper cabinets and ceiling," he said finally. "Think you can handle the rest?"

"I'm sure I'll manage."

"How long do you think it'll be before you can whip up something else for lunch?"

The look she gave him nearly speared him to the wall. "Within an hour."

Mike nodded, a little more relieved than he probably should be. But for now, getting lunch on the table without further incident was about all he dared hope for.

"WHAT'S THAT?" Lola slowly sank into the floral-upholstered dining-room chair Howard held out for her. With small creases drawing her brows together, she peered closer at the plate Jolie had just set before her.

"Shrimp salad." Jolie's tone was dulcet. Her blood pressure, however, was sky-high.

"Is it *real* shrimp?" Lola picked up a fork and poked one of the mangled crustaceans.

Jolie opened her mouth to deliver a sarcastic answer, but caught her husband's warning look. He was standing at the door. No telling how long he'd been there.

Lola had invited them to dine with her and Howard. Jolie had wanted to turn down the offer. Mike had over-ruled her.

"Yes," Jolie said, forcing a smile. "Real honest-to-goodness shrimp."

"Why are they shaped funny?" Lola squinted from her plate to Jolie. A blur of false eyelashes fluttered as she noticed Mike at the doorway. "There you are," she said, a smile softening her pinched features.

"Oh, good." Howard sat across from his wife and studied his plate. "We're having crab."

"Shrimp, honey buns," Lola corrected automatically, then gave a final suspicious glance at her food before gesturing Mike to the chair beside her. She gave a little shimmy, the tops of her breasts mounding over her flimsy bikini cover-up like two ripe melons. "Are you all settled in?"

Jolie disappeared into the galley. She couldn't stomach another slobber-all-over-Mike session. Lola sucked up his attention better than a commercial vacuum did dirt.

Besides, Jolie had enough to worry about. She picked up a fork and stirred the shrimp salad. Well, maybe it didn't look like a dish from the pages of *Gourmet,* but it tasted great. She took a nibble.

Midswallow, she reached for some mineral water. *Great* might be pushing it, she conceded, and got the mayonnaise out of the refrigerator.

She stopped, and stared at the strange assortment of spices contained in the oak rack, trying to remember which ones she'd already used. She couldn't. So she lined up the small glass jars by color of contents and chose two.

After doctoring up Mike's portion, she returned to the dining room with their salads.

Mike stood over Lola's shoulder, while pouring her some wine. She smiled up at him, her shoulders thrown back, her cleavage directly under his nose. Howard was refolding his napkin into a swan.

"Will you need anything else from the galley?" Jolie asked. She set Mike's plate down with a little too much enthusiasm. One of the mangled shrimp popped up and onto his chair.

No one noticed but him. He briefly eyed the white glob before raising his gaze to hers in warning.

Lola took the wine from him. "I don't think so. Not until dessert, anyway."

"Dessert," Jolie repeated unhappily, groping for her chair.

Mike rounded the table and pulled it out for her. When she started to sit he bowed his head near her ear and whispered, "Nice job, sweetheart."

She slid him a look as he took his own seat, unable to

gauge whether his comment was sarcastic or not. His expression revealed nothing.

Lola took Howard's napkin from him, shook it out and laid it across his lap. Then she picked up her fork and waited for her husband to do the same. Mike followed suit.

It took another minute, however, before Lola dipped into her salad. The men waited, too, though whether they were being polite or cowards, Jolie wasn't sure.

Lola nibbled daintily. A frown puckered her eyebrows but she blinked it away. She stopped chewing and reached for her wineglass.

With a fair amount of enthusiasm, Howard dug into his lunch. He chewed, smiled, chewed.

Jolie exhaled. Then she braved a small bite herself.

And wished she hadn't.

A sharp tang bit her tongue. Followed by a mini-explosion in her mouth that filled her eyes with tears. Her watery gaze darted to Mike. His fork was in midair, heaped with salad, aimed for his mouth. The mixture was liberally sprinkled with red spice. Far more than hers. What *had* she dumped in at the last minute?

It took all of her willpower to choke back the cough erupting in her throat as her thoughts scrambled for a way to stop Mike.

Too late. His fork disappeared between his lips.

"Any more salad left, Jolie?" Howard asked.

Her attention instantly riveted to the older man and his half-empty plate.

"I believe this is the best crab salad I've ever eaten," he said, continuing to scoop up the unappetizing concoction.

Mike coughed into his napkin, a dull red creeping into his complexion.

"Have mine, honey buns," Lola said quickly. "I've barely touched it."

"You're not dieting again, are you?" Howard frowned at the plate she readily pushed at him.

"Just saving room for dessert." She glanced uncertainly at Jolie.

"Me, too," Mike said, his voice hoarse, almost strangled as he nudged his salad aside.

"Got a sweet tooth, have you?" Lola's smile was pure cotton candy.

He barely managed to smile back, but his color was returning to normal. He picked up a yeast roll and a butter knife. The steel tip scarcely dented the hard dough. He casually returned the roll to his plate, and skewered Jolie with a menacing look, his hand still clenching the knife.

Jolie jumped up. "I'll see to dessert."

"I'll help you." Mike pushed back from the table.

"No—" she began, but he was beside her in a heartbeat, hustling her through the galley door.

"Put that knife down," she said, glancing at the gleaming steel. She knew it was too dull to do any bodily damage but he looked mad enough to try.

"You're right. Using my bare hands would be far more satisfying." Mike threw the knife into the sink and backed her against the counter.

She was angry at herself for allowing him to corner her, angry for wanting to cower under the furious sparks coming from his eyes. She lifted her chin. "What is your problem?"

He gaped at her. "You purposely screw up the salad and you have the nerve to ask that? Why the hell are you trying to sabotage this job?"

"Howard loved his lunch." She tried to duck away, but he bracketed her with his arms, his hands firmly gripping the counter on either side of her body. Nearly eye level to her, beneath the sleeves of his polo shirt, biceps bulged with his intent on keeping her right where she was.

"What are you up to, Jolie?" he asked in a low, ominous voice.

He wouldn't give an inch. Herding over her, compelling her to arch back against the steel counter, he was so close that she could see the tiny spot near the cleft in his chin he'd missed shaving. She forced herself to stare into his eyes, no longer sky blue but gray and cloudy and...fixed on her mouth.

She moistened her suddenly dry lips.

He started to smile. A slow, confident smile. "Don't bother trying to distract me."

Her laugh was short and haughty. She tried to back up again, but remembered that she was trapped. "Why would I?"

He ran a lazy gaze from her mouth to her eyes. His gleamed wickedly. "Because you think you can."

Something between a gasp and a snicker formed her response. Not sure if she should be amused or indignant, she tried to cross her arms. There wasn't enough room between them.

"You're crazy," she said, the words sounding lame as she dropped her hands to her sides.

His arms slid in toward her and he leaned impossibly closer. "About your little sabotage effort—"

The door to the galley opened. From the corner of her eye, she saw Howard's bright red blazer...a second before she noted the sudden wariness in Mike's face.

And then her husband's broad shoulders swamped her vision as he leaned down and pressed his lips to hers.

She slid her hands up between their bodies, pressed her palms against his chest. She meant to shove him away, meant to bite down on the lips that were trying to part hers.

But her fingers curled until she fisted his shirt, the heel of her hand pressed flush to the steady beat of his heart, and she no longer knew if she was pushing or pulling.

The tip of his tongue moistened her lips, requested entry. And despising herself, she laid out the red carpet.

Somewhere in the fog, she heard chuckling, then Howard's voice. "Forget it, Lola. We're on our own."

Then the galley door closed.

Mike's lips stopped moving.

He straightened, looked at her for an indifferent second. She thought she heard a relieved sigh before he calmly strode to the refrigerator.

As if the world hadn't stopped spinning, he opened it, and asked matter-of-factly, "What's for dessert?"

Chapter Nine

Mike didn't get it. If Jolie really had her own scam going, why would she have served that crap at lunch today? And that dessert? Entering the cockpit, he shuddered, remembering the unappetizing blob of pea green she'd called pistachio mousse. Why was she deliberately trying to get them fired?

He peered blindly at the controls. On the other hand, if she really did need the job...why would she have served that crap at lunch today?

Damn it. He reset the automatic pilot and stared off at the last remnants of dusk. Patting his pocket, he searched unsuccessfully for a cigarette, a straw—anything to keep his mind off her. She had him so tied up in knots he couldn't even think straight.

Except for random streaks of salmon-colored clouds, the horizon was beginning to darken. Around the ship the water rippled, its velvety, glassy depths already mirroring the onset of night.

He loved this time of day. Especially out on the ocean. Surrounded by nothing but nature and his own inner reflections. He had a lot to be thankful for. His was the proverbial rags-to-riches story.

He grinned wryly. No matter that some people didn't approve of how he'd acquired his wealth. Like Angela.

He tamped down the old anger.

He didn't have time for it. He had a more immediate problem. Jolie. His irritation swelled. If he didn't figure out what she was up to, he could damn well be getting a taste of poor again. And that idea was about as digestible to him as her lousy, so-called shrimp salad.

When in a more reasonable frame of mind, he'd pretty much dismissed the possibility that she was working a scam. She wasn't smooth enough to pull it off. She was far too impulsive. A poker face was beyond her grasp. He smiled. She lacked the temperament to be a con artist.

Unbidden, the memory of her hurt look when he'd abruptly stopped their kiss flashed in his mind. When he'd pretended that the whole thing had been a show for Howard.

The recollection made him cringe. He banished it.

"Mike?" Her soft voice floated out from the shadow of the cabin.

He turned to look at her. The last golden rays of twilight filtered around her windswept hair. She pushed it out of her face, her finger catching on the small gold hoop she wore in her ear. The pregnant silence stretched a moment too long and her eyes started to widen.

In that instant, Mike knew he was in trouble, that she'd made a shambles of his well-ordered scheme.

And if she knew what a vulnerable picture she made or what he was thinking, she'd probably give him an uppercut to the jaw that would send him overboard.

Tough on the outside, she was as soft as a toasted marshmallow on the inside. Not soft when it came to resolve or determination. She had enough firepower in that department to blow them all to Barbados.

But there was something else that seemed to undermine her controlled facade. Something that caused her eyes to widen when she was uncertain, that made her fidget with her earring way too often. Something that made her stick to the shadows.

"Come here," he said, offering her his hand. "There's only a few more minutes of sunset."

"Only for a second. I'm working on dinner."

"You didn't leave the stove on, did you?"

"Knock it off. The fire wasn't my fault." She stepped out farther onto the deck and lifted her face to the breeze. "Besides, we're having finger sandwiches for dinner."

He groaned. "Does Lola know that?"

"She ordered it. What's wrong with sandwiches?"

"*Finger* sandwiches? I didn't know this was a diet cruise." His stomach rumbled on cue.

Jolie smiled. "We're having fruit salad, too."

"Oh, good," he said, his voice laced with sarcasm. "I won't have to worry about gaining any weight."

"That's right." Laughing, she reached out and patted his stomach. His eyes met hers, and she quickly withdrew her hand. She rubbed her palm. "I'd better get back."

"Wait a minute." Mike grabbed her arm as she started to go. "About tonight."

"Tonight?" Abruptly, she pulled away.

"The sleeping arrangements?" Lowering his voice, he scanned the length of the deck to be sure they were alone. When his gaze returned to her, he noticed that she'd stepped closer in order to hear him.

"Yes. I've been thinking about that." A soft pink infused her face and she briefly looked away. "I'm going to sleep with FiFi."

"The dog?"

"Shhh. Keep your voice down." She glanced over her

shoulder. "She's got the stateroom between ours and the Longfellows."

"Forget it."

"You've got a better idea?"

"You're sleeping with me."

"Excuse me?"

"We're supposed to be on our damn honeymoon, for God's sake. What'll they think if they find out you've chosen a dog over me?"

She grinned. "That you aren't very good?"

He grinned back. "Good at what?"

Jolie sighed loudly. "Let's get back to the matter of sneaking me into FiFi's room."

"Have you met that miniature Hitler yet? She's a yappy little mutt."

"No, she's not. She's just a tad high-strung."

"Yeah? So am I." He hauled up a coil of rope and slammed it out of the way, not much caring for the fact that she preferred sleeping with a dog. "Can't handle sleeping in the same bed?"

She folded her arms across her chest. "It simply isn't necessary when there's a perfectly good bed next door."

He gave her a biting sidelong glance. Which she pointedly ignored. She was too busy looking all high and mighty as she sometimes did, her arms crossed, chin lifted. As if *she* owned the bloody yacht.

Damn, he wanted to kiss her.

"Look, we don't need any more screwups," he said. "Between the fire and lunch, we're inviting a mutiny."

"You were the only one who complained," she said, surprise etched between her brows.

Was she kidding? "Okay, one small disaster. It's not the end of the world. I'm sure dinner will be better."

"Was the salad that bad? I mean I know I put too

much..." She frowned. "I think yours was the only one I messed up."

If he hadn't already sampled her cooking, he'd be very worried about now. "Let's wait until we get into our cabin, okay? We'll discuss sleeping arrangements after dinner."

"There's nothing to discuss." The stubborn twist to her mouth gave way to a grin. "I've got a plan."

Mike sighed. *This ought to be good.*

JOLIE HAD THOUGHT it was going to be easier than this.

The flashlight slipped, the beam bouncing off the hall wall and landing on the Longfellows' door. All was dark but for a thin stream of light along their bottom door frame. Quickly, she flipped off the switch. Then she lowered the tote she was carrying, which was far too heavy and causing her so much trouble.

She shouldn't have tried to take so many things in one trip, she realized now. Only she'd been trying to avoid another confrontation with Mike.

So, feeling like a thief, she'd grabbed as much as she could as soon as he'd left to talk to Tom on deck.

Abandoning her bag for now, she switched on the light and crept toward FiFi's room, only a blanket draping her arm.

Bless Howard and his allergy to dogs. FiFi's door remained closed. Slowly, Jolie turned the knob.

A cross between a whine and a growl hummed through the silence.

"FiFi, good FiFi," she whispered as she slipped inside the door. She eased it shut and sank against it.

The dog whimpered.

She directed the flashlight toward the sound. The illumination met the Yorkie's large black eyes, peeking out from under a pink floral quilt. FiFi growled.

She flicked the beam at her own face. "It's your aunt Jolie, you stupid mutt."

Unimpressed, FiFi growled again.

Sighing, Jolie reached into her shorts pocket for a piece of one of the finger chicken sandwiches she'd made for dinner. She unwrapped it and extended the peace offering to her new roommate. FiFi pushed forward, sniffing.

When her nose got within a foot of the sandwich, she whimpered and dived back under the covers.

Jolie snorted. "Very funny, you little worm." Taking another look at the flattened bread, she sniffed it herself. Making a face, she stuffed it back in her pocket and swung the beam across the room.

Her heart somersaulted. She staggered back against the door, staring at the wavering light.

Lola stared back.

Well, not Lola exactly. But a large head shot of her that took up half the wall.

Jolie swept the beam to the next wall. A collage of Lolas stared back this time, some sultry, some smiling. All of them looking directly at her.

She groaned.

The door creaked.

Switching off the light, she dropped to a crouch.

The door creaked again, this time opening several inches. A tentative growl escaped from under the quilt.

"Jolie? I know you're in there." Mike's voice was low and unamused. He poked his head inside.

She grinned, and flashed on the light. Lola's face loomed at him from across the room.

"Jeez," he murmured, rearing his head back.

"Gotcha." She stood, startling him again. "What do you want?"

"It's what you might want." He twisted around and produced the overstuffed tote she'd left in the hall.

She reached out for the bag but he held on to it.

"You're acting childish about sharing a room," he said. "I'm not going to touch you."

"Actually, I haven't given you a thought." Having heard amusement in his voice, she felt a pang of hurt. It wasn't that she thought anything was going to happen. If he were any more indifferent toward her than he'd been this evening, she'd have to jump-start him just to have a conversation.

"Really?" He glanced around. "Where's the pooch?"

"Under there." She inclined her head toward the bed. With the frilly pink shams and decorative satin pillows strewed about, it was difficult to tell which lump was FiFi.

He glanced at the heap, then skimmed the rest of the room. A small night-light in the far corner of the floor illuminated a silver water dish.

Jolie panned the flashlight along the wall, past an upholstered chaise longue to a box. It was rectangular, almost antique looking with detailed engravings. And it was filled with sand.

Mike laughed. "A litter box?"

She nodded, unsmiling.

"I thought only cats used those."

"Don't you have some place you have to be?"

"One of your duties, huh?" He chuckled again, then returned his attention to the box, his grin fading. "The rich really are something, aren't they?"

She followed his gaze, and frowned. "What do you mean?"

"Look at this room." He grabbed the flashlight from

her and pointed it. Silk plants stood in the other two corners. A rich mahogany chest housed FiFi's dog food. Wealth and pomposity fairly scented the air.

He let out a sound of disgust. "A bit much for a dog, wouldn't you say?"

"Oh, I don't know..." Her mother had two poodles who had their own fur-lined car seats in the limo.

He looked at her as if she were from another solar system. "That damn litter box alone probably costs more than what they're paying us for the month."

"I didn't think this job was about money for you."

"That isn't the point."

She laughed. "What is?"

He didn't crack a smile. "You don't think there's something a little wrong with this picture?"

She shrugged, not sure what he wanted her to say. "Everything is relative," she said finally and calmly, because although his voice had leveled rather than raised, his irritation was obvious. "The cost of the box simply doesn't mean that much to the Longfellows."

"No kidding. Just like people's reputations."

She knew he hadn't meant to say that by the way he swung his gaze away. It was clear she should let the subject drop. But she wondered about it. "Are you talking about the Longfellows, or the rich in general?"

He returned the flashlight to her and raked a hand through his hair. "Come on. Let's get out of here."

"I'm staying."

"This isn't part of our bargain."

"Getting the job was our bargain. Sleeping with you isn't."

"You really are afraid, aren't you?" His face was shadowed but his amusement came through loud and clear.

"Actually I figured there wasn't enough room for your ego and me in the same cabin."

He laughed. "So, it's only a swelled ego you're worried about?"

She blinked into the darkness, then squinted at his veiled face. There was no mistaking his meaning. "You are really sick."

"Just tired. Let's go." His warm hand circled her arm.

She opened her mouth to protest just as a sharp noise came from the Longfellows' stateroom. She held her breath.

Mike's grip tightened. "This isn't the time or place to discuss this, Jolie," he whispered.

Although she knew he was right, she didn't care for his dictatorial tone. But when FiFi growled, she caved in.

"I get the bed," she said haughtily and turned to the door.

After a brief and disturbing silence, he said, "No problem." Then his soft chuckle haunted her swift trip down the passageway.

JOLIE UNCURLED her cramped body and stretched her arms toward the teak cabinetry that served as the headboard. As soon as she straightened, warmth cupped her backside. Mike threw an arm around her waist and she froze, her eyes flying open to stare at the white wall facing her side of the bed.

Heavy with sleep, his palm rested on her bare inner thigh. Slowly she scissored her legs together. One wrong move and he'd have a handful of explaining to do. But she succeeded without waking him, and his hand thudded to the mattress, his arm still firmly circling her.

This was their third morning at sea. And this was the

third time Mike had slipped into bed after she'd fallen asleep and he'd completed his watch on deck.

And darn it. She was starting to like having him there.

The first morning had been a shock, waking up with his warm breath on her neck, his body a scant inch from hers, and she'd nearly jerked them both off the bed. By the second morning, she'd waited almost five minutes before quietly slipping out of his unconscious embrace.

Today she waited seven.

Confident now that his hand was no longer near her thigh, she took small even breaths and enjoyed the weight of his warm bare arm rising and falling against her midriff.

Glancing at the alarm clock, she was about to remove his hand, when he made a sleepy noise and nuzzled her ear. His beard-roughened chin tickled her neck and she had to press a fist to her mouth to keep from giggling aloud.

She lingered another moment before gently lifting his arm and easing herself from between the sheets. Tugging down the hem of her shorts, she managed to scoot out the door without waking him.

After a quick shower she reluctantly yet dutifully entered the galley. Kitchen duty had not improved. Sighing, she reached into her hiding place behind the spices and withdrew a cookbook. She leafed through several pages, stopping to study glossy pictures of omelets and frittatas.

She smiled. Perfect. How could she botch an omelet? She flipped on the oven switch, then started scanning the list of recipe ingredients.

"So what gastronomic disaster are you plotting today?" Startling her, Mike's sarcastic question ended with a yawn.

She slammed the cookbook shut and pushed it under a

hand towel before turning to glare at him. His eyes were sleepy-blue and entirely too close. Dark stubble accentuated his jaw and made the skin behind her ear tingle. She rubbed the spot that had a memory all its own.

"Don't you have something to do on deck?" She flung open the refrigerator door, and he hopped back to keep from getting slammed in the belly.

Then he peered over her shoulder into the fridge, frowning when she reached for the eggs. "Let's keep breakfast simple."

Rolling her eyes toward the ceiling, she nudged him aside and set the eggs on the counter. "Omelets, okay?"

His gaze followed her movements warily, coming to rest on the lighted oven switch. His eyes narrowed. "What else?"

She made her irritation known with a loud sigh, but knew from the past couple of days that she'd have to answer him or he wouldn't go away. "Toast," she said tightly.

"And?"

"Fruit. That's it."

One dark brow lifted. "Why is the oven on?"

Damn. She could never get that straight. "A soufflé. I thought I'd try an omelet soufflé." Proud of herself, she smiled. She knew for certain soufflés were made in the oven.

"Oh, no, you don't. We had *pancakes* yesterday."

The stark fear in his eyes made her all the more indignant. She planted a hand on her hip. "Those were not pancakes."

"My point exactly. Stick to eggs...scrambled...no frills. Got it?"

"I thought you and Lola *wanted* frills," she said through gritted teeth.

"Do you know how hard it is to keep a soufflé up?"

She blinked, her thoughts skittering at the line he'd just handed her. She was tempted. Really tempted. Instead, silently, with an arched brow, she raked a gaze over him.

He shifted uneasily and her lips curved in satisfaction. He glared back. "Eggs, toast, fruit. No screwups."

She jumped when he slammed the oven switch to off before storming out the door.

BY THEIR FIFTH MORNING at sea Jolie was thoroughly sick of kitchen duty. Although since her lost battle with scrambled eggs, her breakfast repertoire now consisted simply of cutting up fruit and setting out ready-made bakery items. Mike figured she couldn't mess that up.

Jolie hoped he was right.

After washing and drying the breakfast dishes, she made up the Longfellows' room, then changed into her swimsuit, intent on preserving the light tan she'd acquired in Tahiti a few weeks earlier.

So far Jolie had taken little advantage of the free time the Longfellows had offered. If she was busy fiddling below deck, she didn't have to run into Mike. And the less she saw of him, the better off they both were.

Not that he made a point of spending time with her…dinner supervision excepted, she thought sourly as she twisted around to check out the back view in the mirror. The legs of the new bikini bottom were cut higher than she normally wore them. She plucked at the elastic but couldn't get the yellow fabric to cover any more of her fanny.

Backing up, she inched closer to her reflection to look for cellulite. She gasped when she saw a tiny dimple. Gulping a breath, she told herself it was only a shadow, then grabbed a towel and hurried out before she lost her nerve.

Everyone was atop deck already. But Lola was the first person Jolie saw. As if she could have missed her.

As she did every morning, Lola stood near the helm, practicing her kicks. Showgirl kicks, as Jolie liked to think of them, wondering if Lola was beginning to miss the bright lights of Las Vegas.

"Did you see that one, Howard?" Lola called out. But it wasn't her husband she was looking at. Her gaze strayed to Mike standing at the wheel. "I think it's a record."

"I believe you may be right, my dear." Lounging in the shade, Howard saluted her, then sipped his Bloody Mary. FiFi lay curled in a ball a few feet away.

Lola stretched out one leg while smoothing a palm up her calf. Her skin glistened with the beginnings of a tan and coats of cocoa butter. Pointing her toe, she raised her leg. And sneaked a sidelong glance at Mike. He only briefly looked her way before returning his eyes to the horizon.

Jolie's annoyed sigh must have been louder than she thought. Howard turned to look at her. She smiled sheepishly and took the last step up onto the deck.

Howard chuckled. It wasn't an altogether pleasant sound. "You needn't worry, young lady. Your young buck doesn't have enough money." He went back to sipping his drink, his attention redirected at his youthful wife.

If it hadn't been for the cagey gleam in the man's eyes, or his perverse laugh, she might have thought she'd misunderstood his meaning.

"I understand we should be reaching land some time tomorrow evening," she said instead of responding.

"That's what they tell me." He patted the chaise beside him. "Lola will be at it for another hour. Have a seat."

"Can I get you another drink?" she asked, not anxious to engage in any further conversation.

Howard reached beside his chaise and produced a small thermos. His lips curved into that goofy smile that at times made Jolie wonder if he weren't three French fries short of a Happy Meal. "How about I get you one?"

Jolie laughed. "No thanks." She nodded toward the stern. "I think I'll get some sun before I make lunch."

"Good idea." He started to lean back in his chair. "Hey, when are we having that crab salad again?"

She knew there was something she liked about him. "How about tomorrow?"

He nodded, smiling, his eyes drifting closed.

Seeing a sunny patch of deck near the mast, she grabbed a chaise and headed toward it. She didn't look at either Lola or Mike on the opposite side of the ship. Although Lola paid no attention to her, Jolie felt the weight of her husband's stare as she shook out her towel and draped it over the lounger.

Brave behind her dark glasses, she twisted around to settle onto the lounger and get a furtive eyeful of Mike.

Her heart throbbed a beat off rhythm. Her mouth went dry. He had a stunning rear, especially in his white shorts. Without a shirt, his broad tanned back had just the right amount of muscle, rippling and flexing as he controlled the wheel, then tapering nicely at his waist. And his thighs...

Jolie reached for a nonexistent drink. She started to look around, then realized that she wasn't on Grandfather's yacht, and that she was the waiter and not the waitee.

She sighed. God, but she didn't want to be poor. She wanted to sail around all day in luxury, avoiding kitchen

duty, drinking piña coladas and watching Mike's
back...and tush.

Not that she could actually spend her time so idly. He
glanced over his shoulder at her and she busied herself
with rearranging her towel. But then again... She sneaked
another peek at him.

Sighing with a mixture of guilt and bliss, she closed
her eyes and lay back, wondering how Father Martin was
faring at the shelter. She hoped he was able to adequately
cover her shifts. She'd felt bad about giving him such last-
minute notice, but she knew she'd feel a lot worse not
knowing where her next dollar was coming from.

"I don't remember that swimsuit."

Mike's voice startled her. Wrapped up in her thoughts,
she hadn't heard him approach. She kept her head resting
against the chaise, her face tilted up to the sun. Behind
the sunglasses, she opened one eye. He was a little to her
right, his broad, bare chest blocking out Lola and Howard.

"I'm surprised you noticed." Her voice sounded churl-
ish. She bit her lip.

"Who wouldn't?" He drove an impatient hand through
his hair and glanced at Tom, who'd taken over on the
flybridge and seemed to be dividing his attention between
Lola, Jolie and his duties at the controls.

Jolie's other eye popped open, and then they both narrowed on her husband. "Excuse me?"

"How much material did that thing take? A whole
square foot?"

She nearly pulled off her glasses to get a better look at
him. If she hadn't known better, she'd have thought he
was jealous. "You're on my time, Mike. What do you
want?"

He didn't say anything at first. He just stood there staring at her, his unreadable gaze covering every inch of her exposed skin until she wanted to scream.

"Are you going to be up here a while?" he asked.

"About an hour. Why?"

He shook his head. "No reason. I'm going below while Tom's relieving me. You take care of the Longfellows, okay?"

She rolled her eyes as he turned and disappeared down the stairs. She could have predicted how this morning would go. If she came up top, Mike went below. If she was in their room or the main salon, Mike headed for the deck. The only time he stuck around was in the galley where she'd just as soon be rid of him. Although he *had* bailed her out of one or two sticky scrapes with melted cheese.

She took little consolation in the fact that he equally ignored Lola and all her subtle hints. Jolie wondered again why he'd even wanted to come on this trip.

She flopped over onto her stomach, and tried to chase away the feeling of disappointment. But her thoughts continued to go haywire. She didn't know why she felt slighted by his lack of attention. This was a business arrangement, after all. It didn't help, however, that his moods seemed unpredictable. Sometimes she thought he was actually attracted to her. She hated him most for that. Because deep down, she knew that was absurd.

Lola concluded her kicking exercises earlier than usual, joined her husband in the shade, and they settled down to their morning game of cards. Jolie knew that meant she had another thirty minutes before she had to start lunch. She wondered how many more days she could get by with serving salads or sandwiches. Kitchen disasters were minimized when she stayed away from hot food.

The warmth at her back began to fade. A shadow eased

toward her on the deck. Glancing up at the sky, she noticed a pesky gray cloud playing cat-and-mouse with the sun. Another band of dense clouds streaked its way toward them.

She sighed. She could outwait the interruption to her suntan. The delay would only last minutes. But she was too restless.

Gathering up her things, she decided to go below and leaf through cookbooks. Dinner would be another challenge, and she was on pretty thin ice in that department already.

She had made it past FiFi's room when she heard a noise coming from the Longfellows' stateroom. She slowed down, craning her neck, and saw that their door was slightly ajar. She could have sworn she'd closed it after making their bed.

Frowning, she edged closer. Everyone was on deck. Except Mike. But he wouldn't be in there. She frowned again, then padded softly to peek into the narrow opening.

His back was to her, Lola's dresser drawer pulled open in front of him. He ducked his head while he riffled through the contents. In the mirror in front of him, all she could see was the top of his head.

Several seconds later, he withdrew a pink teddy, and after a cursory look, cast it aside. His movements were quick and economical as he inspected several other pieces in the same manner. He paused, and instinctively, Jolie dropped to a crouch and held her breath.

Furtively, Mike looked over his shoulder toward the door. Apparently appeased, he resumed his rummaging, but at this new angle, his profile was now clearly visible.

For the next minute, she watched, wide-eyed, while he examined the rest of Lola's lingerie with a look of such resolve that it totally floored her. She was about to back away, when his steely look gave way to a slow smile.

Reaching into the drawer, he pulled out something filmy and black, and shook it out in front of him. It was a negligee, long, with a feather-boa collar. His smile broadened as he ran his hands over the gossamer fabric. It was an odd smile—a strangely expectant one. She didn't know quite what to make of it.

"What's going on here?"

Lola's incredulous voice, coming from behind her, almost landed Jolie's rear end on the floor. Attempting to recover her balance, she fell against the door and it opened the rest of the way.

Mike looked up. He didn't turn around, but Jolie caught his surprised expression in the mirror. His eyes met hers for an instant as he fumbled with the negligee. Then, as if unaware of his audience, he calmly tucked the nightie under his chin and solemnly regarded his reflection.

"Oh my God," Lola whispered in shocked amazement. "He's...he's—"

Howard frowned over his wife's shoulder. "I like the red one myself."

Jolie only stared.

Then Lola turned to her with wistfully sympathetic eyes and said, "What a waste."

Chapter Ten

Mike never thought he'd be so grateful to Howard. But after Mike's feeble attempt to explain and nearly a half hour of Lola's theatrics, it was the older man who'd diffused the sticky situation by demanding his lunch.

That request sent Lola running for cover. No one saw her the rest of the afternoon. And she hadn't surfaced for the usual cocktail hour, or for dinner either.

Mike didn't think she'd bought his explanation that he was making sure their room was picked up. And that was about the best thing he could say about the entire evening experience.

Clearing the rest of the dinner table, he cringed, thinking about how he'd done everything but pirouette with the negligee tucked under his chin. The vivid image of Jolie's shocked face as he preened in front of the mirror flashed in his mind, and he nearly sent an entire bottle of expensive cabernet to its death. Just maybe he'd have been better off getting busted looking for the diamonds—instead of acting like a damned fruitcake.

He managed to carry the last of the dishes into the galley without incident. That is, until Jolie turned from the plate she was scraping to give him that disbelieving, wide-eyed look he'd been treated to since *the incident*.

Quickly, he slid the tray of dishes onto the counter and safety. "Howard took his coffee and brandy to his stateroom. He doesn't want dessert."

"I know." She'd turned back to furiously scraping a plate that had not a shred of food on it.

"What do you want me to do?"

"Nothing. You go ahead and..." She paused. Although she wouldn't look at him, he could see the color climb the side of her neck. "Do whatever it is you do."

Mike heaved an annoyed sigh and reached into his pocket for a straw. "How long are you gonna give me the business?"

"What do you mean?" She darted a look at him before returning to her duties.

"Oh, hell."

She glanced up again, abandoning the plate and reaching for a dish towel. "I'm a very broad-minded person. What you do in your personal life is none of my concern."

Mike leaned back against the counter and folded his arms, defensiveness settling in every joint in his body. He hated to admit it, but his ego was at serious risk here.

"I mean..." She shrugged, vigorously drying her hands, refusing to meet his eyes. "It's really none of my concern. Our arrangement is strictly business. In fact, I've been around a lot of artsy people who, uh—" she glanced up, before resuming her brisk drying "—who prefer alternate life-styles. I'm very liberal about that sort of thing."

"It's not what you think."

Her lips curved in a tiny, sad smile. She looked small and a little deflated, like a child who'd just been told there was no Santa Claus. "It's okay, Mike. You don't have to hide it anymore. I understand."

"Damn it—" He stopped. He was shouting. He uncrossed his arms and realized he'd crushed the straw in his hands. Tossing it aside, he gripped the edge of the counter. "I'm not hiding anything. Appearances can be deceiving, you know."

Her eyes widened and she ran a gaze down his white denim jeans to his deck shoes. "No kidding."

He snorted a loud sound of disgust. "No. I mean what you saw in the Longfellows' stateroom."

She frowned. "You mean you like dressing up *and* women, too?"

He laughed. He couldn't help it. The way her nose scrunched up while she digested this new information she figured she'd discovered made her look so cute.

And then he remembered what she was reacting to. "That is not what I mean. Yes, I like women. No, I don't like dressing up in their clothes."

"But I saw—"

"Yeah. I know." He passed a hand over his face. Obviously he couldn't tell her what he'd really been up to, that he'd been searching the Longfellows' drawers for the diamonds. So, why did he have to tell her anything anyway? What did it matter what she thought?

He peered back at her suspicious face and all but tripped over his ego. And then she scrunched her nose again.

Sighing, he stepped forward and cupped her shoulders. She didn't flinch from his touch or try to back away as she sometimes did. She just stood there looking up at him, a myriad of questions in her wide brown eyes.

"Can you trust me on this?" he asked.

"Sure. I just wish you'd told me sooner." She shook a few unruly strands of hair away from her face and stared up at him. "I wouldn't have worried about…things."

Mike's hold on her shoulders tightened reflexively. He could easily shake her. Instead, his hands loosened their grasp and slid down her arms.

She blinked, and tugged her lower lip between her teeth.

He stopped above her elbows, and pulled her to him. She didn't resist, but her carriage was stiff, unnatural as she continued to watch him, her head tilted back. The ship rocked suddenly and she sagged against him.

When she would have righted herself, he held her to his chest, imprisoning her arms, and pressed his mouth to hers. She swayed a little, her lips rigid with surprise, before they parted in even greater shock.

He gained entry with his tongue, teasing her, tasting her. Then she relaxed and her hands rose to cradle his hips.

Leaning back against the cold refrigerator, he brought her with him until her thighs nestled between his. The impact of the chilly metal pressing through his shirt was enough to rouse his good sense, but not enough to stop him from hardening.

He broke the kiss, and stared down at her.

Her eyes were glazed and locked on his. She blinked, slowly, as the fog lifted. He saw the movement at her throat when she swallowed.

She righted herself. "What are you trying to prove? I already told you I understand."

"Prove? You think I—" He shook his head.

"You don't have to pretend with me." She laid a hand on his arm, then quickly snatched it back.

Her reaction reassured him. She felt the attraction, too. He grabbed her arms again and refitted her against him, moving his hips a fraction. The moment she felt his straining fly, color blossomed in her cheeks.

"You think I could pretend this?" he asked.

She lifted her chin, but the rest of her remained as stiff as a gangplank. "*Under* the right circumstances."

"Actually, I'd prefer you on top."

She stared blankly at first, then as his meaning sunk in, she flushed with renewed indignation. "Let go of me."

The ship rocked again, making a mockery of her words. She stumbled, and her chest flattened to his. His arms promptly circled her.

As she squirmed to get her balance, Mike groaned at the friction. Immediately, she stilled.

"No one *has* to actually be on top," he whispered into her hair.

It was difficult to keep from laughing, when she threw her head back to glare at him and he saw the daggers in her eyes. Her mouth moved but nothing came out. She was as mad as he'd ever seen her, and he could tell she didn't know what to do about it.

Jolie? Speechless? He grinned.

Confusion abruptly replaced the irritation in her face. "I don't know what to think anymore," she grumbled as she extricated herself from his hold. Her actions were slow, almost reluctant, he noted with satisfaction.

"You might think about going back to the room with me." He leaned against the refrigerator. Cold metal didn't come close to a cold shower. And from the way Jolie's attention strayed to points south, she was acutely aware of that fact.

When her gaze finally made it back to his face a fresh surge of color rushed her cheeks. "I'm moving in with FiFi."

"Because you don't think I'm interested?" He shifted against the uncomfortable snugness of his jeans. "Or are you afraid I'm too interested?"

She crossed her arms. "I think we need some space."

He shook his head. Between his getting caught in the Longfellows' room this morning, and Jolie's less than stellar cuisine, they were skating on thin ice. "Not a good idea. Someone may catch you."

"If they do, I'll handle it." She gave him a flip smile and turned back to the dishes. "Besides, what are they going to do? Dump us overboard?"

Mike frowned, thinking about Howard's measuring silence at dinner. If they suspected him at all, they probably wouldn't hesitate to do just that.

JOLIE LUGGED the two picnic baskets up from the galley and onto the deck. She tried dragging them to the tender, but her hands were shaking too badly. She wasn't sure if that was a result of carrying too much weight, or the aftermath of last night's disaster.

She shuddered, half from nerves, half from anger. Had Howard discovered her in FiFi's bed by accident, or did Mike have something to do with her getting caught?

It was awfully coincidental that last night of all nights, Howard would have wandered into FiFi's room, that he would have unknowingly crawled into bed beside her. The man was allergic to the dog, for heaven's sake. He normally stayed clear of her.

Jolie pressed two fingers to her temple. Her head ached from too little sleep, from Howard's startled shriek that had awakened the entire boat. If they didn't get fired by the end of the day it would be a miracle.

Sighing, she kicked at one of the baskets. A sloshing noise brought her back to her senses and she quickly peeked inside for damage. Everything looked okay.

She had spent extra time preparing the lunch Lola had requested. Since they didn't expect to reach the first scheduled port until this evening, Lola had suggested they picnic on one of the smaller islands along the way.

Jolie shaded her eyes from the sun and scanned the small, deserted island still several hundred yards away. The beach on the southern tip was nice, partially shaded by three large coconut trees, but the interior looked horribly overgrown and not very appealing for a hike. Stopping only for a picnic sounded like a lot of trouble, especially since they would be docking for the night only hours later, but right now, she was in no position to argue. She had to reserve her energy for begging. She shuddered again. Lots and lots of begging.

Time was growing short. If she didn't keep this job, she wouldn't have a prayer of seeing her inheritance.

Jolie bent to drag the baskets of food the remaining way when FiFi bounded up the stairs, becoming temporarily airborne off the last step in her excitement. She started barking before she hit the deck.

"Did you tell on me, you little rat?" Jolie mumbled as the dog started fervently sniffing the basket. Within seconds, nose turned up, she trotted away.

"Gee, that's a good sign."

From behind her, Mike's sarcasm was like a blast of icy air. Jolie gritted her teeth. She liked it better when he wasn't speaking to her, which had been most of the morning.

Ignoring him, she dragged the baskets to the tender that would take them ashore. When she started to hoist the food over the side, he stepped up and wrestled it from her.

It was then that she noticed he was bare-chested, and that his swimming trunks rode low on his hips. His skin was smooth and brown except for a smattering of dark golden hair that glistened in the sunlight. It arrowed down to a thin pale strip of skin around the waist of his shorts. Releasing a slow breath, she raised her gaze to his chest...where a nipple started to bead. Quickly, she unhanded the basket and allowed him to swing it easily aboard the small vessel.

When he leaned over to properly secure their cargo, his arms and back muscles tensed with the effort. She stared at the interplay between tan skin and sinew, down to the firm curve of his buttocks, nicely filling out the red trunks.

Without warning, a picture of the black negligee formed in her mind. She blinked at the incongruous image. Lola was right. What a waste.

He turned at the sound of her too-loud sigh. For a second, he looked past her, and then she was in his arms, the sweet smell of cocoa butter surrounding her, his lips finding hers.

His move had been sudden, and she allowed the swift contact of their mouths more from surprise than desire. But at the first lick of his tongue across her lower lip, heat erupted in her belly.

Before she could even think to struggle, he whispered, "The Longfellows are coming up behind you." Then he dragged his lips along her jaw, nipped at the fleshy part of her ear.

Foolish disappointment doused the spark. Silently she cursed him, cursed the goose bumps that had betrayed her. "One giant step for manhood," she murmured and arranged her expression into one of bored indifference only he could see.

He pulled back slowly, heedless of the other couple's approach. No match for the sparkling blue Atlantic, his eyes glittered with temper. "Careful, sweetheart. If I want to prove anything in that department, it won't be up here on deck."

She gave him her dirtiest look. Out of the corner of her eye, she caught a glimpse of Tom, looking tanned and fit at the helm, and she thought seriously about taking another whack at her husband's ego. She stopped herself. She was being intolerant of his preferences because of her own frustration. As if she'd ever had a chance with him in the first place.

She took a calming breath and managed a small, conciliatory smile. She was just so damn tired. Last night had been a disaster, leaving her with little sleep. Add to that the acute disappointment she'd love to deny.

Mike had made it clear he wasn't interested in Lola or her flirtations, and fool that she was, Jolie had sown a seed of hope. Although she hadn't consciously nurtured the idea of any relationship developing between them, she'd forgotten one basic truth. She was not like her sisters. The only thing she had going for her was her trust fund, and if she wasn't careful, she wouldn't even have that.

She forced a broader smile. Even if her act was for the sake of the Longfellows, she found comfort in knowing that Mike's disinterest wasn't entirely personal.

Nevertheless, she was glad they were docking tonight. She needed the distance.

"Hate to interrupt you two lovebirds, but are we all set?" Lola asked.

The woman's curt tone snapped Jolie out of her mental gymnastics, and she stepped to Mike's side, giving the Longfellows her full attention. Obviously, Lola was still peeved over last night's debacle.

"The food's ready," Jolie said pleasantly.

"Good." The malice in Lola's eyes sharpened before it vanished. Her gaze stalled on Mike for nearly a minute, her brows puckering, lips thinning. Then she smiled at

Jolie. "Tom will take you both over to the island to set up."

Jolie blinked. Lola wasn't angry with her at all. Mike was her target. Was this the "woman scorned" syndrome? Or was that pity she saw flash in the woman's eyes?

The thought lent no comfort. "Sure," Jolie said. "We should have everything ready in about fifteen minutes."

Lola barely listened. She'd headed for a chaise.

Howard cast a quick glance after his wife, and in a low voice, he said, "Better take jackets. It might get chilly."

"Jackets?" Jolie looked skyward. The bright sun made her squint.

"Good idea," Mike said. "Jolie, why don't you run down and get them?"

Nodding thoughtfully, Howard hurried after his wife.

"Jackets," Jolie repeated.

"Damn it. If he wants us to wear boots, we wear boots. Indulge him, would you? We're in no position to argue."

"God, but I hate to agree with you," she muttered, as she headed below, ignoring Mike's grunt of annoyance.

She grabbed two windbreakers from the tangle of clothes in the closet, a result of her hasty reinstallment in their room early this morning.

By the time she returned, Mike had equipped them with blankets to sit on, an ice chest of drinks, along with one of the picnic baskets.

Tom told them he'd bring the rest of the food when he came back for the Longfellows, and they all climbed down the ladder into the tender.

The men took turns steering while Jolie shaded her eyes, searching the shoreline for a spot to set up their picnic.

There wasn't much from which to choose. Apart from

the small clearing with the three coconut trees, the rest of the island was overgrown with mango and other strange trees and a wild assortment of ferns. But she did notice a semigrassy area shaded by a leafy breadfruit tree and pointed them in that direction.

They quickly unloaded their cargo and set out the blankets. Tom was halfway back to the yacht when Mike finally spoke to her again.

Well, he didn't exactly speak. She was down on her hands and knees leveling the sand beneath the blanket when she heard a groan coming from the vicinity of the picnic basket. Half-expecting him to make another crack about her cooking, she sat back on her heels and turned to give him a warning look. "What did you say?"

Mike frowned. He stacked the last plate, the brief clang of china piercing the silence. "Nothing."

More silence. Then another soft groan.

The tropical March air was hardly chilly, but a shiver lifted the hair on Jolie's arms. She stared at Mike's unmoving lips. His frown deepened as he reached for the picnic basket.

He flipped open the top. A pair of tan and black pointed ears sprang out, twitched, then sank backward. FiFi's eyes seemed to roll in her head, as it lolled back. She blinked, then cut loose a king-size belch.

"How did she get in there?" Jolie dropped her hand from her mouth and hurried over on her knees. She took the limp terrier from Mike's hands.

"So much for lunch." He snorted, poking around the picnic basket.

"Do you think she's okay?" Jolie dabbed at the frothy mayonnaise coating the dog's whiskers.

"With your cooking?" Sighing with disgust, he rubbed his eyes. "Maybe this is a blessing in disguise."

"Knock it off, *Duval*." She grinned when he scowled. "Besides, that was only the appetizer. Lunch is in the basket you left for Tom to bring."

She squinted past him in the direction of the yacht.

The smile froze on her face, and her pulse skidded. She squinted harder. "Hey, does the *Lola* look like it's moving to you?"

Chapter Eleven

Mike spun around. He watched for several moments as the *Lola II* gained speed toward the open sea.

He drove a hand through his hair. "Son of a—"

FiFi's excited bark drowned him out.

"Shut that damn mutt up." He poked a finger in Jolie's direction as she cradled the dog to her breasts. FiFi cowered at his tone of voice. Exhaling sharply, Mike felt no relief from the volcano threatening to erupt in his chest.

"It's not her fault," Jolie said, rubbing the dog's small ears. "Don't snap at her. Besides, they're probably just turning around or something. I mean, they wouldn't just leave us." She frowned at the retreating ship before returning wide eyes on him. "Would they?"

He'd have loved to reassure her. "They're gone."

"But why?" She shook her head. "We didn't do anything *that* bad. Besides, Lola wouldn't leave FiFi."

"She doesn't know about FiFi. *We* didn't know about FiFi."

"I still don't believe they'd leave us. Even if they're mad, they could have fired us when we docked tonight."

Mike silently agreed. Which meant they knew he was after the diamonds. He'd have a hell of a time explaining that to Jolie. "Maybe they couldn't face another one of your culinary masterpieces." He glanced pointedly at the pathetic-looking terrier.

"Wait a minute." She set the dog on the blanket and scrambled to her feet. "You're not blaming me for this."

He held up both hands. "Of course not." The smirk in his voice could have been heard clear back to New York.

"After all, Lola's lingerie was safe with me," she said, lifting her chin.

"I was *not* trying on that stuff, damn it."

"Of course not."

He crossed his arms. "Nor was I the one sleeping with the dog...and Howard."

A hand flew to her hip and she opened her mouth. Then she closed it again and shook her head. Bending down, she scooped up her jacket, picked up FiFi and marched off toward the trees.

"Where are you going?" Mike called out when she approached the first pocket of vegetation.

He didn't really expect her to answer, and she didn't. Watching her white shorts and lightly tanned legs disappear into the brush, he kicked at the blanket until it bunched against the breadfruit tree. The stacked china clattered into the sand. Two crystal goblets collided and shattered.

And still he had enough tension bottled up inside to send a rocket to the moon. Or a small watercraft to Jamaica.

He scanned the horizon. Blue skies met blue ocean, without any trace left of the Longfellows. The short, jagged stretch of sandy beach showed no signs of human inhabitation.

"Great. Where's the bane of civilization when you need it?" he muttered, pulling on the shirt he had grabbed at the last minute. And then it occurred to him that not only were they stranded, but they had no money on them. He shook his head, squashing the urge to punch out a tree.

A broken hand wouldn't do him any good. Especially now that he was responsible for Jolie. As much of a pain as she was, she wouldn't be in this mess if it weren't for him.

Not that he intended to let her know that, he thought as he approached the mouth of the jungle and easily picked up her trail. Broken branches and splintered twigs scratched his arms and legs and pointed him in her direction.

But after following the trampled vegetation for the next ten minutes, Mike still saw no sign of her and started to worry. With his longer stride, he should have caught up to her by now. Yet he hadn't heard so much as a yap out of FiFi.

Crouching, he checked the ground for footprints. He hoped Jolie was better at surviving than she was at cooking.

JOLIE SLAPPED at the wayward branch. Visualizing Mike's arrogant face within the broad flat leaves, she gave it an extra cuff. When she started to cross the slippery rock path to the pool, the limb sprang back and about knocked her over. She teetered uncertainly for a moment, one arm reaching out for balance, the other safely cuddling FiFi. The dog was still drowsy from its gluttony, and probably a little sick.

She sighed as she aligned her body with her feet, then hopped off the rock. So, she wasn't a great cook. No big deal. She was good at…at…

The thought was too depressing to contemplate. Kicking off her tennis shoes, she sat on the side of the pool and set FiFi down. What the hell *was* she good at?

Had Monique or Nicole been asked that question, they would have run out of fingers to tick off.

FiFi growled at a movement on the opposite rock. A green lizard darted across to disappear under some twigs. FiFi's growl dissolved into a whimper.

Jolie laughed and petted the dog. "You're bigger than he is, you baby. You probably scared him half to death."

Dipping the tips of her toes into the pool, she found the water cooler than she'd expected. But of course, she hadn't expected to run across any fresh water either. She'd bet her inheritance Mike hadn't been so lucky.

So, she had done that well, hadn't she?

As much as she tried pushing the thought away, it bothered her that she couldn't readily come up with something she excelled at. On top of that, she'd gotten fired *again.* And this time with flourish.

She eyed the dog speculatively. "What do you think, FiFi? Could I still be considered employed while baby-sitting you?" The dog barked and shot across the rocks.

"Oh, no you don't." Jolie slipped and slid, trying to gain her footing, then scrambled after her potential meal ticket. Fast and determined, FiFi was out of sight within seconds.

If not for the little terror's insistent barking, no telling if or when she'd have found her. But it was fairly easy to stay on the dog's noisy trail as Jolie dodged clusters of ferns thick from humidity and the absence of human intrusion.

Vaguely she noted several low-hung mango tree branches, dense with plump ripe fruit and looking a lot like lunch.

The barking stopped. "FiFi? Come here, girl."

The squawk of a strange bird was her only response.

"FiFi?" The vegetation was so dense, all she could see was straight up. She peered at the nearly obscured sky. It looked like rain. When had that happened? "FiFi! Come here. Now."

Another noise. Dog...no. Animal...yes. Of the human variety...possibly. Drawing a shaky hand up her bare arm, she swallowed.

"FiFi? You want a treat? I've got a treat for you." She offered the lie without compunction, hoping the little sucker was too greedy to remember that she had nearly overdosed on deviled eggs.

That got a small bark out of the dog, but still she didn't appear. Jolie took a tentative step in the direction of the noise. She continued calling out, half-afraid of what she was calling out to. The island was supposed to be uninhabited. It certainly looked that way.

There'd be no reason for a person to be here. Unless they'd been shipwrecked...or abandoned, she thought wryly.

Or if they were hiding out.

Her steps faltered. Fanciful visions of pirates, escaped convicts, desperadoes traipsed through her overtired brain. Her hand fluttered to her throat, and she laughed nervously.

"It's not funny."

Mike's voice startled her. It came from somewhere to her left, followed by FiFi's growl. Quickly, she scanned the trees and shrubs.

Several yards away, he was backed up against the trunk of a breadfruit tree, his tan T-shirt blending in with the bark, his gaze riveted to something on the ground. Not once did he look her way. From the same vicinity, FiFi whimpered.

Parting the leafy branches, Jolie pushed her way toward them. "What's going on? How did you find me?"

He blinked, and with great hesitation, tossed her a lightning-quick glance. "Uh, you were easy to track."

"Really? I bet you didn't find the water yet." She stepped out into the small clearing. Out of the corner of her eye, she noticed movement on the ground to her right.

FiFi barked. Jolie whipped around. Nothing was there but the terrier wagging her tail.

She turned back to Mike. He looked pale for a second, before color flooded his face. "Are you okay?"

"Fine." He took a deep breath and stepped away from the tree. "Why the hell did you run off like that?"

"Sorry, Dad, I didn't know I had to check with you." She bent down and scooped up FiFi. "What were you doing?"

"Never mind. What did you say about water?"

She frowned, glanced around, then tucked the dog under her arm. "I found a fresh pool if you want to follow me."

"Great." His gaze bounced to the path, but he made no attempt to move. "Good."

Jolie scratched FiFi's ears, wishing the dog could explain what the heck was going on. The terrier squirmed. Then her sudden loud bark made them both jump.

A scaly brown lizard darted out from under a bush, and Jolie barely managed to keep the wriggling ball of canine fur contained. She looked to Mike for help and was astonished to find that the color had again fled his face, leaving behind a mask of sheer terror. He was afraid of lizards.

She tried not to gape. She tried not to laugh.

But he was so wrapped up in keeping tabs on the small reptile, that he was unaware of her interest. Biting her lip, she looked away to give him some privacy.

After a moment she tried to push past him, but he halted her with a hand on her shoulder. She looked up and saw that his color was returning, that his morning shave was nothing but a shadowy memory. The cleft on his chin broadened with a slow smile that gallantly tugged at his lips.

"Let me go first." He cast a quick glance at the path, then sidestepped her into the thickening brush. A limb scraped his arm. He snapped it in two, ignoring the long scratch it left across his bicep.

He continued to plow ahead, shoving aside the wild tangle of green and brown leaves and gnarled branches. He made sure that she cleared the area behind him before letting go, and thanks to his care, she made it to the next small clearing without even the tiniest scrape.

And with startling clarity and a small catch in her heart, Jolie realized she more than liked this man.

"Which way?" he asked, stopping to glance over his shoulder at her.

"Well…" Her gaze darted from one tree to the other as she pulled herself together. *This is nothing more than physical attraction,* she told herself sternly as she concentrated on the landscape. Everything yet nothing looked familiar. She peered up at the darkening clouds.

He dragged a forearm across his brow, and squinting, followed her line of vision. "Looks like we're going to have all the fresh water we need."

"You think so? I mean, if it does rain, it probably won't last long. It doesn't usually." At his curious frown, she shrugged. "At least, not when I've been here before."

"Here?"

"The Caribbean," she said. He narrowed his gaze. "On vacation. With my grandfather." She didn't owe him any explanations. Why did he make her feel so defensive?

"The jeweler?"

She nodded, and looked away.

"Where specifically do you *vacation?*"

"I thought we were looking for water."

"I didn't know we needed to look for it."

She pressed her lips together and peered past him through the throng of trees. "Keep going straight."

He nodded, looking far from convinced. Mopping his brow one last time, he pushed forward.

Ten minutes later, they found water. Only it wasn't exactly what Jolie had hoped for. One fat drop landed on her cheek. Another clipped the tip of her nose.

"Damn." Mike stopped abruptly in front of her.

Too busy ducking the rain to react, she collided with his broad, unmovable back. Coarse leg hair brushed her bare thighs. His powerful male scent rushed her. She threw up a hand to brace herself, and thinly sheathed muscles bunched and pressed against her palm.

Startled, she looked up into his eyes. He'd swiveled around at some point during the collision, and she found that it was his chest cupped beneath her hand.

She started to let go, but FiFi squirmed under her other arm, throwing her off balance. So instead, she clung to him as the heavens opened, showering them with cool spring rain.

Mike swore. Then he slipped an arm around her, hunching his body to shield her and the dog from the worst of the downpour. Huddled together, they hastened toward a tree with a sweeping crown of large flat leaves.

Once he had them safely beneath the protective branches, he dropped his arm from around her shoulders and stepped back. Wiping the water from his face, he released a lusty breath. His T-shirt was soaked to his skin, the thin fabric clinging to each well-defined muscle, to beaded nipples.

Jolie couldn't look away. "I think there's a shallow cave at the pool I found. Enough to offer some shelter."

His disbelieving look made her instantly regret the stupid remark. Obviously, it was a little late to be worried about shelter. Swiping the thick coating of moisture from her arms, she steeled herself for his sarcasm.

Mike chuckled. "Still think you can find your way? You must have one hell of a sense of direction."

"Yeah." She stared uncertainly at the mass of trees and vines being pelted by the rain. Dampness gathered in her lashes and blurred her vision. She swiped it away. Tree limbs twisted and bent, their glossy, green leaves being pummeled under the force of the downpour.

Yet the rain was no longer the problem. The wind had picked up considerably, and what had initially seemed like a warm tropical shower now chilled her to the bone. She shivered.

"Hey." He captured her hand and tugged her toward him, drawing her and FiFi into the circle of his arms. "I'm pretty wet, but body heat has to count for something."

"Aren't you cold?" She tilted her head back to look at him.

He didn't answer, but stared down at her, his gaze lingering on her quivering lower lip. He was going to kiss her. She sucked in a breath.

Slowly, he shook his head. "Not now."

"Oh." She didn't know quite what to do with her free hand, the one not spoken for by FiFi. She fisted it around her soaked shirttail, which had managed to come loose.

"I hope the stuff we left on the beach manages to stay partially dry," he said, transferring his gaze briefly in the direction of the beach.

"Did you cover it up?"

"Not exactly." His mouth dipped in a wry twist. "I left everything under a tree, sort of wrapped in the blanket."

"Your jacket's in there."

"That's kinda what I was hoping stayed dry."

"Me, too."

A lopsided grin lifted one side of his mouth. "It's not that hard being nice to each other, is it?"

"Of course not," she said, and when he raised a brow, they both laughed. "Do you think the Longfellows got caught in this?"

His hold tightened for a moment, his eyes glinting with a dangerous gleam. Then with obvious effort, he relaxed.

She waited for her earlier fears to rush back. Fear because she didn't know this man, or why he was really here. But not even a vague doubt threatened. She smiled up at him.

"I hope so. Maybe it'll slow them down," he said, his palm starting to roam her back. The heat of his gaze warmed her. "Then again, maybe we shouldn't be in such a hurry."

Jolie's heart burst into an erratic beat. She was certain he could feel it, with her breasts pressed against his chest as they were, the pressure of his hand crushing her closer. "Yeah. Give them time to realize FiFi is missing. Then they'll turn around."

"I wouldn't count on that."

She held her breath. "Why not?"

He stopped the gentle kneading, but his gaze continued to hold hers. His hand traveled up to cup her nape. "I'm sorry I got you into this."

His eyes were so beautiful, so intense, she wanted to look away. She couldn't. "Into what?"

He stared hard, as if trying to make a decision. "The rain is starting to taper off. Let's head back to the beach."

She wanted to know what he'd meant. But he dropped his arms to his sides, and she knew she'd not get her answer.

"We should keep looking for the pool," she said. "There was a small waterfall feeding it, so now's a good time. After all that rain, we should be able to hear it."

He gave her a funny look, then grinned. "Good work, detective. You're probably right."

She smiled back, absurdly happy. "Yes, that was good detecting, wasn't it?"

He shoved a large branch out of their way. Another one that had tangled with it sprang forward, its wet leaves dousing them.

The full effect of the spray hit Jolie directly in the face. She blinked and sputtered, trying to catch her breath. FiFi whined, then sneezed.

"I'm sorry, kid," Mike said, sounding anything but contrite. Laughter shook his voice.

When she was finally able to focus, she saw the corners of his eyes crinkle. She swiped at her moist cheeks. "Don't call me 'kid.'"

He lifted an amused brow, but as his gaze drifted down the front of her shirt, all amusement vanished from his face. "Right. Let's get moving."

She frowned at the sudden gruff tone he'd adopted and cast a furtive glance down the front of her. Both nipples were perfectly outlined, and protruded against the thin pink cotton of her shirt. Casually, she tried to peel the wet fabric away from her body.

But she needn't have bothered. He'd already turned back to the path and was several feet ahead of her, savagely whacking at the tree limbs and vines that got in his way.

She smiled, her brief shyness forgotten. She'd gotten to him. And Mr. Confidence wasn't responding well at all.

"Slow down, will you? I doubt there's a fire," she called out, trying to keep the smile out of her tone.

He came to an abrupt halt, and faced her. She stopped, too, wishing that she'd kept her big mouth shut. She had no trouble wiping the grin from her lips and voice now.

His eyes were the same stormy blue that she imagined the ocean surrounding them was at the moment, and his mouth...God, his mouth inched into a lazy, sensual curve.

"What?" Dipping her chin, she hid her nervous hands under FiFi's wet fur.

He grabbed the hem of his sodden shirt, yanked the fabric over his head and took a step toward her. "So, you wanna start a fire?"

Chapter Twelve

Mike frowned when Jolie backed up. What did she think he was going to do to her? He reached for FiFi and practically had to pry her from Jolie's cold hands. The poor mutt was about to get the life squeezed out of her.

FiFi growled softly at him as if she knew he preferred big dogs, and not small, yappy, spoiled ones. He tucked her into the crook of his arm, and asked, "Do you think you could do that?"

Jolie flexed her fingers, her gaze settling on his bare chest, before lowering to his stomach. Something had startled her. He could see it in the glimmer in her eyes, the way her tongue darted out to moisten her lips. Her breasts rose and fell with the deep breath she took, her nipples still hard as she quickly schooled her expression.

He squashed the urge to check his fly. Hell, he didn't even have a zipper.

"Do what?" she asked.

"A fire, Sherlock. As in start one."

Her chin came up. "Here?"

"No. Back on the beach. I figure we ought to split up, and I'll start looking for shelter." Angling his watch, he glanced at it. "We have a few hours before dark, but if we have to build anything it's going to take a while."

"Build something? You really think we'll..." Her voice trailed off as she stared out into the dank vegetation obscuring their path.

"Don't fall apart on me now, honey."

"Me?" She huffed her impatience. "I'm totally capable of taking care of myself, *sweetheart*." She held out her hands. "*And* FiFi."

He handed her his wet shirt. "Once you get the fire started, hang this nearby, will you?"

She flung the soggy fabric over her shoulder. "Now, give me the dog."

"The pooch stays with me. Can you find your way back?"

"FiFi and I will do just fine."

"I don't want the little princess darting away from you. You'll end up chasing her and getting lost."

"Who died and made you dictator? Give me the dog."

He grinned at the stubborn way she scrunched up her mouth. "No can do, Sherlock. Now, I suggest you get your fanny moving before we have another downpour."

Her gaze narrowed before taking a quick inventory of the sky. "It won't rain again. Not this afternoon, anyway." She wiggled the fingers of one hand impatiently, the other she placed on her hip.

It was then he noticed that her white shorts were drenched, and plastered to her thighs and hips like a coat of fresh paint. Something brief and rosy was outlined beneath, the color seeping through the transparent cotton. A misshapen triangle, the phantom pink suspended by lacy twine cut high over her hips...hips that seductively curved toward a waist he could span with one hand.

He stared, his appreciation of her image no less than if she were an expensive watercolor.

"What's wrong?" Jolie took a step back, her teeth

catching at her lower lip. The fingers of her outstretched hand curled into a nervous fist. She lowered her arm, her gaze faltering as it met his. Then she blinked, her eyes drifting toward the visual path he'd blazed.

He shifted FiFi from one arm to the other, while he watched Jolie's eyes widen in horror at the view she got of herself.

"You ready to start that fire?" he asked, the impatience he'd strived for lost in the hoarseness of his voice.

"I think we already have." Her gaze moved to the front of his swim trunks.

Mike didn't have to look to see what she was talking about. The pressure had started building much earlier, with the way she'd looked at him, her eyes glowing with both fear and excitement, telling him her sensual thoughts in a way that would have infuriated her had she known.

He shifted against the hardness cramping his trunks, and did the only thing he could. He laughed.

She blinked again, and slowly raised her eyes to his. They widened a fraction, before she shut them tight. Clearly, she hadn't meant to vocalize that crack about the fire. Now as she mouthed something, she did so silently. Though it wasn't hard to make out the earthy word she used.

He laughed again. "Hell of a honeymoon, huh?"

Her eyes flew open, chocolate-brown, ringed with panic. "Don't even think it."

"What?"

She took another step back, and stumbled before jerking around, and plowing through the thick, wet foliage.

"What's wrong?" He started to go after her, but she'd managed a large lead in the direction of the beach, FiFi long since forgotten.

He stopped, shook his head. "What did I say?"

The terrier growled, her dark eyes large and accusing, the silly pink bow askew against her wet, black fur.

Mike frowned. "I only joked about the honeymoon...." He stared off after his wife, understanding starting to dawn. Grinning, he absently patted FiFi's head and continued to gaze in Jolie's direction. "Too late, honey. I've already been thinking about it."

MIDRUB, ONE STICK snapped. Surprised, Jolie lost control of its mate, and the switch flew from her hand to spin high into the air. She scooted back to avoid its fall. It missed her by a hair.

Not so, the clump of wet sand that worked its way up her shorts leg and wedged itself under the elastic of her bikini panties.

"Damn it. Damn it. Damn it." Dropping the useless stick, she jumped to her feet, shook and shimmied, stomped and swore. And found a lot more sand in inconvenient places.

"Sure, a fire," she muttered as she reached under her shorts to pull the elastic away from her body. What seemed like half the beach slid down her leg to the ground. She let the elastic snap back into place, and shifted uncomfortably.

So she wasn't a darn Girl Scout. Certainly neither Monique nor Nicole could do any better under the circumstances. But of course, her sisters wouldn't have found themselves in this dismal situation.

Out of nowhere, a memory of Mike and *his* obvious predicament presented itself. The image of him was in Technicolor, so real in her mind that she could see the outline of his problem straining against the wet, red swim trunks. She could almost feel the solid strength of his chest as he'd shielded her from the rain.

She shut her eyes against the flashback. And still the heat assaulted her body. The tingling crept up her thighs and competed with the annoying sand.

She didn't want to think about him, think about possibilities that didn't have a snowball's chance in July. Possibilities that only existed because she was, for the next few days, the proverbial last woman on earth.

Most of all, she didn't want to be second-best.

Hovering in the shadows had been acceptable for most of her life, but for some reason it wasn't okay now. Not here. Not with Mike.

She kicked the useless sticks to the side. With the movement, another clump of sand dislodged and plopped down on her other foot. Wishing she could shake her other problem so easily, she stared miserably out toward the rain-shrouded horizon.

Waves capped and rolled, spreading white foam like birthday-cake icing. Once hitting land, they lapped gently as if in invitation.

It took only a second for Jolie to decide. After a brief glance over her shoulder, she kicked off her shorts, shrugged out of her jacket and pulled off her shirt. Although she didn't think Mike would be returning anytime soon, she left her gear near the water's edge.

Not that he hadn't already gotten an eyeful, she thought wryly, as she tugged her bikini panties into place, adjusted her bra straps and charged the receding surf.

The water felt cooler than she'd expected, and tiny bumps surfaced her skin about the same time she surfaced an exceptionally choppy swell. She wasn't sure if it was the spring temperature chilling the ocean, or merely the contrast of her own heated nerves. Sucking in another breath, she dived under again.

After about fifteen minutes of vigorous swimming, a

pleasant lethargy infused her limbs as she lumbered out of the water. She was glad Mike had insisted on keeping FiFi. The swim had done her good. Maybe even more than a cold shower, she thought, and smiling as she swiped the water from her face and reached for her clothes.

They weren't there. She blinked at the mound of sand where her clothes should have been.

Quickly, she spun toward the stretch of beach. Pristine white sand extended as far as she could see. Something brown caught her eye, but it was only a piece of driftwood.

She looked the other way. Several dried clumps of seaweed dotted the shoreline. Nothing else. Clenching her teeth, she turned back for a closer inspection of the spot where she'd left her clothes.

A couple of feet away was a footprint deeply embedded in the sand. It was large, almost twice the size of hers. The heel of another was a stride away, and although the toe portion was obliterated by drifting sand, it was enough to tell her which way he'd headed.

Irritation bubbled in her chest and evolved to a low growl. She flexed her fingers in anticipation of closing them around his conniving neck and took a determined step. And stopped when she realized that she had a clear view of the spot where they'd left their things. The clothes weren't there. Neither was the blanket. Or anything else.

A shiver slithered down her spine. The skin puckered on her arms. She looked down and realized that, wet, her pink underwear was so transparent that it might just as well be nonexistent.

She shivered again. Resisting the urge to cover herself with her arms, she looked back up, doubt nipping the edge off her annoyance. Maybe they had been wrong to assume there was no one else on the island. Maybe the Longfellows had docked on the other side. Maybe.

Maybe she ought to get out of view.

Quickly, she headed toward the trees, her arms creeping up to cross over her chest. She didn't know what she should be hoping for...to find that Mike had played a practical joke on her, or that someone else was on the island. Either way, she'd literally been caught with her pants down.

The thought inspired a healthy dose of anger. She approached the tree where their things had been stored, and glimpsed something blue through the trees. Before she could screw up her courage to investigate, she heard FiFi bark. She spun toward the sound.

Mike stepped out of the foliage. He was still barechested as she'd left him. His trunks were unsnapped. "Have a nice swim?" he asked, his voice low and emotionless.

"Where are my clothes?"

One dark brow lifted as he ran a deliberate gaze down her body. "Not on you."

She realized that she had, at some point, dropped her arms. She crossed them again. "I want them now."

"Do you?" He walked past her. Although his expression remained bland, she could feel the anger radiating from him.

She didn't move. Out of the corner of her eye, she watched him circle her, pick up some twigs and return to the path from where he'd appeared. As soon as he started back, she hurried after him through the trees.

FiFi barked in welcome as soon as they approached the small clearing on the other side. The dog was tied to a tree next to a pile of coconut fronds that looked to have been freshly harvested.

"I want my clothes, Mike."

"I bet you do." He didn't look up from the collection of twigs he was arranging in a circle. "I was kinda thinking it would be nice to have a partially dry shirt."

Jolie shivered, as much from the ice in his voice as the increasingly cool trade winds. The problem was clear now. He was upset because she hadn't lit a fire. She glanced over his head, searching in vain for signs of her clothes.

She sighed. "Most of the sticks were wet. I couldn't find two that worked."

He did look up then, and frowned.

She shifted from one foot to the other as his gaze fell to her shoulders, her breasts, her belly, her... His frown deepened. He sat back on his haunches, his eyes moving up to her face. "What are you talking about?"

"The fire. I tried starting it. I really did. But the sticks—" She mimicked the rubbing motion to reinforce her claim, and noticed the splinters, the small blister bubbling near her thumb.

He saw them, too, and stood. "What the hell did you do?" He grabbed her wrists and held both hands up for inspection. "You were playing Girl Scout?" he asked incredulously.

"Playing?" She tried to jerk her hands free, but he held firm. "I was trying to start the fire you asked for."

He shook his head, a wry smile curving the corners of his mouth. Using one hand, he held both her wrists together. She shrunk back but he pulled her up against him. His eyes met hers for an instant. Danger shone from their depths. And her well-honed common sense quivered with foolish anticipation.

He bowed his head. She held her breath. He was going to kiss her.

He plucked a splinter from her finger. Gently, he probed her skin, his fingers softly trailing the creases over her knuckles.

His hands were so much larger than hers, his movements should have been awkward. Only they weren't. He found another small piece of bark and removed it with a featherlight touch.

Jolie hadn't realized she was still holding her breath until it came out in a whoosh. His hooded gaze leaped to her mouth, and she sucked the air back in so fast it made her dizzy.

He smiled, steadying her, keeping her wrists imprisoned. Dragging his attention away from her face, he returned his eyes to her hand. He brought it closer, inches from his lips, his touch so gentle she thought she'd die from the sensation. She waited, her palm itching for the inevitable kiss.

"What a beauty."

She swallowed, forgetting to breathe altogether. Gazing up at the earnestness in his face, she reveled in the huskiness of his voice, in the words she never expected to hear. She wanted to hear them again. "Mike?"

He peered closer. "The blister."

It took several seconds for reality to sink in. Then she stepped back, pressing her trembling lips together.

Stupid. Stupid. Stupid. What was she *thinking?* She gave a hard twist with both arms, stumbling backward with the force.

Clearly surprised, he let her go.

"What's wrong?" He recovered and tried to catch her from falling.

She dodged him, nearly tripping. A broad-leaved shrub cushioned her. "Don't touch me."

He spread his hands. "I was only trying to help."

"You can do that by starting the fire."

He looked as though he had more to say, then thought better of it. Frowning, he moved to their small stash, then crouched to withdraw a book of matches.

Without thinking, Jolie moved closer and glared at them. "Why didn't you tell me about those?"

"All you had to do was look through this kit."

"You did that deliberately, didn't you?"

"Don't be childish. We have more important things to worry about." He struck a match, touched the flame to a twig and threw the lighted stick in with the kindling he'd collected. "I'm starving. Why don't you go find something for us to eat?"

Childish? She was mad. Mad because he'd made a fool out of her. A fool to believe she had anything he wanted.

"You're the one starving." She stooped down and took over rooting through the pile he'd abandoned, and found her jacket and shorts all wadded up. She pulled them on with jerky movements, then returned to her search.

He sighed with disgust. "Are you going to be totally useless?"

Her head snapped up. She glared into his mocking face, the confident tilt of his strong jaw. "I am not..."

The words caught in her throat. Maybe she was useless. Maybe... Lifting her chin, she slowly stood up.

She had to get away from him. Away from the reminder that her best was never good enough.

MIKE SHOOK several branches of the lean-to, checking its sturdiness. One good, strong wind and their temporary shelter would be history, but at least for the night, it would give them a sense of security, no matter how false.

He glanced at his watch. She'd been gone for almost two hours. And it was his fault.

Fifteen more minutes. That's all he was going to give her before he'd go after her. He knew that it shouldn't have taken more than ten minutes or so to find some fruit. He had seen plenty earlier dangling from trees.

And then the sickening thought occurred to him. What if she couldn't reach any? What if she'd tried climbing a tree, fallen and hurt herself? He wouldn't put it past her. She'd already demonstrated her persistence by trying to rub those damn sticks together to the point of blistering herself. While he admired her tenacity, it did a number on his guilt quotient.

He ordered himself to calm down. She hadn't fallen out of a tree. He would have heard her scream. Wouldn't he?

''Damn.''

He made some minor adjustments to the lean-to, then laid out the blanket on the sheltered side. When he stepped back to check his handiwork, a branch scraped his bare belly. He cursed a blue streak, then glanced around to make sure Jolie hadn't approached suddenly.

Somehow he didn't really expect to see her. And deep down he knew why. She wasn't staying away to find food, or because she had hurt herself. She was staying away from him.

He'd wanted to kiss her. Really bad. Hell, he wanted to do a lot more than kiss her. And although he'd held himself back, she knew.

And she wanted no part of him.

It was a new experience for Mike. A very depressing one. He didn't know which hurt worse, his ego or his libido.

He chuckled wryly to himself. He knew damn well which hurt worse. That was a no-brainer. Then he remembered the incident with Lola's negligee. Maybe Jolie still wasn't convinced that he liked women?

That was probably it. Smiling, he rubbed relief into his temples. Sure. And there was one perfect way to straighten out that idiotic notion.

His grin fell to a sigh. What if he was wrong?

This was crazy. Why was this woman getting under his skin like this? Was it because he felt guilty, responsible? He should be worrying about the damn diamonds.

He scooped up his jacket. That was the only reason he was going after her. So he didn't have to think about her anymore.

"Here's your dinner."

She startled him from behind. He turned around just in time to catch the mango she hurled at him. He missed the second one, and tensing his muscles too late, he felt the sting of the torpedo-shaped fruit hitting his belly.

He looked down at the red mark "dinner" had left then at the battered mango lying on the ground. Slowly he raised his eyes to her don't-mess-with-me expression. She threw another small round yellow fruit straight up into the air and caught it without looking away.

And here he was worried about her hurting herself, about having hurt her. Guilt and atonement went the way of the swift sea breeze chilling his chest and legs. "Knock it off, Jolie."

She spun the fruit up into the air again as if it were a kid's baseball. "Yeah? Or what?"

Now that he knew she was okay, he remembered how hungry he was and that she was messing with his dinner. He stuffed the mango into his jacket pocket, and draped the garment over his arm. "Well, let's just say that if you act like a child, I'm going to have to discipline you like one."

He looked meaningfully at her bottom. It was small but

round. And he already knew it was nice and firm. He flexed his hands. Hell, he wished she'd call his bluff.

The fruit had already left her hand, headed for the sky. This time she nearly missed catching it. "You wouldn't—" Narrowing her gaze, she tossed back her hair. Then extended her hand. "I'm not sure what this is. It looks like some sort of passion fruit, doesn't it?"

Passion fruit? He shook out his jacket, trying to decide whether he should let that opening slide or not. He started to slip on the jacket in order to free his hands and to ward off the cool late-afternoon wind kicking up off the ocean. But something wasn't right. The sleeve felt too tight.

He jerked the jacket off his forearm and stared at the unfamiliar tan fabric. Now that he focused on it, he realized it was far too small. "This isn't mine."

She frowned, stepping closer, and fingered the collar. "It's mine."

Mike let his incredulous gaze drift to the cream-colored jacket she wore, then back to her guilt-stricken face. "You brought two for you and none for me?"

Her eyes reluctantly met his as she began shaking her head. "It wasn't like that. I didn't think we needed them. I brought them just to appease Howard, remember?"

"I don't believe this."

She let go of the jacket and laid a hand on his arm. "It wasn't intentional."

"I'll bet."

"Of course it wasn't. Don't you remember we thought it odd that Howard suggested we—" She stopped. "What are you looking at?"

He smiled. He was going to enjoy this. "I guess you'll have to keep me warm."

She dropped her hand. "You're crazy."

"No question about it." Sighing, he caught her wrist before she managed to pull away. "I need to talk to you."

"You can talk to me without touching me."

"That's what I want to talk to you about."

Her eyes widened comically. She made a nervous swipe at her hair. That was when he smelled the strawberries. Strange. He hadn't associated that scent with her before.

"I don't understand," she said while attempting to back up. "I'm not sure I want to, either. We had a deal. We're simply supposed to—"

"Did you shampoo your hair?" The question sounded absurd even to him. But the aroma of strawberries was so strong....

She laughed. "How could I have done that?"

"I must really be hungry." Shaking his head, he laughed, too. "You smell like strawberries."

The color drained from her face. When it abruptly returned, she was far redder than the elusive berry. "I think I'll go cut up these mangoes."

She grabbed as much fruit as she could and nearly tripped in her haste to get away from him. Interestingly, along with her went the phantom aroma.

He watched her fish out a knife from the picnic basket and immediately get to work on their dinner. It was the most enthusiastic he'd seen her around anything that resembled cooking.

Yet her attention continued to dart his way, her attempts at furtiveness failing miserably. When Mike realized that she was trying to keep him in her sight, he knew it wasn't strawberries he smelled any longer, but a rat.

"I'll be back in a few minutes," he called out, and made a show of slipping off into the jungle.

He waited a minute, then doubled back and sneaked up on her from the opposite side of their small camp.

Crouched by a low bush, too busy to look up, she continued to unload something from her jacket pockets.

"What's that?"

She jumped at the sound of his voice. Her precarious balance upset, she landed on her fanny while trying to restuff her pockets. "Where did you come from?"

"What are you hiding?"

"Nothing."

"Let's see it."

"Dinner's ready." She sprang to her feet and tugged at his forearm.

He didn't budge. Squinting down at her, he got another distinct whiff of strawberries. "What's in your pockets?"

"Nothing. Not that it would be any business of yours if there were anything." She let go of his arm. He caught hers.

"Then you won't mind turning them inside out."

"Back off."

"Not a chance." He encircled her waist and easily pulled her against him.

She tipped her head back to look at him. Her eyes were wide and a little fearful. "Okay. I'll give you what you want. Just let me go."

"A kiss?"

"I'm not on the menu."

He smiled. "It's just a kiss, Jolie. But if you really want me to, I'll let you go."

Her lips parted, but no sound came out.

His smile broadened, then he lowered his head and accepted her response.

Chapter Thirteen

This was stupid. Jolie knew that even as her neck arched back from the pressure of Mike's mouth on hers.

Still, she clung to him, drinking in the warmth of his arms around her, the urgency of his lips on hers. She felt his blossoming desire press against her belly, and found some small consolation in the modest amount of power she held.

When his tongue swept her lower lip, she hesitated only a moment before allowing him access.

He was gentle at first, his mouth slanting for a better fit, his tongue exploring her hidden recesses. But she felt the fever growing in his hands as they stroked a restless pattern against her back, the curve of her buttocks.

Despite the cooling air, his flesh was hot beneath her hand. Coarse chest hair tickled her sensitive palm, his nipple beaded against it. She shifted her position, allowing her hand to roam across his shoulders.

A low groan rumbled in his throat. And although his mouth left hers, he never lost contact, dragging his lips across her jaw, down her neck. He licked at her collarbone. Then pushed aside the front of her jacket.

She took a deep shaky breath. "You said only a kiss."

"Is that all you want?" He nibbled at her ear.

"No. Yes." She felt his slow smile against her throat. "Tell me to stop."

"Okay." Sighing, she let her head loll farther back. For a second, she panicked, thinking she would fall, and she clutched at his shoulders.

He scooped her up in his arms. "The lean-to," he whispered hoarsely.

Her mind was foggy. Her whole body was foggy. She wasn't sure what he meant. So she wrapped her arms around his neck and held on while he shifted her to a more manageable position. His eyes, hypnotically blue, stared down at her, and his mouth was stretched in such a seductive smile that she decided right then and there that she didn't care what he meant. As long as he never let her go.

She smiled tentatively back, and brushed a lock of sun-kissed hair from his brow.

With her arm elevated, her jacket flapped open. The left pocket gaped and a flurry of small packets fell to the ground. One triangular-shaped package targeted Mike's toes.

He squinted in confusion, then looked down. His gaze slowly scanned the handful of miniature, restaurant-size packets of preserves littering the ground. He kicked the one off his foot, his eyes meeting hers. "Strawberry?"

The heat of guilt replaced that of desire in her face. She twisted to be free of his grasp, and he all too eagerly allowed her swift descent to the ground.

She waited until her feet were safely planted, and said, "Grape, too."

He said nothing. He merely folded his arms across his chest...his bare chest. The chest that only moments ago had pulsed rapidly under her palm.

"They must have been left over from when I used my jacket before. I found them when I was out walking."

He barely moved a muscle.

"It wasn't like I was *hiding* them. I was saving them. As a surprise."

He lifted a brow.

"Look, I had this French fry attack and obviously I wasn't going to find any out here, but then I found these in my pocket by accident and..." She stepped away, feeling cornered. "Okay, so FiFi and I pigged out on the suckers. Sue me."

"FiFi? You gave some to FiFi?"

"We *are* responsible for her." When his scowl deepened, she added, "I don't know about you, but I plan on taking good care of this little darling. She may still be our ticket out of here. Besides, I consider myself employed as long as I have her to look after."

His stomach growled. He ignored the sound, shaking his head, an incredibly sad look on his face...a disappointed look.

She could handle annoyed. She could handle angry. She couldn't take disappointed. "You don't understand—"

"Yeah, I do." He passed a weary hand over his face, then started off toward the lean-to.

"Here. Take these." She reached into her pocket and brought out the remaining packets of grape jelly.

He kept walking.

"Don't be so stubborn. You can have these."

He stopped. She saw his shoulders rise and fall with the deep breath he took. Then he turned around. "Screw the preserves. I don't care about that."

She swallowed. "Then what's wrong?"

"Nothing. Chalk it up to foolish expectations." Half

under his breath he added, "You're no different than Lola or Angela." Then he headed toward the lean-to.

"Who's Angela?"

His steps faltered. "What?" he asked without turning around.

"Angela. You said Angela."

Silence stung the air. Then he turned to her. "Look, you're so damn fond of establishing territory, his and hers, all that crap. So, I'll tell you what."

Purposefully, he walked over to the mango tree and picked up one of the blankets. He draped it over his arm, then yanked a couple of knives and plates out of the picnic basket. After gathering several other items, he marched back to her and shoved the bundle into her arms.

"You don't believe in team spirit." He threw up his now empty hands. "Okay by me. You're on your own. Have a great life."

Too stunned to say anything, she stared at him. The blanket unfolded, a flap of wet pungent wool slapping the ground. A couple of items slipped from her overburdened arms and she stumbled trying to recover them.

He blinked, a look of regret crossing his face. Letting out a sound of disgust, he shoved his hands through his hair. Then he reached for the bundle. "Give me those things."

Still a little numb, she started to let go. Until he murmured, "You'd never make it."

She pulled back. "Excuse me?"

"I'm sorry. I overreacted."

"No. What did you say before?"

He heaved a weary sigh. "It's going to be dark soon. Let's get settled in."

She shifted her load and wrapped her arms more tightly around it. "Then I suggest you get *your* camp secured."

"What?"

She backed away, and his hands fell to his sides.

"This is crazy." The shadow of a coconut tree frond fell briefly across his face. It gave her a moment's respite from the sudden gleam of amusement in his eyes. Then his voice lowered. "We were kissing only ten minutes ago."

Damn him for reminding her. Her gaze automatically moved to his mouth, before she forced it away and started to turn. "My mistake."

"At least take this."

Curious, she paused, and out of the corner of her eye, saw him grab the chaise longue.

She held up a hand when he headed back toward her. "No, thank you."

He kept on coming until his chest ended up flush against her palm. "Don't be so stubborn."

It was his lower chest actually. Right above his waist, and thinking about how only moments ago the coarse hair there had tickled her palm made her want to scratch. Preferably at his eyes.

She gazed up at the eyes in question. They were only several inches from her own and breathtakingly blue. Bedroom blue. Who the hell was she kidding?

She snatched back her hand, stepped back and stuck out her big toe. And with it, slowly, careful not to drop anything, she made a long sweeping line in the sand.

"This," she said, pointing one foot at his side, "is your half of the island." With a graceful sweep she'd learned in ballet class years ago, she drew back her leg and directed her perfectly pointed toes toward the ground beside her. "And this is my side."

Then she spun on her heel, half-dragging the waterlogged blanket behind her.

JOLIE SCRAPED the bark of the breadfruit tree with the same fat twig she'd used yesterday and the day before that. After being certain the new mark was even with the other two lines, she stepped back to appraise her primitive calendar.

She didn't know why she was being so anal about keeping a record like this, except she'd seen someone do it in a movie when she was a kid and thought it looked pretty romantic.

Sinking to the ground, she leaned against the tree, stared out at the ocean and decided that notion was a crock. Being stranded was no fun. She was sick of mangoes, bananas and whatever the heck those little yellow round things were. She'd readily give up her trust fund for a single order of fries. Extra crispy. Lots of salt.

Sighing, she kicked at the shredded coconut husk near her feet. Last night's dinner had been okay, and different, but what was the chance of her finding another coconut that was already cracked open. She'd failed dismally at trying to split one herself.

She took a deep breath and, shading her eyes against the midday sun, she scanned the horizon for at least the hundredth time. Nothing but blue-green sparkling water. This should have been paradise. It felt like hell.

She sighed. Three days stuck here without shelter was long enough. She'd have to finally break down and rig something. The Longfellows obviously weren't coming back, and who knew when anyone else would show up. Mike didn't count.

The thought of him sent a fresh wave of annoyance and determination through her lethargic body and she straightened. Half of her was glad she hadn't seen him since their abrupt parting, the other half seethed that he'd not made the attempt to find her.

She knew she'd been too sensitive and impulsive. But he'd called her useless, thought she couldn't take care of herself. And something inside of her had short-circuited.

Her consolation was that he'd been wrong. She'd managed very well. She'd even managed to abduct FiFi. And had kept herself and the ungrateful mutt both well fed. So, as far as she was concerned, she was still employed.

They had plenty of fresh water—for both drinking and baths. She'd quickly rediscovered the pool she'd stumbled upon that first day, had even found a second one. And although she'd not yet bothered to construct any shelter, she'd found a bunch of fallen coconut fronds that would do the trick.

She threw a stick at an incoming wave. It barely reached the water, but as the tide receded, so did the stalk. She watched it until it disappeared beneath the foam.

She wished she could rid herself of shame and guilt so easily. Mike's disappointed look popped into her mind at the least expected times. She hadn't really been hoarding the jellies. But how could she explain that after finding them in her pocket, she had unthinkingly scarfed most of them. And that she was embarrassed about it.

She knew she should have waited, been fair, divided the jellies evenly with Mike. But she hadn't.... When she discovered them in her pocket, they'd been as tempting and irresistible as...Mike himself.

Grimacing, she struggled to her feet, took one last useless glimpse toward sea, then shoved and slapped her way back through the thick tangle of leaves and vines.

She'd made the short trip from her so-called camp to the beach so often that the path wasn't nearly as overgrown as it had been, and she reached the snoozing FiFi in minutes.

She peeked in the dog's water bowl. "What do you think, FiFi? Are you about ready for another water run?"

The terrier's large black eyes opened with grudging slowness. She lifted her head a fraction before letting it drop down between her paws again.

"You are the laziest—" Jolie stopped, and looked around. She sniffed the air.

A tantalizing whiff of roasted meat nearly brought her to her knees.

It couldn't be. She shook her head, certain she'd only imagined the heavenly smell.

FiFi's head bobbed up, her tiny nostrils quivering. She barely took time for a stretch, her nose stuck up as far in the air as it would go as she strained against her makeshift leash of vines and woven coconut fronds.

Jolie unfastened her and tucked the dog under her arm. The dog started to whine. "I'm hungry, too, but you gotta be quiet if you want to help me investigate," she whispered.

As if she understood, FiFi immediately quieted down as Jolie crept through the vines and trees in the direction of the smell.

The clearing was only a dozen yards from her camp. It was a small area and she would have missed it if not for Mike's shirt hanging from a low-hung branch. The shirt flapped in the gentle afternoon breeze near a small stack of firewood. Beside that was a crudely made barbecue pit.

Suspended over the fire by two forked sticks was a large golden brown fish.

Jolie swallowed. Although she normally liked her fish filleted and poached, the woodsy, smoked aroma was driving her over the edge.

Staying hidden behind some bushes, she surveyed the area. Mike was nowhere to be seen. She wondered where he could be while she let a minute or two pass. He still didn't show.

Taking another swift glance around, she poked one foot out. She'd already stooped to thievery by snatching FiFi. Of course, that hadn't really been stealing.

She advanced another couple of feet. And neither would this, really. After all, she *was* entitled to half the matches, *which* she didn't get. Surely she deserved a piece of the fish.

Besides, technically, he was on her half of the island.

The fire crackled. The fish sizzled. Her stomach growled. FiFi squirmed. Jolie took the last few steps.

"Oh, my." She licked her lips, staring down at the gastronomic delight. It was golden perfection.

After making sure the squirming dog was securely tucked under her arm, she bent toward her surprise snack.

"Good afternoon."

His voice came out of nowhere. Before she could pull back her guilty hand, he swung down from a nearby tree and landed on his feet in her shadow.

She recoiled at his unexpected nearness. "What the hell are you doing?"

He lifted a brow at her compromising position, amusement lurking at the corners of his mouth. "Supplementing dinner and breakfast." He tugged at the end-to-end cloth napkins he had tied to his waist and a bounty of mangoes spilled out.

She grinned smugly. "I haven't had to climb any trees. I've found perfectly good ones on the ground. Lots of other kinds of fruit, too."

He seemed unimpressed. He kept unraveling the napkins and carefully stacking the fruit. "They must be bruised."

"Not in the least."

"Lucky you."

"I've even found a coconut already cracked."

Finished with his task, he pulled the last napkin from the waist of his trunks. The elastic snapped back at a lower place on his stomach, although the skin there was just as tan. The hair around his navel was a dark golden against the deep bronze his belly had turned. The deep hue traveled down to cover the well-defined muscles tightening his thighs. He looked as if he'd been sculpted by an artist.

When she finally dragged her gaze back to his face, he was smiling.

"Can I help you with something?" he asked.

She tossed back her hair. "Actually, I'm doing remarkably well."

He laughed, dusting his hands. Then he dropped down to turn the fish. "You hung around Lola too long. You sound like one of those snotty little rich girls."

She made a face over the top of his head. That hairtossing move was her best Monique imitation. "Don't you know it's politically incorrect to use the term 'girls.'"

"That's what they are when they act like that. I see you're taking good care of the little princess." He inclined his head toward FiFi.

"Somebody has to."

"Oh, no you don't. She was doing fine with me."

"Right. And you were so worried when she turned up missing that you scoured the island for her."

He squinted suspiciously. "Is that why you took her? To get me to come after you?"

"In your dreams."

"Come on. Haven't you missed my company just a little?"

"Actually, I'd prefer the company of a burrito."

"Ah, a burrito." His tongue appeared at the corner of his mouth to make a slow pass over his upper lip. "Beef and bean, extra cheese. Melted, stringy, dripping."

She wondered what law this small island was subject to, and whether she could get away with strangling him. Giving him a dirty look, she started to leave.

He laughed. "Hey, wait a minute." He gave the fish another turn, then pulled a piece off with his fingers. "Whoa! Hot." He tossed the morsel from one hand to the other, while blowing at it. Then he held the tidbit up to her. "Tell me if it's done."

Her mouth watered. She swallowed the urge to grab it out of his hand. He waited a moment, then withdrew it.

A protest hovered on the tip of her tongue. He put the flaky piece once more to his pursed lips, and blew, his magnetic blue gaze snagging hers.

"Here."

Out of her peripheral vision, she saw his extended hand and she blinked, forcing her eyes to break contact with his. She cleared her throat. "Oh, no thank you. My dinner is…will be ready at any moment."

He shrugged and popped the morsel into his mouth. Briefly closing his eyes, he licked his lips. "Hmm. Nothing like a little sea salt to jazz things up." He stood and looked at her. "Of course, you've already discovered that."

"Of course."

He nodded, and using one of the linen napkins, plucked the fish off the wooden sticks. "You sure you won't join me for dinner?"

She took one last longing whiff. "Positive."

"Okay." He kicked sand on the fire, and Jolie had to bite her lip to keep from begging him to leave it blazing. He smiled at her. "Guess I'll see you around."

"Sure." She watched him swathe the fish until each crisp, golden little inch was wrapped in the white linen. Then he rolled the mangoes onto his shirt, drew it up knapsack style and, whistling, sauntered into the jungle.

She wanted to scream. After she beaned him in that taut, enticing behind. She settled for jabbing her foot into the sand and sending a spray of the fine white stuff through the air. It reminded her of sugar. Which brought to mind sugar cookies.

Groaning, she dropped her chin to her chest and closed her eyes.

When she opened them, she saw the matches. They were on the ground near her feet. Instinctively, her lips parted and she started to call Mike back.

She clamped them shut again. What the hell was she doing? She deserved these matches, too. He'd already used his share.

Quickly, she snatched up the book. Picking up his tune, she whistled all the way back to her meager camp.

MIKE LEANED back against the breadfruit tree and patted his stomach. He shouldn't have eaten the entire fish. Although it wouldn't have kept long in this heat.

He was amazed at how hot it could be during the day yet turn so cool at night. Not really cold by any means, but cool enough that Jolie's warm body next to his was all he could think about most of the time.

He sighed and slumped farther down, briefly closing his eyes, imagining the smell of her shampoo. A grin tugged at his mouth, his nose twitched. The scent of strawberries was what his hapless brain came up with. He tried to push the sensation aside and vaguely considered a short nap before he patrolled the beach again.

They shouldn't be split up this way, he thought. They

should be working together to make sure one person was on the lookout for passing ships. He'd planned on having that discussion with her over dinner this evening. But not even the enticing aroma of the fish had persuaded her to join him. He knew she had to be sick of fruit. The woman was just too damn stubborn for her own good.

He had already apologized for his overreacting. He didn't know what else he was supposed to do. Apart from strategically cooking food under her nose, that is.

Besides, she had overreacted, too.

And he wondered why she had. Hell, he wondered why old baggage from Angela had set *him* off again. He hadn't given his ex-fiancée a thought since…well, since he'd… met Jolie.

He shifted positions, uncomfortable with the implication of that enlightening piece of truth. And like a thorn in his backside, readily pricked him.

In retrospect, it didn't take a Ph.D. to figure out that his aversion to rich, self-centered women had obviously played a role in his reaction the other day. Yet Jolie was not in that category. Certainly not rich, and as far as self-centered…

He thought back to the bum she'd slipped money to, the sparse wardrobe that hung in her closet, her friends Byron and Gail, who, knowing her, were so loyal he had no doubt they'd cut his heart out if anything happened to her.

Which made him wonder what the little darling was up to now. Keeping tabs on her was taking up a lot of time. Time he should be using to worry about how he was going to get his hands on the diamonds.

He pushed himself to a standing position. He was losing sight of his goal, and for that reason alone he should be madder than hell. But he wasn't. Maybe a little.

Stretching his neck from side to side, he headed for the beach. Besides needing to scout the water for ships, he kind of had an idea what she might be up to.

Within five minutes of skirting the south shore from the privacy of the bordering jungle, he spotted her.

Standing in the middle of a large tidal pool, water up to midthigh, Jolie stood frozen. Her hands spread just above the surface, she bent slightly forward, peering into the seawater, a fierce frown on her small oval face, looking like a warrior prepared to do battle.

Mike had to suck in his breath to keep from laughing out loud. He flattened himself against a tree, safely out of view and breathed out slowly.

She must have seen this approach in a movie, he figured. But it wasn't going to work. It took a lot of practice and speed to catch a fish by hand. All she was doing was scaring them. If she caught anything at all, it would be because she gave her victim a heart attack.

He continued to watch her for several long minutes as she hovered motionlessly over the water. She was patient. He'd give her that. More than he could afford to be.

He was about to return to his patrol, when suddenly, the top half of her body pitched forward. Her arms shot below the surface.

Seconds later, she came up, no fish, but with two handfuls of water, which she splashed directly into her eyes. Sputtering, cursing, she teetered backward, straightened, then wiped the moisture from her face. He noted the furious jut of her profile right before she again lost her balance. Arms flailing useless circles in the air, she fell unceremoniously into the pool.

Chapter Fourteen

Jolie stared at the bananas, trying to decide how hungry she was. What she really wanted to do was mash them with the two fallen mangoes she'd found, throw in some thick, gooey coconut milk and treat Mike to a face full of fruit salad.

She sighed, pushing aside the entire bunch, careful not to bruise them. As sick as she was of all this disgustingly healthy fruit, they'd probably still be her dinner.

She knew she had no right to be angry with Mike because he could catch fish and she couldn't. But that didn't soothe her irritation.

Shaking off the ever-present sand, she stood and picked up the spear she'd fashioned from a branch. Her resourcefulness had probably ruined her only knife, but she didn't care. She wasn't giving up on her fish dinner yet.

Besides, she was rather proud of the crude weapon. The small net she'd managed to knot together from scraps of blanket material and strips of tree bark had already proved useful, too. All in all, she was quite proud of herself. Period.

She wondered what Grandfather would think?

And damn it, even though she didn't want to, she wondered what Mike would think, too.

Sighing, she headed back toward the tidal pool. Pink and orange hues streaked the cloudy horizon, marking the end of another day in paradise. She hoped the fish were as tired as she was.

She eased over a cluster of black rocks, wet and shiny from the tide. Using the spear as a balancing cane, she crept to the edge of the pool.

The fading sunlight made it difficult to see at first, but as soon as her eyes began to adjust, movement snagged her peripheral vision. In a smaller, shallower pool, closer to shore, something jumped.

Careful of her footing, she hopped over the two rocks necessary to get closer, and peered into the sandy water. Something jumped again, startling her, and she had to drop to a crouch to keep from slipping.

Although getting this close wasn't what she'd had in mind, excitement consoled her when she realized the culprit was a fish. Long and dark gray, it flapped helplessly in the too-shallow water well within her reach.

Jolie stared at it, her initial elation dimming. Could she really do this? Cleaned, filleted and cooked was one thing…

Barely peeking through slitted eyes, she extended her shaky thumb and index finger and reached for its tail. It jumped again. She snatched back her hand.

"Oh, God." She took a deep breath. "This one's for you, FiFi."

Before she had a chance to chicken out, she reached in, grabbed the tail and slipped the wriggling fish into her homemade net. Making a face, she held her catch as far away from her body as she could, then gingerly made her way across the rocks to the sand.

She had mixed feelings as she trudged through the jungle to the small waterfall she'd found that first day. But after taking a brief, uncomfortable glance at her resigned captive she swallowed back her queasiness over what she was about to do. After all, she had a lot to be thankful for. She was surviving on her own, taking care of FiFi, providing food and shelter for them both.

Thinking of her newfound self-reliance curved her lips as she approached the pool. She heard the light gush of water cascading over the small cliff even before she caught sight of the falls. Last night's rain had ensured a fresh supply of water. Although she couldn't take credit for that piece of luck, she was in such a good mood she felt like claiming responsibility anyway.

She'd taken the final leap over a trickling wayward stream when she saw Mike's red trunks spread out on a rock near the falls.

Jolie froze, her gaze darting over the landscape. Creeping backward, she ducked behind a tree. She knew for a fact he had only one pair of trunks with him, which meant...

The fish slipped, and she had to make a grab for it.

She caught it before it hit the ground. Trying to bunch the net more securely, she kept her eyes on her hands.

What was he doing on her turf? This was where she and FiFi got their water, found most of their food, played, napped. What was he doing here? And without his clothes?

Her fingers slipped and she stabbed herself with her own nail. Muttering under her breath, she peeked over the bush she was using as her shield.

She had every right to look. This was her pool. She was certain that he'd been using the other one, the first one she had located. The one on the other side of the island.

But she'd obviously been wrong.

Mike's head surfaced the water. He shook the excess moisture from his hair, then passed a hand over his face. It was hard to see. Besides the approaching twilight, the density of trees and vines obscured much of the fading sunlight. That was why Jolie told herself that it was okay to gape the way she was as he slowly made his way toward the rocky bank where his trunks lay.

He didn't look the least bit wary or self-conscious as the water ebbed from his chest, to his belly, to his....

She closed her eyes, her pulse roaring in her ears. If she had a shred of decency she wouldn't look. She'd be furious with him if the situation were reversed. She'd count to ten.

She got to three. *Oh, hell.*

Opening her eyes, she blinked several times when she saw no sign of him. Her gaze did a frantic search, bouncing from rocks to trees. Then she saw him, his naked back facing her, as he wrung out the trunks.

She'd always known he was perfect. He had a model's face, thick glorious hair, a nicely muscled chest. But the taut, sculpted curves of his buttocks stole her breath.

They flexed and tightened as he shook out the trunks. The genius of Rodin couldn't have created greater perfection. There was little difference in color between the curved muscles and the bronze of his back. It was obvious he'd done a lot of nude sunbathing in the past few days, and Jolie experienced a pang of regret for having driven the wedge she had between them.

They should have spent those days in the sun together.

She shook her head. The lusty part of her brain was doing a number on her, making her think crazy things. She begged and pleaded with herself to look away. She couldn't do it.

Mike settled her dilemma. He slipped on his trunks,

then faced her direction. Guilt made her jump, even though it was impossible for him to see her.

She heaved a soft sigh, waiting for relief to set in. It didn't. And she knew why. She still wanted him.

The scary thing was, it had little to do with physical response. Yeah, he was drop-dead gorgeous. And he probably had the best tush this side of the equator. But the feelings he was beginning to inspire went much deeper.

He had been kind to her. Even when she was at her obnoxious worst, he'd been patient and accommodating, even making sure she got home when she'd been stupid enough to make herself sick on wine. He'd even braved the lizard world for her, she thought, smiling.

Above all, he kissed her as if she were the only woman on earth.

Oh, God. She was in trouble. All he had to do was crook his finger and she'd be his. And she'd undoubtedly regret it in the morning. Because after all, she was still plain-Jane Jolie.

She watched him continue toward the path she herself always took. It made her a little nervous that he would pass not more than six feet from her. Not that she feared being discovered. She was well hidden and it was getting duskier by the minute. But she didn't know if she could stop herself from jumping his bones.

The uncharacteristic thought made her gasp. Her hand flew to her mouth to cover the sound and she squinted in horror. But he kept threading up the path as if he hadn't a care in the world.

It was odd, she thought, that he seemed so unconcerned, as though he either didn't care that she might discover him, or that he was confident she wouldn't be around.

Because of his lack of concern, it was tempting to show herself, to clear the air, to not waste any more time. But she hesitated, and then something even more curious happened.

Mike slowed and looked over his shoulder. Then he craned his neck to look down the path ahead of him. When he came to a complete stop, she got a good shot of his face. He looked guilty as hell.

She frowned. This didn't make sense. She quietly shifted positions in order to keep him in her sight when he suddenly charged a particularly thick mango tree. Grasping the trunk in his hands, he climbed up to the first branch.

She almost cried out then, to stop him, to tell him it wasn't necessary, that fruit fell in abundance here. But something made her keep silent.

Planting himself firmly at the juncture of the branch, he sprawled out along the limb and flexed his fingers toward the fruit. She cringed, watching his bare skin make contact with the rough bark. But still she said nothing.

Within seconds he had plucked two plump mangoes from their stem, then shimmied down the tree. He was careful not to drop the fruit, and when he got to the bottom, he laid them undisturbed beside the path.

He glanced once more over his shoulder, straightened, then resumed his carefree pace in the direction of his camp.

Confused, Jolie started to stand, but her thigh muscles cramped and she eased her rear end onto the sandy dirt. What was he—

She stared at the inert fish lying in the homemade net...the far too convenient fish. The two cracked coconuts she'd been so lucky to find wormed their way into her thoughts. And the mangoes, dozens and unbruised, that she'd found practically waiting at her feet each day.

Her reluctant gaze strayed to the two latest mercy offerings so strategically placed, and humiliation slapped her with a swift hand.

HE WAS GETTING TIRED of this game. There was no reason for him and Jolie to be working apart. He had to talk to her tonight. Hopefully, after her fish dinner, she'd be more agreeable, Mike thought as he reinforced the thatched roof of his lean-to.

He stepped back to inspect his handiwork.

The first rock hit him in the shoulder. The second nailed him in the butt. He stumbled with the impact. The thud sounded worse than it actually felt, but caught off guard, he nearly plowed into his newly renovated shack.

"What the hell?" He spun around. No one was there. Long evening shadows played tricks with his vision, until he saw the mango lying several feet away and realized it hadn't been a rock at all that had hit him.

"I think you lost these." Jolie stepped out of a shadow. She picked up the second mango that had bounced off him and landed near her feet. "I'm returning them."

"Why did you—?"

She took a second to aim, then beaned him in the arm again.

Although he was still pretty stunned, he caught it on the rebound. She turned to go, and he charged her.

She realized what he was doing only moments before he reached her, and too late, she started to run. He grabbed her around the waist and tackled her to the ground.

"Get off me." She twisted around and shoved hard at his chest.

He shackled her wrists with a firm grip. "What the hell are you doing?"

"I already told you." The words barely made it out of

her clenched teeth. She writhed beneath him, kicking without much regard for where her knees or feet landed.

He rolled over to her side. "You attack me like some crazy person and you don't think you owe me an explanation?"

She tried wrenching her wrists free, then speared him with a look of such fury, that for a moment he felt as if he didn't know this woman at all.

Suddenly her breath seeped out as though it had been locked tightly inside her chest. Her shoulders sagged. The anger deserted her face. From the nearby light of his campfire, he saw the dried tearstain on her cheek.

"Let me up," she said in a small voice.

He stood, then offered her his hand. She ignored it and lumbered to her feet, dusting sand from her legs and arms, avoiding his eyes.

"What's going on, Jolie?" He brushed a tiny shell from her cheek.

She shied away from his touch. "I didn't need your help." Her gaze finally met his. It was accusing. "At least I don't think I did. But now I don't really know, do I?"

She blinked, swallowed. Her eyes looked suspiciously bright before she glanced away again. And he realized the accusation masked hurt.

"Tell me something. Did you purposely *lose* the matches, too?" she asked, sarcasm warring with pain.

He didn't have to answer. He was sure his expression gave him away by the proud lift of her chin, the flash of new hurt in her eyes.

"Never mind," she said breezily, wiping her palms on her thighs. "I am sorry, though. I shouldn't have hit you." She hesitated. "But I'm even sorrier you thought I was truly that inept. Or useless."

When she started to leave, he grabbed her arm. "Don't, Jolie."

She tried to shake his hold. He let go. And put both arms around her. Her eyes widened on him. She opened her mouth to protest. He kissed her.

She started to struggle, but when she realized it was a gentle kiss meant to soothe, she stilled. His lips pressed softly against her lower one, the seam, the corners. She didn't respond.

He pulled back and stared into her crestfallen face. He wanted her to start kicking him again. He wanted to kick himself. He was guilty, but not of what she was accusing him. She'd gotten it all wrong.

Yeah, he'd been leaving fruit for her, the fish…the lousy matches. But it wasn't because he thought she was incapable. It was because he felt so damn guilty about getting her stranded here in the first place. His quest for the diamonds had caused her all this trouble. It was his responsibility to take care of her.

Who was he kidding? Although all that was true, there was more to it. Whenever he'd imagined her climbing a tree, or doing something dangerous… Oh, hell. He *wanted* to take care of her, period. The thought clenched his gut. The whole notion was really stupid. She didn't need him.

The hand he raised to cup her cheek was a little shaky. "I don't think you're incapable *or* useless."

"That's not what you said."

He frowned, trying to think back. "If I did it was probably just angry words. I didn't mean them. You have to admit, you have a way of goading me."

She didn't return his smile. But neither did she try to back away from him. She narrowed her eyes skeptically before looking away. "It doesn't matter. I'm sorry I overreacted."

She didn't believe him. And yeah, he thought maybe she had overreacted, too. But there was a reason, and although he was interested in why and how her self-esteem had taken enough of a whack for her to react that way, he was more concerned with the fact that he'd hurt her.

"It matters to me," he said. "How can I get you to believe me?"

She smiled. It failed to reach her eyes. "I believe you, okay?"

He held her chin with his fingers when she would have pulled away. There was a way he could convince her. He could tell her about the diamonds.

Damn. He didn't want to do that. She'd probably really hate him then. But at least she'd understand. She'd know this had nothing to do with her. Damn.

"We need to talk." He released her chin and circled his fingers around her upper arm, steering her toward the fire.

She glared at the flames as if seeing them for the first time. "You have more matches?"

He shrugged.

"So, leaving me the others wasn't charity." She jabbed him in the chest. "You owed them to me."

"Yes, ma'am." This was the old Jolie. Chuckling, he wrapped his hand around hers and brought the attacking finger to his lips. He kissed the tip.

A slight smile tugged at the corners of her mouth, and he was sorely tempted to forgo his explanation. Except the hurt in her eyes had already branded him.

He plumped up the folded blanket. "Here you go."

"No, thank you." She lowered herself to the ground opposite him across the fire.

He sighed and took the makeshift seat. "I've got to tell you the reason I wanted the Longfellows' job."

A frown creased her brows, but she said nothing. Drawing up her knees, she rested her chin on them and waited expectantly. The fire threw dancing shadows across her face, making it difficult to read her expression.

He didn't want her sitting across from him when he gave his explanation. He wanted her in his arms. And after he told what he had to tell her, she'd probably be retreating to her side of the island.

"We could share the blanket," he suggested.

"I'm fine here, thank you."

He grimaced at her formal tone. "I don't suppose I could get you to promise not to be mad."

Her eyebrows shot up.

He needed a cigarette. Or a stick of gum. "Okay. It's my fault we got dumped here. I think the Longfellows know I'm after the diamonds."

Her brows lowered and drew together in confusion.

He stretched his neck from side to side, trying to rid himself of the sudden tension tightening his muscles. "I own a security company and we were recently hired to wire the Longfellows' estate. About a month after we installed their system, they were robbed. They claim more than a million dollars in diamonds were taken."

She frowned, and it was clear she was trying to digest what he'd just told her. After a meditative silence, she said, "Claim?"

Mike's temper sizzled. "No way did *anyone* get past that system. I designed it myself."

The corners of her mouth softened. "Those things happen, Mike."

"Not to me they don't. I have a sterling reputation in the industry. Or had." He picked up a twig and hurled it into the fire. "The insurance just paid them off. Biggest claim in three decades. I'm surprised you hadn't read about it in the papers."

The wry tilt of her lips told him she had. "So, you think it was an inside job?" she asked.

"No question in my mind."

"Not to sound unkind, but I don't think Howard is capable of pulling off something like that."

"Don't be too sure. People like that are cagey suckers."

She shook her head. "They don't need the money."

He snorted his disgust. "It doesn't have to be about money. The rich don't need a reason. When they get bored, they play head games."

Her hand shot to her hair and fluttered in a nervous gesture, and Mike immediately regretted his bitter tone. She licked her lips.

He edged the blanket to the side, careful not to get too close to her and reached for her hand. It was ice-cold. "Are you still speaking to me?"

"Are you kidding? I've got at least a hundred questions."

He nodded, a faint grin relieving the tension around his mouth. "I'm ready."

"Is that what you were doing with Lola's lingerie? Looking for the diamonds?"

He laughed at the unexpected question. "You got it."

She grinned, looking pleased all of a sudden. Then she wrinkled her nose. "Wouldn't the Longfellows have known who you were from the beginning?"

"No way. I was never personally involved with converting their system."

"But they'd know your name."

"Only if they'd made an effort to find out who owned the company. We've been in business long enough, with such an impeccable reputation…'' He sighed. ''Anyway, they wouldn't have had any reason to check me out as an owner. Besides, I'm using your name.''

She straightened, pulling back her hand. ''That's why you were so agreeable.''

He shrugged.

''You rat.''

Grinning, he scooted the rest of the way to her side, and slipped an arm around her shoulders. ''Cold?''

''I'm not done yet,'' she said, removing his arm and placing it on his bent knee. She reared her head back and narrowed her eyes on him. ''Where do you live? And how do you know Byron?''

He answered the easy question first. ''I spend part of the year in Maine, the rest in Hawaii.'' He paused when her eyebrows lifted, wondering what he'd said wrong. He was being truthful. When she made no comment, he said, ''I've known Byron since high school.''

''You were a preppy?''

''God, no. I went to the public school down the street.''

''Then how did you hook up with Byron? He was such a snob back then.''

''That was Byron all right.'' Which made him wonder how Jolie knew their mutual friend. He sifted a handful of sand through his fingers, trying to decide how much he needed to tell her. ''I was his bodyguard.''

''His what?'' She started to laugh, then stopped. ''Had he been threatened, kidnapped?''

He did laugh. ''Nothing like that—''

''It isn't funny, Mike. Two of my friends were kidnapped. One was eight and the other twelve at the time.'' A shiver danced across her shoulders. She hugged her knees closer to her chest and leaned toward the fire.

This information renewed his interest. He angled his head to look at her face. "How do *you* know Byron?"

Her hair acted as a curtain, hiding most of her profile. She said nothing for a moment, then turned to him with a victorious twinkle in her eye. "You're the one in the hot seat, Duval. Tell me about this bodyguard business."

He groaned. "Technically, that has nothing to do with us getting dumped here."

"Too bad." She tilted her head expectantly.

This was the part he hated. "I was a thug back then. I guess he figured I was better on his side than against him."

Her eyes rounded. "He paid you protection money?"

"It wasn't like that."

"Tell me." Her eyes glowed with curiosity. She shook the hair away from her face and gazed at him with such earnest interest that he felt his defenses begin to crumble.

"I was a pretty rowdy kid, real rough around the edges. The crowd I hung with was fast, and I was big for my age. I got into a little trouble here and there." He shrugged, hoping she wouldn't ask for details.

She clapped her hands together and hooted with laughter. "I bet Byron's bow tie unraveled just looking at you. Take him out of his element, and..." She snapped her fingers. "He tried to date my sister Monique, but even *she* thought he was a snobby brat."

"Was she the one in the limo?" He didn't know what made him ask that question. It was absurd to think Jolie had family who paraded around in limousines.

She turned back to the fire and stared at the flames. "He's changed a lot, of course. Well, you know that."

It was clear she wasn't going to answer him. And he certainly wasn't going to push her. He wanted out of this conversation. So far, he'd gotten off easy. He wasn't proud of some of the things he'd done back then, when it was far easier to be a bully than a pretty boy. He cringed inwardly, flashing on the blackened eyes and spilled blood he'd caused through his teen years.

"So let me get this straight. You didn't think I was incompetent," she said. "You just felt responsible."

"Well, yeah. I mean, hell no, I've never thought you were incompetent." He laughed. "Lady, I don't know how, by any stretch of the imagination, anyone could accuse you of incompetence. You know, for a while, I thought you might be running some kind of scam."

"Really?"

That information seemed to make her happy. Her smile made him glad to be alive. Its brilliance surpassed the finest diamond and zapped him right between the eyes. He didn't understand it, but he didn't have to either. It occurred to him that he was in deeper trouble than he thought.

"Look at that." She laid a hand on his arm.

He glanced up from his musings to find her pointing up at the darkened sky. Her head was tilted back, her hair tumbling wildly about her shoulders.

"Is that the Big Dipper?" she asked.

When he was too busy looking at her to answer right away, she lowered her hand and turned large questioning eyes to him. He brushed her cheek with the back of his fingers.

Her tongue darted out to touch the corner of her mouth. "Do you think anyone else can see it?"

He smiled at the absurdity of the question, and slowly shook his head. "Only us."

She smiled, too, then leaned toward him. He turned his hand so that his palm glided across her jaw to the back of her neck. He cupped her soft skin, massaging gently with his fingers.

When their lips met, she put a hand on his chest. As the kiss deepened, her hand curled over his shoulder, pulling him toward her. Her shirt rode up, exposing her midriff. Although clearly not wearing a bra, she ignored it.

Her urgency turned him on like nothing else could. Sure, she'd responded to him before, but it was different now. This was more than a mere response. She wanted him. He could feel her desire in the sensual clawing of her fingers, taste it in the silkiness of her mouth.

Overwhelmed by her obvious need, he silently cursed the adolescent trembling that threatened his fingers as he circled his palm over her exposed belly, as he smoothed the indention of her waist, as he grazed her nipple.

She shifted, and he thought she was going to pull away. Instead, she angled herself so that his palm fit perfectly over her unbound breast. Then she sighed.

"Jolie..." He forced his lips away from hers. He was way too old to let his hormones get to the finish line first. But, damn, if she kept this up...

"I have another question," she said between sighs.

It took a second for his brain to kick in. He used the moment to circle her hardening nipple with his palm. "A what?"

She shuddered. "Who's Angela?"

Lord, but she had a long memory. He pulled away, trying to gather his wits about him. He knew better than to look at her, to get caught in those beautiful brown eyes. If he did he'd probably end up squealing like a stuffed pig. And he did *not* want to talk about his ex-fiancée. Not now.

Instead, he looked past her into the blackened night.

And found the Big Dipper. Only it was lower than before. Much lower. And there were more lights.

"Jolie?" He gently pushed her aside in his struggle to get to his feet. Surprised, she ducked her head and tugged her blouse down. He grabbed her hand, pulled her up beside him and pointed through the trees toward the ocean. "Tell me I'm not seeing things."

Her gaze followed his arm until her eyes widened and her mouth gaped. In the middle of the sea, looking like a giant, suspended Christmas tree, a string of white lights started up one side, peaked, then angled off to form a triangle.

"That's a mast, honey. A ship." Feeling his pocket for matches, he started toward the beach, tugging her along with him. "That sucker is huge. Probably a freighter. Not much chance it'll stop here tonight. We'll have to act fast."

"I can't believe it." Jolie kept shaking her head, her eyes glued to the string of lights—the ship's only evidence in the inky black union of sky and sea.

Mike squinted, trying to make out the true shape of the vessel, but with the slivered moon behind the clouds, it was too dark to see. Luckily, the ship had just come abreast of the island, and they were only a matter of yards from the open beach. There was still time to light an SOS fire.

As soon as they broke from the jungle, he realized his mistake. Although he'd prepared isolated piles of firewood for this sort of opportunity, none of them would be seen once the ship rounded the island's southernmost tip. Right where the ship was headed. He'd foolishly forgotten about the odd formation of land that extended toward the reef.

His feet lagged, sinking into the sand, as he mentally

kicked himself for his stupid oversight. He'd been too busy worrying about Jolie instead of getting them off the island. And now, it looked as though he'd cost them their escape.

"What are you doing?" She tugged at his hand. "We need to get their attention."

"Right." Of course they'd give it a try. He started to veer left toward the nearest pile. She nearly jerked him off his feet.

"Not that way." She let go, reached into her pocket and withdrew some matches. Then she pointed to the jutting land. "I've piled some kindling over here."

He reared his head back in surprise. "Good girl."

They both broke into a run. She pulled ahead of him, her tinkling laughter sailing back on the wind. "I told you that term's politically incorrect."

He tried to swat her bottom but she zipped out of range. Slipping and sliding in the sand, he overtook her as they approached her impressive mound of twigs and branches. Gasping for breath, they both flipped open their matches.

Moonlight made a brief appearance. Jolie's hands stilled. She looked up, her expression confused, questioning. Their eyes met, and he couldn't seem to get his fingers to work either.

This was crazy. Every second counted.

But he knew what she was thinking. He was having the same thoughts. This new bond they'd just forged was so tenuous, fragile. The smallest interruption could snap the thread of uncertainty weaving the connection together.

He put out a palm and she laid hers on top. Their gazes stayed locked for a moment, then slowly drifted toward the retreating ship.

Chapter Fifteen

Jolie accepted the young dark-haired seaman's hand and allowed him to assist her onto the pier. Even before her feet touched Jamaican soil, old anxieties began to fester.

For much of the past thirty hours, she'd spent her time and energy trying to communicate with their rescuers. Although she spoke both French and Spanish fluently, her skills helped very little. With the exception of two officers, the entire crew of merchant seamen spoke nothing but Greek.

The only thing she'd managed to accomplish was the myriad questions in Mike's eyes...ones she wasn't crazy about answering. She knew it was only a matter of time before he asked what her stake was in accepting the Long-fellows' job. And with his obvious contempt for the rich, she suddenly wished she had a more noble cause.

As soon as her feet were firmly planted on the dock she tried to withdraw her hand. Flashing her a brilliant smile, the young man brought the back of her fingers to his lips for a brief kiss.

Behind her, Mike sighed loudly.

From under thick black brows, the seaman peered over her shoulder at her husband. Quickly he dropped her hand.

Mike had told the first officer they were married. And

from what she could tell, news had spread swiftly. When, in a fit of panicked uncertainty, she had asked for a separate stateroom, it had caused a second wave of stares and whispers. And a whole lot of unexpected attention.

Men usually didn't pay her any mind, so for the most part she'd been flattered by their attentiveness. Especially when it seemed to irritate Mike. She glanced over her shoulder and gave him a smile.

He cupped the back of her neck possessively with one hand and saluted the young seaman with the other. The sailor shot her a bewildered look before heading up the gangway.

She switched FiFi to her other arm. "Nice to travel light, isn't it?"

"Yeah, right." He gestured for her to precede him down the narrow, rickety walkway leading to the parking lot. "I don't suppose you know where the nearest wire service is."

"As a matter of fact…" She wrinkled her nose at the stench rising from the stagnant water on the left. Oblivious to them and the odor, an older man wearing a hot pink baseball cap scrubbed barnacles off a small tugboat.

"You do," Mike finished for her, shaking his head. "Point the way and I'll get my office to wire us some money. You call around and find us a hotel room while I do that."

She nodded slowly, trying to decide if now was the time to 'fess up. There were only two hotels on this side of the island. It would be so much simpler to stay in her mother's penthouse overlooking the marina.

"Make sure it overlooks the water. That'll make it easier to keep tabs on what ships are coming and going."

She cringed. The penthouse would be perfect. "If you

think the Longfellows are suspicious of you, do you really think they'll stick to their itinerary and show up here?''

"Why not? There's no way they could guess we got a ride this far. Besides, I don't think they actually know who I am. They probably think we're a couple of jewel thieves they've outsmarted.'' He chuckled.

Jolie bit her lip. She hadn't thought of that. She cast a sidelong glance at Mike's determined profile. What if he was a thief? What if there was no security company? He was too damned handsome, too charming. Was she being a fool? "Okay. I'll find a couple of rooms," she said slowly. "You get some money.''

He rubbed his jaw. "One room would be simpler.''

"Why?''

"We'll be on watch for the Longfellows. It'll be easier to relieve each other if we're in one room.''

"We?" She choked on the word.

He stopped at the edge of the road and faced her. "I'll pay you the same thing the Longfellows were paying us no matter what happens. If I get my hands on the diamonds, you get a bonus.''

She frowned, not happy with the way he phrased that. Maybe she was just being paranoid. She knew him. He couldn't be a jewel thief. Besides, the deal was tempting. It would mean that she was still employed. "Well, maybe we should call the local police in the meantime.''

"And tell them what?" His laugh was humorless. "No police. We do it my way. Are you in or out?''

She didn't answer. As much as Lola irked her and as flaky as Howard was, she didn't believe they were thieves either. Money wasn't a motive, she knew, because despite her earlier assurances to Mike to the contrary, Jolie had crossed paths with Howard Longfellow before. Their association had been too brief for him to adequately remember, but long enough for Jolie to know he didn't need to steal anything.

She looked up into Mike's stone-set face. And saw the muscle ticking at his jaw.

Impatiently, he pushed back a stubborn lock of dark, sun-streaked hair that fell across his brow. "I'll even pay your rent for the next six months."

And then the impatience was gone and what remained stole her breath. Rare uncertainty clouded his eyes as his gaze fell to her mouth. "Jolie?"

"Deal," she said, not to save her trust fund, but because she couldn't bear to part with him yet. And what she'd just seen made her foolishly hope he felt the same way.

He took her hand and started to speak.

She cleared her throat, and briefly looking away, inclined her head toward the southbound road. "Town should be only a mile this way, but there's not much to it. Today is Sunday. I don't know that you can get money wired."

He gave her an indulgent smile. "I'll take care of it."

SHE'D SPARED no expense, Mike noticed as he stared out the suite's sliding glass doors. They had a perfect view of the harbor from the top floor of what was probably the best hotel on the island. The vantage point was ideal for monitoring incoming ships, and he supposed he should be glad she'd had no trouble spending his money.

He winced. Her money.

He still didn't know how she'd done it, gotten money wired when he couldn't. But she had. He glanced around at the original artwork, the stately furnishings. And she'd apparently gotten lots of it.

Damn, he was curious. But she'd offered no explanation. Which upset him more than he cared to think about. Although he'd opened up to her, she continued to carefully guard her privacy. Not that he'd revealed all that much, he admitted, but he had decided to trust her. Which was a major step for him. Did that make him a fool? Was he alone in thinking that they'd made some kind of connection?

He'd been flying solo for some time now, and doing just fine. Why did he have this sudden compulsion to be with Jolie? Anticipate her next wisecrack? Look forward to her next smile? He shook his head, amazed that he'd actually offered to pay for her company.

Exhaling loudly, he pulled up his T-shirt and yanked it over his head. If she left this minute, he'd still owe her for having had enough sense to light the fire, for having gotten them off the island.

He should be grateful. He wasn't.

He wanted her to be as confused as he was. He wanted her to have all those silly romantic notions that he'd had. Like being stranded there together, away from outside influences and social demands. Like making love on the beach in the sun, under the stars.

Tossing his shirt on the chair, he rubbed his bare chest with disgust. He was getting stupid and sappy when he should be worried about locating the damn diamonds. He would have lit the friggin' fire, at the last minute, when the chips were down. He knew he would have.

The latch clicked and he turned to watch her emerge from the bathroom, her freshly scrubbed face glowing with health and vitality. The smile actually started in her eyes, then turned up the corners of her mouth, lighting her face and hair. And all that warmth was directed at him.

Gratitude zapped him like a bolt of lightning. She was

safe and dry and out of harm's way. And he wouldn't trade that for all the diamonds in the world. Or unrequited feelings.

He slid open the glass door and sucked in the salty sea air.

"You can have the bathroom now," she said quietly.

Slowly he turned back to her. The smile was gone. Wariness flashed in her eyes as they lingered on him, and she bent to scoop up FiFi. She cuddled the dog to her breasts, whispered something in its ear. A pang of ugly jealousy sliced through him.

He scrubbed at his eyes. Jealous of a dog. He was truly pathetic. "You wanna call room service while I'm in the shower?"

"Sure. What would you like?"

"Anything but fruit or fish."

She laughed. "Me, too. Although the crab-stuffed avocado is heavenly."

He gave her an inquiring look that she promptly avoided. They were going to have to talk, he decided. She needed to be straight with him. He was her new employer.

He clenched his teeth. When did he get to be such a horse's ass? She didn't have to tell him squat.

"We need to talk," Jolie said, her fingers probing her ear for the gold hoop that wasn't there. "After your shower. Or maybe after dinner."

"How about now?"

"It's no big deal." She gathered FiFi closer. "I shouldn't have brought it up. After dinner is fine."

"Okay." He should be hungry. He wasn't. "Order right away. I shouldn't be more than fifteen minutes."

Mike hurried through his shower. He didn't need fifteen minutes. Not to shower, anyway. But he did need the time to gather his thoughts.

He wasn't sure what he was expecting her to say, but he had a feeling the news was going to be big. After shampooing his hair, he used some of the liquid to wash out his trunks. Not until he hung them on the towel rack to dry did he realize what a dumb move that had been. He didn't think she'd appreciate him wearing a towel to dinner.

The thought gave him a hot flash. He grinned, thinking about how expressive her face was. She might verbally deny that there was at least some physical attraction between them, but her eyes said it all. And her mouth and the way her tongue always darted out to nervously moisten her lips…

Hell. If he kept up this line of thinking, he'd be wearing a tented towel, he thought wryly as he tied the burgundy terry around his hips. It was so thick and plush that it was going to be tricky keeping it wrapped as it was.

He continued to mess with the towel until he got it just right, while he considered how vain it was of him to think she'd fall for this age-old ploy. But he was a desperate man. And if it worked out in the end, screw the means.

She was sitting on the high-backed couch surrounded by plump cream and gold pillows when he finally entered the parlor. She set aside the magazine she was reading and looked up.

Her eyes widened. Her tongue darted out to dab the corners of her mouth. Her fingers grabbed for her phantom earring.

Mike smiled. Rubbing his hands together, he asked, "Hasn't dinner arrived?"

Her gaze snagged on the action, then drew lower to his hips. "There's a robe in the closet."

"Really?" Damn. "How long did room service say it would take?"

"Twenty-five minutes." She rose and disappeared into the room. Within seconds she was back, a gold-trimmed burgundy robe draped over her arm. She held it out to him. "It's been twenty since I placed the order."

"You go ahead and take it," he said, pushing the garment back toward her. Their hands met beneath the thick velour, warm skin rubbing warm skin. She jerked back, leaving the robe to spill from his hands.

"There's another one." She rubbed her palms down the front of her shorts, and her gaze strayed once more to his hips. He wondered if she could see what her brief touch was starting to do to him. "Anyway, I'm having some clothes delivered."

He lifted a brow.

"For both of us," she added. Her eyes did a quick pass at his chest. "I guessed on the size."

"Oh?"

"On the colors, too. I think I know what you like. Although I told the concierge to make one set of shorts white, so there's no risk there." Her fingers fluttered in a nervous gesture. "Anyway, I told her to send only two sets for each of us. We can pick out something else later."

Grinning, he caught her hand. "You're babbling."

Her shoulders sagged. "I'm babbling."

"You look very pretty doing it though." Closing his eyes, breathing in her clean herbal scent, he kissed her palm.

She yanked it back, one of her nails scraping the side of her jaw.

His eyes opened. She looked as if he'd struck her. "I prefer to do that with a razor," he joked, rubbing his skin and watching the wariness darken her eyes.

"Sorry," she mumbled and started to turn away.

"Jolie?" He tried to recapture her hand.

She danced out of reach, holding her clasped hands to her breasts as if to protect them. "Look, I'm not Monique or Nicole. And I don't care that I'm not. Nor that I'm not even cute on my best day. So you don't have to say it."

"No." He tightened the towel. "No, I don't *have* to. Who are Monique and Nicole?"

She ducked her head, clearly embarrassed at her outburst. "You make me nervous."

"Me? You scare me to death."

Her chin lifted. Her eyes narrowed suspiciously. Then she laughed. It was a small, tense sound, but it was a start. "You're teasing me."

"I wish I were," he said, exhaling sharply.

She nibbled at her lower lip. "How so?"

She wasn't supposed to do that…ask him outright. How big a fool did she want him to be? he wondered, cursing under his breath.

Even as he folded his arms, he recognized the defensiveness of his posture. "Because I want you, Jolie. And I'm afraid you don't feel the same way."

Her normally expressive face went blank. She stared at him for a long minute, her gaze intense, measuring. She could burst out laughing at any second, or she could jump into his arms and tell him that she did feel the same way. He couldn't tell.

She lifted her hand, and he thought for a moment that she might slap him, but it settled near the collar of her blouse. She slipped the button loose. "What about room service?"

After his stunned look, the smile Mike gave her was the last assurance Jolie needed. His face lit up brighter than the Christmas tree at Rockefeller Center.

Right before his eyes darkened to a shade of blue that should have been labeled *sex* on the color chart.

Before she could have a second thought, he lifted her into his arms. "Screw room service."

Looping her hands around his neck, she found that her fingers didn't tremble quite as much even though her heart threatened to leap through her chest.

"Shouldn't we call them or something?" she asked as he carried her to the bedroom.

She thought he said "or something" but she wasn't sure, because his lips were on hers and his heart was pounding against her right breast and she wasn't certain about anything anymore.

So she kissed him back, licking and tasting and drinking in the urgency he did nothing to temper.

He laid her on the bed, then followed her down, his towel hanging on by its final resolve. His fingers worked deftly at her buttons, while his mouth nipped at her jaw, her throat, making mush of her common sense.

She barely realized that he'd slipped the shirt off her shoulders until he was urging her slightly off the bed to shuck the garment altogether. He pushed it to the side, letting it topple to the floor, then he leaned back to gaze at her.

The urge to cover her small bare breasts didn't emerge. She should be wary, she knew. She should be concerned that she wasn't up to par. But the feelings just wouldn't come. They couldn't. Not when he was looking at her like she was not only the last woman on earth, but the most beautiful.

"Did I thank you yet?" he whispered as he covered a nipple with his mouth.

She sighed. His tongue punctuated the sound. Curiosity didn't have a chance. Shifting so he'd have better access, she figured she'd ask him what he meant later.

He transferred his attention to her other breast, and she

switched hers to his towel. One thigh extended from the overlap. She ran her palm over the long lean muscle that started just above the knee and stretched to heaven.

His breath grew hotter and ragged over her flesh as she reached deep under the folds of burgundy terry. His heat seared her fingertips, the coarse leg hair grazed her palm. She stopped short of her target and slowly withdrew her hand.

His sigh was gravelly, his laugh hoarse.

He pulled back to look at her, a smile lifting one side of his mouth. "You're right. We need to slow down."

Her lips parted in protest, but when he unhooked her shorts and slid his hand down her belly, only a gasp broke the brief silence.

"But we can go slow naked," he said, his grin reaching full bloom as he slipped her shorts and panties down her hips and tossed them with the shirt.

She couldn't help the little shiver that jiggled across her shoulders and down her spine. Lying there, totally naked, and watching him study her with his stunning blue eyes, a flurry of nerves reminded her that she was out of his league.

He picked up her hand and placed the palm against his chest. His skin was warm, his nipple taut against the fleshy part below her thumb. "Do you feel that?" he asked.

Unsure what he meant, she managed to give a small shake of her head.

"You don't feel my heart pounding?" He lowered himself beside her but kept her palm pressed to his skin. "You do that to me."

He was trying to reassure her. The fact that he'd noticed her nervousness was almost more embarrassing than being here where she didn't belong. She started to push away and caught the hem of his towel. One small, unintentional tug, and it fell open.

Mike glanced down before leveling his amused gaze with her incredulous one. "You do that to me, too."

He put an arm out to draw her to him. Jolie swallowed and shrank against him, burying her face at his shoulder. "For my ego's sake," he said, "I hope you're just having an attack of shyness."

She forced herself to look at him and was surprised to find uncertainty puckering his brows. She wanted to laugh at the sheer absurdity of it. She wanted to cry. "I'm not very good at this."

He pressed several tiny kisses to her temple. "I don't buy it. Superwoman? You're good at everything."

"Me?" Discomfort slid into surprise, then crashed into disappointment. He was feeding her a line. Nothing deeper than he'd use to pick up a quick date in a bar.

"Okay, your cooking stinks." His tongue traced her ear.

She smiled, in spite of the fact that she had a humbling decision to make. She'd accepted being second-best most of her life. Would she do it again? To have this one time to love Mike?

He nibbled her earlobe. "Okay, so you don't know how to catch fish worth a damn, either."

She blinked. "You saw me do that?"

He pressed his lips to hers and swept her surprised mouth with his tongue. Then he drew back slightly, and brushing his thumb across her lower lip, he said, "But you have what counts."

"Mike, I don't want to hear—"

"I know you don't." He held her pinned to the mattress when she would have scrambled off the bed. Half of his much taller body lay across her thigh, her breast, her arm.

His hardness pressed against her hip. He pushed the tangled hair away from her face and stared down at her. "That's part of your charm. You're a trouper. You do what needs to be done. You don't fall apart, you don't talk about it, or wait for someone else to take charge."

His eyebrows drew together, and although his attention focused squarely on her face, she got the feeling that he wasn't really seeing her. He looked as though he were explaining something to himself.

"You had the sense to light the fire. You're a gutsy, independent lady. I don't know anyone like you."

She knew a lot of women like her, but she didn't want to tell him that. His words of praise were like balm to her spirit. She couldn't be second-best anymore, she realized. She needed to be the only one. And right now, for this man, she was.

"Are you going to talk all night?" she asked, drawing her knee up to nudge him intimately.

He smiled, moving his hand to her breast. "No, ma'am." And then his mouth was on her, tasting, nibbling, kissing. He whispered words she couldn't quite hear, kissed her in places that smoldered under his care. He slid a hand between her thighs and fingered the dewiness he found there.

She tried to wiggle away from the exquisite pleasure his touch solicited, but the movement only caused greater sensation.

"Don't, baby," he whispered. "Let me love you."

Jolie was lost. She reached for him, and when he tried to evade her, she pushed herself at him, reaching, stroking, guiding him to her.

"Hey, don't you know what foreplay is?" he murmured between shudders.

"Yeah, four days on an island."

His smile was faint as he hovered above her, massaging a breast, lightly pinching the nipple. He briefly closed his eyes, before slanting them open to gaze at her.

His look told her everything she needed to know. Digging her short, blunt nails into his firm buttocks, she pulled him toward her and pushed up to meet him.

"Oh, God, Jolie," he whispered, his breath ragged. "I knew you'd be good at this."

THE ROOM WAS nearly dark when he awoke. Outside the sliding glass door, coconut tree fronds ruffled in the wind and cast spidery shadows upon the white walls and ceilings. They'd only been asleep for two hours, he figured, after making love for three.

Jolie stirred beside him. Eyes still closed, she uncurled her small body, and shoved at the floral coverlet with an open fist, exposing one perfect rosy breast. Then she reversed the process and snuggled up to him.

He smiled, carefully turning on his side so that he could watch her sleep.

She had a perfect profile—just the right size nose, long thick lashes, a very stubborn chin. His smile widened. Yet none of these things were what made her so special. That particular quality you couldn't see with the naked eye. The goodness that radiated from her soul.

From somewhere outside a light switched on and shone through the plate glass. The beam landed on Jolie's face and she grimaced in her sleep.

He was tempted for a moment, to let the light wake her. The thought of making love to her again was all too tempting. But he couldn't ignore the faint circles under her eyes from those sleepless island nights.

Carefully, he pulled away, pressing a soft kiss to her questing hand and slid out of bed. After fumbling with the drapery cord for a few seconds, he started to yank the fabric across the window when he spotted the *Lola II*. Far larger than any other ship, it dominated the harbor like a boor crashing a party.

Mike stared at the vessel, waiting for his adrenaline to start pumping. The Longfellows had come, just as he'd predicted. He wasn't the least bit surprised. They had only three scheduled stops on their itinerary. And this port was scheduled twice. Chances were that whatever plans they had for the diamonds would be executed here. Maybe even tonight.

Behind him, Jolie sighed in her sleep. He looked over his shoulder as she hugged his pillow. Then he cast one more glance at the *Lola,* and sighed, too.

Surely the Longfellows wouldn't make a move tonight, he thought, replaying Jolie's breathy cries in his head. And if they did?

Turning back toward the bed, he vaguely recalled that the adrenaline rush hadn't come.

As he crawled between the sheets and Jolie wrapped her warm body around his, he recalled the saying he'd seen on a coffee mug, and decided that just maybe, living well really was life's best revenge.

Chapter Sixteen

Jolie had no idea where she was. There were no stars overhead, no waves crashing nearby. And the ground was soft, so deliciously soft beneath her body.

Beside her...

She bolted to a sitting position. The fogginess melted from her brain like a banana split left out in the sun. Slowly, she removed her hand from Mike's bare belly.

He mumbled an endearment in his sleep, and tried to tug her down beside him. A narrow strip of filtered light seeped between the drapes and fell across his face and pillow. The beam caught one closed eye, the deep cleft in his chin, the side of his stubbly jaw.

She knew he was still fast asleep because after the unsuccessful tug, his arm slumped back to the pillow, his skin bronze against the white cotton.

Warm tingling memories rushed her, and her face grew hot just thinking about where that arm and hand had been. She took a deep breath. Then lifted the top sheet and peeked under it.

Her pulse skipped two gears. Heat spiraled from her toes to her fingertips. He was truly magnificent. He belonged on a cover of a magazine or a calendar or immortalized by some sculptor. Yet all that beauty bred no conceit. He didn't think he was anything special.

He thought she was.

A fresh wave of tenderness washed over her, and she smiled. He shifted his leg, and her grin widened.

A scratching noise came from the door and she snapped the sheet back in place. He stirred for a second, before his breathing evened out.

It was FiFi, she realized, when another scratch was followed by a whimper. Glancing at the digital clock, guilt pushed her away from Mike and out of bed. Feeling her way around in the dark, she managed to locate her clothes and quietly slip them on.

She cast a last longing look at him, but FiFi's urgent scratching reminded her how inconsiderate they'd been to the dog. She slipped out of the room, grabbed FiFi, the leash, the parlor key, then let them out without waking Mike.

It was a little scary, walking around the dark perimeter of the hotel at three-thirty in the morning. Except for a couple of streetlights shining on the hotel entrance, only landscape lighting showed her the way.

Since FiFi appeared in no hurry to return to the room, Jolie urged her around to the back where she hoped the lights from the harbor would provide more illumination.

The move proved little help. The pier was mostly dark. The path between the docked boats was lighted, extending the length of the port, but only the afterglow reached the hotel grounds.

It was while Jolie waited for FiFi to sniff what seemed like the millionth blade of grass that she saw the *Lola II*. It was wider and taller than any of the other boats, and when her discovery finally sank in, Jolie's heart nearly somersaulted out of her chest.

She snatched FiFi off the ground, surprising a yelp out of the dog. Shushing the disgruntled terrier, Jolie hopped over a low hedge, anxious to tell Mike about what she'd found. But before she could get to the side entrance of the hotel, she noticed the lone figure hurrying down the deserted pier.

She considered not stopping. If anything she should hurry back to the room where it was safe, where she could tell Mike about the Longfellows. But something in the furtive and familiar way the figure moved made Jolie slip back into the shadows and watch.

Although the yellowish lighting was dim and sporadic, and the figure was cloaked in dark, nondescript clothes, Jolie quickly realized the person was a woman.

And not just any woman. The small quick steps, the exaggerated sway of the hips, the high jutting breasts all added up to Lola.

FiFi started to squirm, and Jolie clamped a hand over the dog's mouth. They were too far away for Lola to have heard the terrier's soft whining, but Jolie was afraid that if the dog recognized her mistress, she'd blow their cover. So she crouched behind a hibiscus hedge, keeping the dog tucked low while she peered between two orange flowers.

Dressed in black from the scarf draped around her neck to the toes of her pointy boots, Lola hurried down the pier, careful to keep out of direct light. The clicking of her heels against the weathered wood barely echoed above the waves slapping the pier's corroded support columns.

Jolie shook her head. Although the woman had tucked most of her hair under the scarf, either vanity or stupidity had dissuaded her from covering the platinum-blond crown that now shone like a beacon.

Not that Jolie wasn't grateful. Even after Lola stepped from the pier onto the deserted, shadowed sidewalk, Jolie could easily keep track of her. She started to follow when FiFi began squirming again.

Quickly, she placed the dog on the ground and looped the leash around the bush. "I'm sorry, FiFi," she whispered, and silently prayed the terrier wouldn't start barking. "I'll be right back, girl."

She crooned and petted as long as she dared but as soon as she pulled away, FiFi let out an angry yap. Without looking back, Jolie hurried in the direction Lola had gone even though she could no longer see the woman. Questions ricocheted through her head. Questions she wouldn't get answered by letting Lola slip away.

FiFi's venting faded behind her as she scrambled to catch up. Blood pounded in her ears and drowned out all other sounds around her. There was only one reason she could think of why Lola would be sneaking around this time of night. It had to do with the diamonds, just as Mike had suspected.

Thinking about Mike, she quickened her pace. One part of her wished she could alert him to Lola's night wanderings, the other part relished the idea that she was about to crack the case for him.

Stubbing her toe against a chunk of ragged concrete, she winced, swallowed a curse. She wasn't going to crack anything but a few bones if she didn't spot Lola.

She slowed for a moment to get her bearings. The street leading to town was narrow and crowded with adjoining wooden structures. A couple of rusted-out taxicabs were parked crookedly at the edge, their tires half on the sidewalk.

On the right, behind the tired storefronts, waves lapped the beach. Behind those on the left, weed-infested fields sloped toward the mountains in inky blackness. Unless

Lola had already ducked into one of these buildings, there was no way for her to go but straight down the street.

Jolie stood perfectly still for a moment, peering hard into the darkness, listening for a door, a creaking boardwalk, anything that would give her a clue.

Water and wind hummed beneath the silence.

And then a light blinked on.

Three stores away, on the right, murky yellow light bled onto the street from behind a tattered blind. Surprised, Jolie threw herself against the shabby wooden building beside her. A splinter pierced her palm.

She ignored it, dropped to a crouch and edged her way toward the light. When she got to the door, she took a deep breath, put her hand on the knob and slowly turned it.

She heard a click, then felt the latch start to give. At the last moment, it stopped. She could tell the lock was loose. The whole knob was loose. But she wasn't sure she could rattle it open without giving herself away.

Slackening her grip, she was about to let go and consider her options, when the door creaked open a crack. Her hand flew to her mouth, her fingers splaying her lips as if that would ease the noise from the door. She waited.

Nothing.

Only voices coming from somewhere inside, so faint she could barely make out a single word.

She wrinkled her nose. Now what? What was she supposed to do? She could go back and get Mike. At least she could direct him back here. Lola had only been in there a matter of minutes. If Jolie hurried, they could still catch her red-handed.

Frowning, she craned her neck toward the crack as far as she dared. What if that wasn't Lola in there after all? What if Jolie was wrong? She hadn't actually seen anything yet, she realized, and cringed at the thought of leading Mike on a wild-goose chase.

You gotta finish what you start, girl.

Her grandfather's words rang loud and clear in her head. As did the reminder that she had yet to keep a job anywhere near the thirty days her grandfather had stipulated.

Glancing around the boardwalk, her gaze snagged on a couple of loose rocks where the pillar was cemented in the ground. She scooped up the stones and slid them into her pocket. As weapons went, they were pretty pathetic, but they reassured her nervous fingers as she briefly closed her eyes and pushed open the door.

"That's not what we agreed upon."

Lola's panicked shriek, coming from somewhere down the cramped dingy hall, nearly sent Jolie to her knees. She caught the door frame and narrowly missed tripping over the threshold. She was certain they'd heard her clumsiness, until Lola's annoyed voice again snaked through the hall.

"Don't play games with me. I can have another buyer in an hour," she said, her voice sounding a tad clearer.

A gravelly male laugh was interrupted by a hacking cough. "Sure, lady," he finally ground out, and Jolie realized that they were moving toward her. "Let me see the diamonds."

"I'm not so stupid that I brought them with me. Do we have our original deal?"

The man growled. "How do I know if they're worth what you say?"

Jolie froze. This was good. The exchange had yet to take place. That gave her and Mike time to call the authorities. But right now, she had to get out of here. Fast. And quietly.

"I brought one ring," Lola said, her voice closer. It sounded as though she stopped, turned away from the door and added, "It's representative of the rest."

Jolie breathed a silent, relieved sigh as she backed out the door, pulling it quietly toward her. Before the latch engaged, she felt something at her back. She shifted a fraction and her fanny met something hard, solid. Swallowing, she straightened. Something warm and decidedly human aligned with her back. She gasped.

A large hand covered her mouth.

"What was that?" Lola's panic melded with Jolie's.

"Shut up." The man's gruff voice broke in. "Stay here."

An arm slipped around Jolie's waist, lifted her off her feet and pulled her onto the boardwalk. The door clicked shut, and she fell against his chest. Mike's chest. His familiar scent had finally penetrated her terror, and comfortingly cocooned her as his arms now did.

She started to turn to him. "How did you—"

"Later." His voice was stern, terse, totally at odds with the warm feeling of his sheltering arms, and her momentary euphoria slipped a notch.

He was right, of course, she reasoned as he tugged her deep into the shadows. Now wasn't the time to discuss how he'd found her.

"Who's out there?" The door flew open.

Mike shoved her behind him. She sank against the same wooden building that had delivered a splinter to her palm, sliding down to the ground and managing to add two more.

From the dark, she watched a man with bronze weathered skin step onto the dimly lit boardwalk. He was stoutly out of shape and a head shorter than Mike, but he'd evened the odds with a sawed-off shotgun.

"I'm here for Lola," Mike said calmly.

The man frowned and leveled his gun at Mike's gut. Jolie stifled a scream and tried to get to her feet. She stumbled into the darkened doorway of the next store.

If the man hadn't started to speak, and ended up battling a coughing fit, he surely would have heard her. The bout lasted only seconds, but Jolie wondered if Mike shouldn't have gone for the gun. Instead, he motioned for her to stay put.

"She didn't say nothing about no one else," the man finally said.

Lola appeared then, swinging the door wide, allowing the murky light to paint the scene with a surreal brush. Her eyes widened on Mike from over the man's shoulder.

"Hey, baby," Mike said easily. "Why didn't you wait for me?"

"You know him?" The man nudged the shotgun at Mike.

Lola blinked. "Yeah." She frowned as she looked from Mike to her cohort. Stunned into a brief silence, her eyes narrowed. Then she smiled. "He's my partner."

"You didn't say nothing 'bout no partner." The man held the gun steady.

Lola reached around him and pushed it aside. "That's none of your business." She leaned back and crossed her arms, clearly deciding to trust the devil she knew. "Unless you want to explain to him how you want to cheat us."

"I ain't cheatin' you."

"No, you aren't." She smiled at Mike, then plucked the ring the man had palmed. "Have the money ready by six this evening and I'll bring the rest of the diamonds. We can't afford any screwups. I can get away only then or my husband will get suspicious."

"What about your partner here?" The man spit on the ground, then tilted his head at a cocky angle.

Lola blinked. She slid Mike a guarded look. "Have the money by six or we go somewhere else."

The man grunted. Lola sidestepped him and slipped an arm through Mike's. Jolie caught his profile and saw a flash of white teeth, but darkness prevented her from seeing his expression.

Her stomach churned, and she did all she could to stay hidden. Mike was putting on a show, she reminded herself. And Lola was playing along because she'd gotten in over her head with the monkey-faced thug.

"Come on, Mike, before Howard wakes up." Lola led him down the boardwalk, while the other man continued to stand outside the store and stare at their retreating backs.

Jolie had little choice but to stay where she was. The man waited a moment longer, spitting twice into the street, his stale whiskey breath infecting the humid tropical air and chafing her nostrils.

She didn't move, didn't even glance at her watch as she longed to do. Then after what seemed like a small eternity, he lumbered back inside and latched the door behind him. She waited for several seconds, then, keeping a stooped position, scurried after the other two.

They were back at the marina when she caught up to them, a few steps from the lighted pier, deep in conversation. She maneuvered her way close enough to hear them.

"I knew you'd come around." Lola lifted a hand to sweep the hair off Mike's forehead.

The blonde's familiar gesture sent a chill through Jolie. It was too dark to see their faces, but a satisfied smile laced the woman's words. What did she mean by "come around"? What had they been talking about?

Although Mike didn't respond, he didn't pull away either. "How are you going to get past Howard?"

She heaved a disgusted sigh. "The man is like glue. He thinks I have a hair appointment. I arranged a massage for him at the same time. An hour is all I'll have. Tops."

"*I* could make the exchange."

Lola laughed. "Sorry, lover boy." She stuck out one of her long scarlet nails and dragged it down his cheek. "Not that I think we won't have a long, interesting partnership. But you know what they say—once a thief, always a thief."

He caught her hand and held it away. "You would know, wouldn't you, Lola?"

She laughed again, unoffended. "I figured it out after the lingerie incident, you know. That you were trying to steal my diamonds. I knew you couldn't possibly be—"

"What I can't figure out is why *you're* stealing them."

She snatched back her hand and waved it in an angry gesture. "Howard doesn't give me a cent. Sure, I can charge all I want, but with that damn prenuptial agreement, I can't even leave the bumbling old fool." Her tone evened out and the smile was back in her voice. "How else could we ride off into the sunset together? Rio is going to be a blast."

"Right. You'd better get back. It's going to start getting light."

Jolie felt sick. If she didn't know Mike better, it would have sounded an awful lot like he and Lola had a history. Like maybe he hadn't been totally forthright. Like maybe Jolie had been a fool.

Did she really know him? She shook the doubt away.

She did know him, enough to know he hadn't lied to her, that he wasn't a thief.

"Okay," Lola said. "We may not get a chance to meet again until New York. I don't want anything suspicious happening before we get there. Tomorrow I'm going to suggest we head back. I'll plead one of my migraines."

"Good idea." Mike stepped back when she leaned toward him.

Jolie shrank behind the hibiscus bush. On the surface, they made a striking couple. And although she knew what a devious twit Lola was, it hurt to look at them.

He turned toward the hotel and Lola laid her scarlet nails on his arm. "Okay, honey, but I can't wait for you to tell me how you got rid of the little mouse. Or why you chose someone like *that* to pretend to be your wife. That was pretend with Plain Jane, wasn't it?"

Mike jerked his arm away. Jolie still couldn't see his face, and he said nothing. He merely headed across the lawn toward the hotel.

Lola frowned after him, then glanced at her watch and hurried down the dock, her boot heels clicking in rhythm with the water slapping the wooden columns beneath her feet.

As soon as she knew it was safe, Jolie raced after Mike. He was traveling a breakneck pace and she was breathing hard by the time she headed him off at the lobby entrance.

He turned in surprise when he heard her behind him, then looked over her head toward the marina. Slowly, he lowered his gaze to her face. "Where were you?"

Her voice was ragged between pants. "Hugging the hibiscus."

"You heard Lola?"

He looked so full of dread that for a moment she got a horribly sick feeling again. "Yeah. Why?"

"She's an idiot. Nothing but a two-bit loser and you can't believe a damn thing she says."

Jolie blinked. She didn't. Okay, so the thought had occurred to her.... She hated herself for having had that fleeting doubt. And the fact that he was so passionately protesting was a little strange, but she did believe him. He wasn't a criminal or a liar. She knew that with certainty, where it counted. Deep down in her heart.

She started to smile, and he grabbed both her arms and pulled her toward him.

"You're not a mouse. You're not a Plain Jane."

She shook her head. Those words hadn't bothered her. Truly. She'd been compared to her sisters all her life.

He forced her chin up and his eyes held hers. "Lola could never be as beautiful as you. Inside or out."

She blinked. The smile faltered on her lips. She'd been wrong. Mike was a liar, after all.

EVEN THOUGH he could sense her resistance, he kept his arm around her shoulders and rushed her past the dozing doorman and through the pale pink lobby.

He couldn't wait to get her back to the room. So he could show her how he felt about her. So that with his mouth, his hands, he could erase Lola's ugly words.

Hell...he loved her. He had to tell her. Even though his palms were sweating at the thought. He dragged one down the front of his new jeans.

There was no getting around the truth. When he'd found her side of the bed empty earlier and ran out in time to see her sneaking down the street, he'd been crazy with worry that she'd get herself hurt. He knew then that his concern meant far more than his sense of responsibility for having gotten her into this mess.

Halfway across the lobby, he was surprised and unhappy to see a group of people near the registration desk and tried to steer Jolie toward the elevator.

"Oh, my God. I forgot about FiFi." She stiffened, then tried to twist away from him.

"She's all taken care of." He kept his arm firmly around her, thwarting her efforts to break free, urging her toward the open elevator doors.

"There she is!"

A single shrill voice screeched across the lobby coming from the group of people standing at the desk. Only they were no longer standing but rushing toward them in a blur of mink and silk. Several pair of high heels clicked rapidly across the tile floor like machine gun fire.

"Let go of my daughter. Police, police! There he is." A beautiful blond woman led the others, as she clutched a long strand of pearls at her chest with one hand and motioned to two uniformed men with the other. Behind them, another whole battalion of uniforms closed in.

"Mother?" Jolie's eyes widened in shock.

Stunned, Mike let her go, and watched as two other blond women nearly collided with the older one as she came to a stop several feet away from him. He recognized one of them as the woman who'd picked Jolie up in the limo in Manhattan.

"Monique? Nicole?" Jolie spread her hands in a helpless gesture. "What are you all doing here?"

"That's the kidnapper, officers." The one Jolie called Mother pointed a peach-colored nail at Mike. On the same hand, a huge diamond flashed like a friggin' lighthouse. The cost of her outfit equaled some mortgage balances.

He turned raised eyebrows to Jolie. "Mother?"

She frowned and looked from Mike to the older woman. "Kidnapper?"

"Calm down, Simone. Jolie, are you all right?" A deep

male baritone came from behind the two tall blondes who were babbling in unison. As soon as the man pushed through and Mike saw his white hair and beard, he recognized Sylvester Pillbury—the eccentric diamond tycoon.

"Grandfather?" Jolie's shoulders slumped.

"Grandfather?" Mike's jaw slackened. He shoved a hand through his hair as his gaze bounced from Jolie to Pillbury back to Jolie. "Grandfather."

She nodded glumly.

"This should be interesting," Mike muttered, dumbfounded.

"You're under arrest," the taller of the first two officers said as the other one slapped cuffs on him. Several others drew their guns and aimed them at his heart.

"No." Jolie threw herself between them and him. "You've got this wrong."

"For heaven's sake, Jolie, move aside." Mrs. Duval's face paled.

Jolie drew away from him and rushed to the woman's side. Immediately, he missed her warmth. Although he knew he was in no real danger, irrationally, it felt like desertion.

"Mother, please. Don't be upset. It's not what you think." She rubbed a soothing hand down her mother's mink-clad arm, then she smiled, a wide, joyous smile. "You came all this way for me?"

"Of course I did," the woman snapped. "What kind of mother do you think I am?"

The joy in Jolie's eyes flickered for a moment. But her smile remained intact. She opened her mouth to speak but a flashing light stopped them all cold. It was followed by another, then another.

"Get those photographers out of here," Mrs. Duval ordered in a low, threatening voice.

The officers jumped to do as she instructed. Mike held up his cuffed wrists. "Uh, guys?"

Jolie turned to him in surprise almost as though she'd forgotten he was there. Several more flashes went off.

"Leave them on," Mrs. Duval said. "Get rid of the photographers."

They all hurried to do her bidding, one of them being the police chief, Mike suddenly noticed.

His patience disappeared as quickly as the uniforms did. "Wait a minute—"

"There's no reason for that, Mother," Jolie cut in. "There's no problem here."

"Really?" Mrs. Duval's maternal anxiety evaporated. She narrowed angry eyes on her daughter. "You don't think the press won't have a field day with this story?" She ran a gaze down Mike as if he were yesterday's garbage. "If you weren't kidnapped, what are you doing shacking up with *him?*"

"What?" Jolie stepped back, gaping.

Mrs. Duval took a deep breath, then put a hand out. "Don't worry about it, dear. Just don't make a scene and I'll take care of everything." She touched the pearls at her throat. "After all, it even happened to Patty Hearst. That attachment syndrome or whatever. A good psychiatrist can explain everything."

Monique and Nicole both murmured sympathetic words of agreement.

Jolie squinted at one of her sisters. "You did this, Nicole, didn't you? When I called you for money." She added sadly, "I *asked* you to keep it quiet. I *asked* you to trust me."

The woman's face reddened.

Jolie shook her head. "How did I ever end up in this family? You were right all along. Gypsies did leave me on the doorstep."

Nicole's face progressed to scarlet.

"Now, don't you be including me in that statement." Pillbury stopped stroking his beard, and the pensive look that had been on his face while he'd calmly watched the interchange disappeared.

Jolie walked over and jabbed him in the chest with her index finger. "You're the one who got me into this mess."

The women exchanged confused glances but said nothing.

Pillbury's eyes briefly met Mike's before his gaze moved to his granddaughter. It looked as if a smile tugged at the corners of his mouth but it was hard to tell with that bushy beard. "So, it's a mess, is it?"

"Well, no kidding." Scowling, Jolie withdrew her finger. Then she too glanced at Mike. She started to cringe, then her gaze fell to his wrists and her scowl deepened. "Kindly uncuff him. Now," she ordered the nearby police officer, her shoulders back, her chin lifting.

She looked and sounded an awful lot like her mother just then. Mike wondered what she'd think about that. Then he wondered why she shouldn't sound like the socialite, and sighed. What a chump he'd been.

"You're overreacting, Jolie." Mrs. Duval discreetly waved a refraining hand at the officer, who promptly obeyed.

Mike held up his shackled wrists, but it was too late. Jolie once again ignored him in favor of her mother.

"Me?" she asked. "You think *I'm* overreacting?"

"What was I supposed to think? If nothing was wrong,

why are you checked into this hotel? Why aren't you staying in my penthouse?''

Jolie's guilty eyes flew to Mike's.

Son of a... She didn't trust him. She hadn't all along. Mike lowered his bound wrists. They dropped like five-hundred-pound weights.

She blinked. Then took a breath so deep her shoulders quivered. "I asked you to release him," she said quietly, without looking at the young officer. Then she calmly returned her attention to her mother's smug face. "I want my husband released, Mother. So that we can finish our honeymoon."

Mrs. Duval's lips parted in shock but no sound emerged. Monique and Nicole gasped. Pillbury frowned.

Grinning, the officer promptly produced a key.

Mike smiled, too. A fresh surge of adrenaline purged the irritation from his body. There was nothing like beating the rich and powerful at their own game.

As the man unlocked his cuffs, Mike's smile found Jolie. But she wasn't looking at him. Her eyes were riveted on her mother's pale face, and he could hardly miss the twinkle of triumph as brilliant as a flawless diamond on black velvet.

His smile faded as he remembered.

He wasn't really her husband.

He was her pawn.

Chapter Seventeen

"You're rich." It wasn't a question, and not quite an accusation. But Mike's eyes told her far more than his words. She was losing him.

"Wanna bet?" She glanced at her grandfather as she shoved Mike toward the elevator. "Let's get out of here, okay? We need to talk."

"Talk? What about the honeymoon?"

Despite his teasing words, there was an edge to his tone and any nagging last-minute thought of stopping to explain to her stunned family vanished. The elevator doors opened and she dragged him in.

"I guess I should be flattered that you can't wait to get me to the room, but I've got business to attend to," Mike said, when the doors reopened on their floor and he stood immobile.

"We need to talk." Using her shoulder and all her weight, she forced him into the corridor. "What business?"

"Lola?" Cocking an eyebrow at her, he pointedly straightened his shirt where she'd manhandled him. "You should have had one of your uniformed henchmen do that."

She started to bristle then reminded herself that it was

good for him to get the anger off his chest. From the look in his eyes, he had a ways to go. She pulled the key from her pocket and opened their door. Grabbing his arm, she jerked him inside.

"What's this about? The game's over. You won. Didn't you see your mom's face?" Mike's laugh was brittle, forced.

"What we have to discuss has nothing to do with my family. Well, in a way it does." She twisted her hands. "I mean, I needed this job because of my grandfather."

"You *needed* this job?" He laughed again, putting up his palms. It was a humorless sound. "You don't have to explain. The deal was, no questions."

"The deal changed, Mike," she said, and when he shrugged indifferently, she took a step closer to him. "Tell me it didn't."

"Look…" Backing up, he splayed his fingers through his hair. "The situation got more, uh, involved than we'd intended, but that doesn't mean we—"

"I know I'm not your type," she cut in. "You don't have to spell it out. My family's—" She paused for a breath. "I just don't want us parting like this." She was making matters worse. She could see it in the tightening of his jaw, the narrowing of his eyes.

"In the meantime, I've got something important pending." He inclined his head toward the marina and hooked a thumb in that direction. "Like Lola and a million in diamonds that's going to get away if she sees all these policemen around here."

"What are you going to do?" she asked cautiously.

He didn't answer. He stared at her a long time as if he were looking for something, a sign, an answer. She didn't know what.

"Turn her in," he said finally.

She knew that. Briefly, she closed her eyes, annoyed at his deliberate obtuseness. When she opened them again, she wasn't prepared for what she saw. She swallowed at the hurt etched around his mouth. It made no sense.

"What did you think? I was going to run off with her?" he asked.

Heat flushed her cheeks. She had for a moment. Earlier. But not now. Now the accusation made her angry. "You don't know where she has the diamonds."

"Probably on the yacht. If the stones don't turn up there, with our statements the police should have enough grounds to search any safe-deposit boxes she may have on the island. That is if you're still willing to be a witness."

"Of course I am. Why wouldn't I?"

He shrugged and headed for the door. "Your kind usually stick together."

"How would you know?" She ordered herself to shut up. She had known from the start she wasn't his type, that they never had a chance. He was out of her league. So why humiliate herself? "Your kind doesn't hang around long enough to find out."

He stopped, his back to her, his hand on the knob. Then he opened the door, and he was gone.

GETTING THE POLICE to take action had taken a lot longer than Mike'd thought. If it hadn't been for pressure from the insurance company, and a phone call from the New York police, he wasn't sure he would have gotten them to act at all.

But as he left the marina, a team of a half dozen officers headed down the pier toward the Longfellows' yacht. He should probably stick around, see what they turned up. He couldn't quite understand why he didn't. After all, this was the brass ring, his vindication…and the Longfellows' humiliation. But somehow it didn't seem so important anymore.

Not when he knew Jolie would be gone when he got back.

He plucked a pink bougainvillea blossom from a vine crawling up the side of a cabana and crushed it. An older woman in a green-skirted swimsuit rounded the corner in time to see and gave him a dirty look. He scowled back and she scurried toward the pool.

Jolie wouldn't have let him get away with that. She would have given him a piece of her mind for destroying the flower. He started to smile. Stopped. Then passed a hand over his face and sighed.

Was this how it was going to be? Was he going to waste time thinking about her? Damn. It was over between them. He'd served his purpose. She didn't need him anymore.

"They find the diamonds?"

Sylvester Pillbury, with his confident air of authority, had been lurking near one of the poolside cabanas. He stepped into view, blocking Mike's path, and Mike suddenly knew why the police had had the abrupt change in attitude.

He shook his head in disgust. Money and influence were strong motivators. "I don't know."

Pillbury frowned. "You didn't wait to find out? That doesn't sound like you."

"You don't know me."

The older man laughed. "I know you better than you know yourself."

Mike stopped. The shrewd gleam in the other man's eyes chilled him. Pillbury'd had him checked out. In the time Mike had tried to convince the police to follow up his lead, Jolie's grandfather had had Mike investigated.

"You're really something." Mike dashed the crushed flower to the ground and walked past him.

Pillbury caught up. Barely. For the first time, Mike noticed the man's limp and, cursing himself for the foolish gesture, he slowed down to accommodate him.

"Let's see." Pillbury stroked his beard. "You started your actual bodyguarding business right out of college. Before that, you...well, one might say, you freelanced."

Mike's head snapped up at the laughter in the man's voice. Recalling the first day he'd met Byron, Mike had to smile, too. He'd come a long way since those days. A long way.

But obviously not long enough. He cast a sideways glance at Pillbury. He wondered how much the old man was going to offer him to get out of Jolie's life.

"You made an instant success of it, too, catering to the rich and famous." Pillbury inclined his head toward him as if he had some secret to impart. "Especially the women. With your looks, that was a good move."

Hearing it put like that, Mike cringed. Yet he knew that his looks had played a part in his success. He didn't necessarily like that fact, but it was the truth.

"What's your point, Pillbury?"

A sly, ingratiating smile turned up one corner of his mouth. "And then there was Angela. Beautiful, rich, spoiled Angela." He shook his head. "I could have told you it wouldn't work between you two. I know the family. Did I tell you?"

Irritation swept Mike like high tide charging the beach. He didn't want to think about Angela, or about their brief engagement, about how he hadn't been rich enough or exciting enough for her.

And then a strange thing happened. He realized he really *couldn't* think about her. Her image was fuzzy. Although he'd replayed the scene when she'd dumped him a hundred times in his mind, right now, he couldn't even summon a clear picture of her face. Or their parting conversation.

"Too bad you didn't know Jolie then," Pillbury said. "She could've given you a lesson in acceptance with dignity."

Mike turned to glare at him, but the man was looking past him toward the pool. Mike followed his gaze. Under the shade of a large umbrella near the bar, Monique and Nicole sat talking to four young men. Tall, golden-haired and tan, the women wore revealing bikinis. They made a stunning picture.

Though they couldn't compete with Jolie.

"It's a funny thing," her grandfather continued, "she wants their approval, her mom's most of all, yet she really doesn't approve of them. Kind of ironic, isn't it?"

Mike swallowed hard as he watched two waiters race to take the women's orders. Something in the man's words made him uneasy. He turned to peer closely at Pillbury, trying to identify his hidden agenda, suspicious that the man was actually talking about him. After all, hadn't he, too, struggled for the approval of the wealthy he seemed to despise? "I still don't see your point."

"That's because you've had it easy, too."

Easy? With an absentee father and a mother who was on and off welfare, he'd battled his way through childhood. Mike shook his head. He'd heard enough of the old coot's fantasies. He had too much to do. He needed to contact his office, get some money, get as far away as possible.

He needed to start forgetting about Jolie.

A knot coiled in his throat. "Sorry you wasted your time, old man," he said, swerving in the direction of the hotel and pulling away from his companion.

"Go ahead and start calling me 'Grandfather.'"

When Mike stopped, turning to give him an outraged look, Pillbury laughed uproariously. "Are you a betting man, Duval?"

Mike cringed. "It's Kramer." He turned away again.

"By the way, not that it matters to you, but her inheritance is safe. It always has been. Although I believe she plans on giving most of it to that homeless shelter she thinks I don't know about. Nah, it was her confidence that was in danger." Pillbury's voice faded as Mike got farther away.

But when Mike didn't acknowledge him, he called out loud and clear, "She loves you. She told her mother to go to hell."

Mike missed a step. He tried to swallow around the lump preventing his next breath, but he couldn't suck in enough air to do it.

Half of him wanted to turn around, to march up to the crazy, delusional old man and tell him that he was sick of his riddles, demand that he not screw with him like this.

The other half wanted to believe the old codger.

Mike hesitated, and peripherally to his left, he saw Lola being escorted off the pier by two uniformed police officers and a dark-haired man in a white suit. Her hands were cuffed. Howard trailed behind, accompanied by another tall, well-dressed man.

Mike felt nothing. Not even a sliver of triumph. He'd been consumed with ensuring that Lola got caught and now that it had happened, all he could think about was Jolie.

He smiled. He didn't have to believe Pillbury. But he did have to believe in himself.

Jolie had. She'd trusted him, he realized. Even when she might not have trusted herself. And her humbling gift would forever change him.

But this wasn't about Jolie, or about how rich she was. This was about him. No one was pointing, calling him that poor Kramer kid. He was the only one doing the pointing now. It was time he grew up and laid the past to rest. Or else he wouldn't deserve her. He didn't think he deserved her now, but that wasn't going to stop him from trying to get her back. She was a funny, giving person who had even risked her life to save his reputation.

Hell. He smiled, his feet trying to keep up with his racing heart. She'd even brought him gum.

Not once had she made him feel like an outsider. Kidnapping was serious business. He'd known that even before she'd explained her fears on the island. Earlier today, when she'd tried to reassure her mother that she was okay, that she hadn't been kidnapped, she was doing just that—reassuring her mother—and not pulling away from him, not making him feel like the outsider. He had done that to himself.

Because whether Pillbury's words had targeted him or not, Mike knew he wanted approval, too…every time he remembered he was nothing more than the thug from the wrong side of the tracks.

But not now. Now, all he wanted was Jolie's approval. And her love.

Damn it. He was going to fight for her.

Even if he had to grovel to do it.

JOLIE REFOLDED her spare set of clothes for the third time and laid it on the bed next to Mike's. She stared at them wondering why she was doing this to herself.

Mike could be on his way to the airport by now.

She bit her lip and yanked up the shorts to refold them. He wouldn't leave without saying goodbye. No matter how upset he was. Would he?

It didn't matter, she told herself, if he did, she'd hunt him down.

The reassuring thought gave her a modicum of comfort, and she smiled. But her joy was short-lived. He was far too good-looking, too charming, too everything for her. It was ludicrous to think she'd actually end up with him.

Unbearable to think she wouldn't.

That was why she was willing to fight for him. Because if she didn't, she'd go back to settling for second-best. And that was no longer an option.

Lovingly, she smoothed the wrinkles from his shorts.

Someone turned the outside doorknob. Grinding out an irritated sound, she threw the shorts in a heap.

"Mother. Go away." She marched to the door, briefly considered ignoring her unwelcome visitor, then flung the door open, hoping to fend off her mother's pleas once and for all.

"Sorry, but I'm not feeling very motherly." Mike lifted a brow, his troubled eyes quickly roaming her face before he slipped past her.

He stopped as he neared the bed, his gaze snagging on the clothes. He slowly repocketed his key. "Are those clean?"

"Yeah." She closed the door and tried to breathe. "I was going to pack them."

He didn't say anything. He barely moved. His attention remained glued to the piles of clothing. Without looking at her, he grabbed the hem of his shirt and drew it over his head. "I need a shower. It's hotter than hell out there."

Jolie stared for a moment, stunned that he was behaving

with such appalling nonchalance, and then she did the most incredible thing. She stomped her foot.

Mike looked up then, his eyes warily finding hers. He balled his T-shirt in his fists. "What?"

"What?" she repeated, her eyebrows shooting up.

He shrugged. "You don't want me to take a shower?"

"Michael Duval," she said, her hands flying to her hips. "Why are you being such a jackass?"

He blinked, slowly smiled, then cringed. "About the name. I was thinking, we're going to have to change it. Call me chauvinistic, but I want Kramer back. Maybe we could use them both and hyphenate them? What do you think?"

"I think you truly are a jackass." She couldn't help the smile tugging at her lips.

"You're probably right," he said, dropping the shirt and walking toward her. "But this jackass loves you."

Her knees threatened to buckle. He reached her just in time and she sagged against him. "I love you, too," she whispered.

"Even though I'm a jackass?" His stunningly beautiful face lit up with a smile meant only for her.

She nodded and hiccuped.

He laughed. "You're supposed to say I'm not really a jackass."

"I'll have to think about that one." Her words came out breathy and ragged as he kissed the side of her mouth, her jaw, her neck.

"Wait. I have something for you," she said when he tried to steer her toward the bed, and he reluctantly pulled back to look questioningly at her.

She reached for the nightstand, pulled out a small velvet box and handed it to him.

Frowning, he flipped it open. A single gold hoop lay against black satin.

"I don't get it." His frown deepened.

"It's for you." She tapped his earlobe. "I noticed the hole."

He made a face. "It's been a long time. I'm not into earrings anymore. Besides, your mother would flip."

"Tough." Jolie slid her arms around his neck. "I don't care what she thinks anymore. I love you."

"Will you still love me if I don't wear the earring?"

She grinned. "I'd still love you if you didn't wear a thing."

He smiled back when she unsnapped his shorts, then his eyes turned serious. "Look, Jolie, I have a lot to explain. I have apologies to make—"

She put a finger on his lips. "Me, too. Plus, there's a small matter of my trust fund. I hope you don't—"

"*Small* matter?" He broke in, laughing. "Your money won't be a problem, Jolie. Especially if you want to spend it on that homeless shelter you're so fond of." When her eyes rounded in surprise at his knowledge of the shelter, he laughed again. "My security business hasn't done too bad. I'm not exactly a pauper myself. Think you can live on a million a year?"

She grinned. "Oh, I think so. Will the rest of our lives be enough time to figure that out?"

"I like the sound of that." He cupped her face and kissed her until the money and name issues both became moot.

She couldn't even remember her first name.